A COTTAGE FULL OF SECRETS

JANE LOVERING

Boldwood

First published in Great Britain in 2022 by Boldwood Books Ltd.

Copyright © Jane Lovering, 2022

Cover Design by Debbie Clement Design

Cover Photography: Shutterstock

A CIP catalogue record for this book is available from the British Library.

Paperback ISBN 978-1-80048-255-5

Large Print ISBN 978-1-80048-254-8

Hardback ISBN 978-1-80415-867-8

Ebook ISBN 978-1-80048-256-2

Kindle ISBN 978-1-80048-257-9

Audio CD ISBN 978-1-80048-249-4

MP3 CD ISBN 978-1-80048-250-0

Digital audio download ISBN 978-1-80048-253-1

Boldwood Books Ltd
23 Bowerdean Street
London SW6 3TN
www.boldwoodbooks.com

To anyone, anywhere, who relates to this book.
I hope you all get your happy endings.

1

I can't bear it. I can't bear that I'm going to have to leave my cosy, lovely little house. I'd done the garden up all nice and got the first harvest of beans in, too.

He's right, I can't be the kind of wife he wants me to be, I forget things, I put things in the wrong places, I can't keep the place clean. Now I don't want to touch anything in case I get it wrong. I'm scared to tidy because it's not right, or I arrange the drawers all back to front and what I clean is not enough or too much or I use the wrong cloth. So now all I can do is walk around, looking at everything I made to turn this into a nice home for us.

I have to make a choice. Stay and keep being wrong all the time, or leave when everyone has done so much for us. I know he loves me. I *know* he does. But last night I was afraid of him, even when I knew what he was saying was right. I can't bear it to keep being like this, but on the other hand I can't keep on letting him down. Everyone's going to be so disappointed in me for not sticking it out. I mean, that's what you do, isn't it? You stand by your man. But I'm making him unhappy and angry all the time.

So I've decided. I've packed up as many of my things as I can, just some clothes and bits, and I've hidden the suitcase down in the ruins of the old house – he'll never think to look there. I'm going to get the bus to Kirkby, just like I would on a normal market day to do the shopping. Then I'm going to go to Jeanette's house. I'm going to tell her *everything* and hope she'll help me – her Dean has a car and he could come up one day and pick up my suitcase if I tell him where it is. I can't take it on the bus. Someone might see and tell him and he might get to me before I can get away. It's hidden, he won't find it and spoil all my best things like he does sometimes when he's in a mood.

Once I've got my stuff, I'll go to Auntie Evelyn's. I can get the bus from Pickering down to York and stay there until Auntie can talk to Mum and Dad. They are going to be so disappointed in me. We've never had a divorce in the family and the wedding was *so* expensive, I'm not sure Dad's finished paying it all off yet. But, in the meantime, I can stop with Auntie Evelyn and she's always saying how she could get me a job up in Rowntree's, with her. She won't mind me being separated from my husband. Dad always says she's far too modern for her own good. But if I tell her how I'm just not good enough to stay married, how I keep letting him down and how I haven't dared ask Dad about the house deeds yet, and if I tell her about the pictures – well, I think she'll be on my side.

But I hate having to leave. I love my little house – the peace and quiet with the birds singing and sometimes the foxes and badgers running out over the fields. I'd got it all cosy and nice. I'd just finished re-covering the settee again. It's funny, but it was the settee that made up my mind; I really liked that yellow stripy material which made the room look all bright and sunny. But he said it was horrible and it made his eyes hurt. He said I'd better do it again in a nicer colour and I was to show it to him first before I started. And I was so busy saying sorry that I forgot that he'd been watching me do all the sewing every evening, making all the covers. It was only when it was finished that he decided he didn't like it. But he could have *said*, could have stopped me wasting all those weeks stitching and making my fingers sore because I can't find the thimble and daren't ask him because he'd shout at me for losing it. That was when I knew...

Anyway, I'd better get my face on before I go. There's a bruise over my eye and Bob will be driving the Wednesday bus and I know he will notice if I don't get my foundation right.

I have to be gone before he gets back and finds out what I've done – I broke open the door to his wardrobe this morning. The door was locked and I don't know where he keeps the key, so I took the little axe that we use to chop up the wood for the fire. I chopped, chopped, chopped my way into that wardrobe until it was splinters and jagged old bits of wood. Then I got the axe again and I chopped into his suitcase, because that was locked as well, and I put the lot down on the fire. I'm not supposed to light the fire, with it being warm, but I've stopped caring what he'll say now. And I burned all of them.

It's a strange feeling, not caring. I've cared so much for the last two and a half years. Cared and tried and tried so hard to do everything right. But now I feel like I'm lighter. Like I'm going to be able to go back to doing all the things I loved before; dancing and seeing my friends and Mum and Dad. So it sort of doesn't matter that I'm not a good wife, because I can go back to being someone's daughter and someone's friend.

I'm going to get my life back.

2

The two cottages stood comfortably together where the track petered out into tyre marks and dust, like a couple of plump maiden aunts at the end of the world. One had curtained windows, a neatly lawned garden and a front door with a large 'No Callers' sign drawing-pinned to it, curling around the edges. I pulled my car onto the verge in front of the other cottage, where the bare windows gave the place a vaguely surprised air, like over-plucked eyebrows. As the car engine ticked itself cool, I looked for the first time at my new home and sighed. From his cage in the boot, Brack yipped impatiently.

'Yes, all right. I'm getting out. Look, this is me, getting out.' I opened the car door and put one foot out onto the mud of the verge. A wind so cold as to almost be brittle snapped around me, and I hastily retreated to the warmth inside the car, carefully built up over hundreds of miles of my tuneless singing, and Mint Imperials. 'In a minute. Just let me take in the scenery.'

In fact, there was nothing particularly scenic about the view. I'd been assured by the estate agents' website that the cottage offered a 'panoramic view of the Yorkshire moors' but this was not, currently, evident. All it offered from here was a view of a gravelled-over front yard containing some pots of dead, dry stuff, the muddy lane, and then, over the other side, a thorny hedge.

'Welcome to Yorkshire,' I muttered. To be fair, my vision of Yorkshire thus far had been gleaned from the tourist brochures, which had mostly featured Whitby and a lot of heather. There had also been quite a lot about fish and chips. Apart from a clump of purple flowers on the far bank, none of these things had so far been in evidence, so I was already inclined towards disappointment in my destination.

Brack yipped again and dug at the side of his cage. I turned around to make sure he wasn't hurting his paws in his desperation to be out of the metal box that had contained him for longer than he was used to, and when I turned back, there was a man standing at my car window.

He had his arms folded in the age-old 'what do you think you are doing here?' posture, and an unshaven face that was not wearing a 'welcome to the neighbourhood, here are fresh baked goodies and a timetable for the local rubbish collection' expression.

His sudden arrival made me jump. Still, there was nothing to be gained by antagonising the natives, so I wound down my window half an inch and smiled cautiously up at him. 'Hello.'

He squinted into the car. 'That's a fox,' he said.

My immediate instinct was to say, 'Oh my God, it was a spaniel when I put it in the car, what kind of witchcraft *is* this?' But I didn't. I just said. 'Yes. I know.' Because I did. And then, because I was worried that I'd sounded a little short, and I'd learned to always account for my movements. 'I've just bought the cottage. I'm moving in today. We've come up from Cornwall.'

Horrible little staccato sentences, but the non-reaction of the man at my window was beginning to worry me. He could be planning anything, from ripping me from the driver's seat and hurling me over the hedge to – well, actually, I had no idea. Apart from the generalised frown, his expression was giving nothing away. Maybe he'd been overcome with Mint Imperial fumes?

I cautiously pressed the button to lock my door and hoped he hadn't seen me do it.

'This is Yorkshire,' he said, finally, as though he believed that I might have taken a wrong turn up the M5 and currently be labouring under the belief that this was Taunton. There was a pause, in which I neither confirmed nor denied that yes, this was indeed Yorkshire, and I was at the correct destination. 'That's a long way from Cornwall.'

'Yes,' I said, again stating the absolutely obvious.

My lack of witty repartee brought our conversation to a close. With another squint into the car, the man unfolded his arms and began to walk away, back toward the house with the unwelcoming sign tacked to the door. He stopped just before the gate, looked back at me and said, 'I hope your furniture lorry isn't going to block the lane. I need to go out in an hour.' Then he was gone, closing his front door behind him with an echo that seemed to indicate that the inside of his house was devoid of anything except him and his attitude.

I looked at Brack and Brack looked at me. 'Well,' I said, but had nothing to follow up with.

From somewhere behind came the sound of a van struggling its way up the unpaved lane, lurching over the ruts and through the winter puddles that were just starting to dissipate under the spring sun. The acceptable bits of the rest of my entire life were heaving into view, rolling like a tea clipper in a gale and probably smashing all my china in the process. I couldn't stall any longer, I had to get out of the car and open the door before the removal men left all my furniture in the front garden.

Brack's amber eyes followed me through the gate, up the mossy path and to the front door, I could feel them. He was pretty sanguine, for a fox, but even he would be wondering what the hell was going on and what I meant by ripping him from his nicely established territory in the back garden of our house near Truro and relocating to the wilds of Yorkshire. I couldn't even begin to explain. Especially not to a fox.

The front door creaked aside and let the rays of sun come past me straight into the room, like an opportunistic salesman. The puff of air that met me smelled old. Of old things in old rooms. Dust and furniture polish and warm wood and the frowsty smell of somewhere that needs the windows to be opened more often. The front door opened directly into the living room; ahead of me was another door which led to the staircase, and was slightly ajar, giving a tantalising glimpse of a steep narrow flight leading upwards. Beyond, on the ground floor, lay the bathroom and the kitchen at the back. I'd memorised the estate agent's particulars, since that had been all I had to go on as I'd bought this place without ever seeing it in real life. Somewhere, out past the kitchen, there was a garden. And, presumably, this much-vaunted 'view of the moors', although, as the estate agent had clearly had to stretch themselves descriptively to cover the ground floor, 'extensive living area leading to private bath and toilet, giving on to comfortable farmhouse-style kitchen', I wasn't holding my breath. There wasn't much else you *could* say. 'Not a right angle in the place' sounded woefully prejudicial, if accurate. All the pictures had been those optimistically stretched ones that had made the place look like a goldfish bowl with impossible perspectives. The external pictures had been taken in deep winter and shown mostly grey skies, a cutting frost, and the cottage, bleakly deserted.

I walked through, surprised at the length of the living room, the location of the 'private' bathroom and the size of the kitchen at the back. The sun shone through and showed me the garden, long and thin, rolling slightly downhill to fields at the back. Over the threadbare hedge, I could see the top half of Mister Misery sullenly pegging out washing on a hideous rotary line, which put me off going out to explore, and I turned around to see the removals men struggling my sofa in through the narrow front door.

'It's all labelled,' I said helpfully, as they tilted the sofa at an improbable angle to get it to fit inside.

The first removal man looked at me over his shoulder with a distinct lack of enthusiasm. It *had* been a long drive, though.

'It's the size of our little 'un's doll's house. I think we'll work it out, m'dear. You put the kettle on, we'll have you sorted.'

I found myself halfway to the kitchen before I remembered why I was here. Remembered that I'd promised myself not to jump to comply with a man's every whim. That was not who I was now. 'I'll leave the teabags and milk here,' I said, sidling past them as the sofa finally slid into the room like a difficult birth. 'You help yourselves. I'm going to get Brack – the fox – out of the car.'

The two men exchanged a look that told me they'd got me down as 'bonkers single woman with exotic pet', and sighed, but I nipped past and back down the slippery verge to the car, where Brack was sitting up in his travel cage, paws neatly together and an expression of patient incomprehension on his pointed little face.

He wasn't a pet. But I couldn't begin to explain the complicated relationship the fox and I shared, not to two men who struggled with three-dimensional geometry and spatial aware-ness. Brack, me, the whole of the past five years – all stuff that I wasn't going to even start to put into words. Not yet.

This cottage was my new beginning. A small, narrow-doored and inconspicuous one, but mine.

3

After the removal men had gone, I was filled with the urge to make the cottage 'mine'. I had spent an unreasonable amount of time and money in the last few weeks on house renovation magazines and interior design websites. Of course, these had all featured eighteen-bedroomed houses in picturesque places like Berkshire, with handy little local emporiums selling exquisite artisan furniture, and usually a stream in the garden. This was more of a bargain basement version, I thought, as I stared around at the bare floors; two bedrooms and a puddle on the patio, but there was still a lot I could do with it.

For example, the fireplace. Someone had fitted a modern log-burning stove with a fire surround in shades of Old Pond-water meets Silage Clamp; with swirly tiles like a muddy Rorschach test. That needed to go, but a few experimental tugs told me that I'd need proper equipment – a bit of rocking and my fingernails were not going to do it. It was so hideous, I was almost prepared to take to it with my shoe and a chair leg, but restrained myself. Then there were the floorboards, they could be treated and polished and, with a few coats of paint more colourful than the present magnolia, the whole place would have more character.

I stood back and stared again. Yep. There was a lot I could do. But then the words I'd heard so often over the previous years echoed in my ears. 'Really, darling? You don't have much of an eye for colour, do you? And that table – far too big for the space. You're not going to buy *that*, are you, it's dreadful!' All said in a tone that I'd heard as loving, as creative. Words I'd reassured myself weren't meant to hurt me, but to stop me making expensive mistakes. But that was then. This was now. I could paint this cottage purple if I wanted to. Take up the floorboards and lay fake grass indoors. Leave the fireplace where it was and decorate it with glitter, hang a disco ball from the ceiling beams.

I thought of the reaction to that, and grinned to myself. Then I went and made another cup of tea.

My first night in the cottage was strange.

I had electricity, the estate agent had arranged to have that turned back on for me, but I couldn't find the stopcock to turn on the water, so I was having to ration the water in the tank in the loft. Once that was empty, that was it. I went to bed unshowered, feeling itchy with sweat from moving furniture into the most appropriate places. While the removals men had put it into the rooms, they'd dumped it all in the middle and I spent most of the evening shoving beds and tables into workable locations. My room, the front bedroom, was so small that, once the bed was in, the chest of drawers had to stay on the landing. The back bedroom, larger and looking out over the garden, was going to be my office as it would, presumably, be quieter.

Quieter. Ha! I lay in bed and listened to the silence whistling in my ears, broken only by Brack's occasional shift and whine. Until I got him a run built outside, he was overnighting in the bathroom, where the easy-clean floor would hopefully not smell too badly. Brack was a wonderful companion, but unhousetrainable, and the smell of fox tended to get everywhere.

There was the odd bump and thud from the wall that connected me with Mr Next Door too. The walls were thick, the cottages were old enough to have been built when two feet of solid stone was put between neighbours, and I hadn't heard a whisper from him all evening. No TV blaring, no resounding farts, no voices muted just below the level of hearing the actual words, so all you heard was a mutter and half-shouted laughter. None of that. Just the isolated clonks from the wall. I wondered, as I lay in the absolute darkness with the familiar duvet pulled up around my ears, what that dark man with the grey-streaked stubble was doing in there and whether I dared knock on his door tomorrow to ask where the stopcock was for my cottage or whether I'd just wash in buckets of rainwater from now on. He hadn't been exactly friendly. And I'd been slightly disconcerted to find that my neighbour was a man who appeared to be single, even if that single status was unsurprising given his general air of unwelcoming irritability.

I pulled the duvet higher. He wasn't anything to do with me. I could just ignore him. Plus, he might actually *have* a wife or girl-friend who'd just gone to visit her mother or was on a shopping trip to somewhere with actual shops. Or perhaps he had a boyfriend? And anyway, I'd probably hardly ever see him – after all, he must work, mustn't he?

I restlessly heaved to face an unfamiliar wall. No street lights. No traffic. It was like sensory deprivation, only dustier, and with more magnolia paintwork. I never thought I would find myself missing the seagulls that had squawked and stomped on my roof at all hours, or the endless trundle of traffic on the hill outside.

And everything else? Did I miss that? I didn't know. A resounding 'no' came first to mind, but then the good things came crowding in, stamping and stumbling over the bad so that my heart ached with loss and my dreams were full of tears.

I slept and woke in stuttered sections through the night to a final waking with the early sun sliding in through the curtains that had been left in the house by the previous occupants, along with some isolated bits of furniture and a stupendously impractical cooker. I sat up in bed and stifled the flash of claustrophobia. This was it now, this five-roomed house perched against its neighbour in the wilderness of fields, with frantically singing birds outside and the rustle of wind in the treetops. Thinking of the neighbour made me realise that I was going to have to grit my teeth and knock on his door and ask about the stopcock. But first I got up and went down to the kitchen, where I used bottled water to make myself a fortifying cup of tea.

Then I went and had a look around my new property.

Both cottages had a patch of land at the side, presumably where previous cottages had once formed a small terrace. The estate agent had called it a 'paddock, with the possibility of extension (subject to planning permission)' but on the evidence, only if you wanted to build a conservatory in which to breed giant carnivorous plants. My 'paddock' had a huge tangle of overgrown brambles in the middle, a skein of ragged twigs menacingly groping for the sky, forming a clump so dense that the whole thing had a look of a *Doctor Who* monster about it. Amid this, there was a hint of a wall still standing, jutting the occasional brick through the tendrils of snagging growth, looking like a drowning arm sticking above the water. I gave it a cursory examination. No doubt it would be a useful space, as soon as I got hold of a flame thrower and weedkiller so strong it was banned on four continents.

The other side, next to the other cottage, the patch of land was cleared, neatly fenced and contained a wooden, open-fronted garage. Funny, I thought. My neighbour hadn't looked like the sort of man who would go in for tidy fencing. He'd definitely given me more of the razor wire-and-landmines vibes, with his anti-social stare and folded arms. Plus his eerie silence last night, that wasn't natural either. I wondered if I'd upset him with my noisy furniture arranging and off-key singing. Although, if I didn't find out about the stopcock soon, it wouldn't be the noise that would be upsetting him, it would be the general air of foetid human and enclosed fox seeping through the brickwork.

Even his back garden looked miserable. No patches of fresh earth newly planted with summer bedding plants or fruit trees beginning to show signs of blossom. Just a glum brick path down the centre of a rather ragged lawn, a washing line and the half-hedge that separated our gardens and looked as though my side hadn't been clipped for several years. His side looked as though he periodically opened the gate and let the cattle in for a chew. My garden at least had a patio set on the flat flagged area near the back door, and a couple of rather truncated rose bushes at the end near the wall. There was still no sign of the moors. Just fields dipping down over the horizon, and then a grey-clouded sky rising up, dappled like the coat of a giant beast.

From where I stood, halfway down my garden path, I could see into the kitchen window of next door. And just at the point I noticed this, Mr Misery walked into the kitchen, glanced up and, before I had chance to turn and look elsewhere, saw me. Our eyes met and I, uncomfortably, noted that his were very dark, almost shadowed. This was not the kind of detail I wanted to notice about my neighbour – I'd have been happy sticking to acknowledging that he seemed short-tempered and oddly silent. I definitely did *not* want physical characteristics to loom to the forefront. But there we were. He was male and he had dark eyes. Awkward, at the observation, as well as being caught in a position to make it, I gave him a weak smile and the kind of wave you do when you know you've been seen doing something horribly embarrassing and sincerely hope that the observer will never mention it again.

He stood for a second right by the window. Unlike my kitchen, he must have his sink there, because he was filling a kettle. I saw it as he swung it out from under the tap, using the opportunity to glare at me. His dark eyes imbued the glare with a degree of menace he perhaps didn't mean, but I wasn't going to risk it.

I stopped waving.

He turned his back and walked out of sight. In case he was going to burst out of the back door waving an iron bar and yelling, I straightened up and hurried back indoors, deciding that I could put off asking about the stopcock for a little while longer. Until he forgot about my bizarre 'staring through his window', anyway. A fortnight might do it. Except that I needed to clean, Brack had sprayed his intent to own the entire bathroom fairly liberally and, even with tiled walls, it needed to be scrubbed off pronto before it sank into the wooden bath surround.

I sighed into the quiet, and loneliness draped itself over my shoulders again, like an enthusiastic old friend saying hello. But Brack at least was pleased to see me when I released him from his isolation, and yipped around me for a few minutes, tripping me up and generally being annoying.

'Get out from under my feet, you crazed vulpine!' I found myself snapping, trying to climb over the excited ball of russet fur to mop at the tiles with some of the disinfectant wipes I kept for the purpose. I might as well have been annoyed with the toilet cistern for all the good it did. Brack had no ability to judge my mood from my tone, my mere presence was enough for him, and the fact that I fed him regularly would keep him twirling his complicated moves until he fell over. Owning a fox, it turned out, was less like a Disney movie and more like having a toddler on a permanent additives binge.

'All right.' I gave in and went through to the kitchen, where I opened the fridge, put some pieces of meat in my hand, and then threw them. Raw meat carved a delicate arc through the air and then met the uncarpeted floor with a splat and a scatter which sent Brack into a fury of chasing, rolling and digging until he had found, worried and swallowed each one. But at least it gave me a window of opportunity for another hunt for the stopcock. I went back into the smelly bathroom, wrenched open the stuck plywood door to the immersion tank and shone my phone torch into the depths.

This was my last-ditch attempt, I'd looked everywhere else that a stopcock might reasonably have been expected to be sited. Inside the cupboard, a modern-looking timer ticked away behind the grey fluff. I leaned further in and poked my torch as far around the squat tank as it would go, and then laughed at the image I had of myself as someone trying to hug R2D2.

The fox, who'd obviously cleared the floor of meat and now regarded my crouching as an invitation to play, leapt onto my back. His little feet, like cushions of needles, dug into my spine and made me jump. Then I dropped the phone.

The torch continued to shine behind the tank, a little beacon in the fusty depths of the cupboard. I could see its light but couldn't reach it, even if I stretched my arm in as far as it would go.

And then, of course... *of course*... it started to ring.

I nearly dislocated my shoulder but couldn't do any more than touch the outside of the casing with the very tips of my fingers and sort of scrabble at it, like a zoo animal struggling for freedom. When the phone stopped ringing, I gave up the feeble rummaging, dislodged the fox who was trying to eat my collar, and went in search of helpful items. Unfortunately, as I hadn't got round to unpacking much more than the vital essentials, all I had to hand was a fork, the packaging from last night's microwave dinner and a cereal box. The tank itself was no help, squatting smugly amid its dust and fluff, as though it were perversely enjoying the fondling. This tank, I thought, gritting my teeth at it, was going to get the same treatment as the hideous fireplace if it wasn't careful.

The phone had fallen face down, so the torch was shining upwards, illuminating the top of the tank cupboard with a fan of light dissipated through falling dust. I continued to poke, stretch and fumble, squeezed tightly in against the tank, which I was sure was smirking over my shoulder, with my arm bent at an improbable angle. The fork was squashed between my first two fingers and I was using it to try to claw the phone close enough to grasp without any notable success. There was, however, a lot of dust and hot piping, and I was alternating sneezing viciously with exclaiming 'ow, ow', which was driving Brack into a state of frenzy.

Eventually I sat back and regarded my illuminated tank with despair. This was not how I'd imagined my first day in my new house. Tears pressed behind my eyes as I slumped against the door to the airing cupboard with a delighted Brack clambering onto my lap to stare expectantly into my face. I'd anticipated walking through rooms, picking out colours from an online chart of expensive paints, rearranging the furniture to give 'room accents' and 'pops of colour' and gazing out at the garden planning a planting scheme. Not one edition of *Ideal Home* magazine mentioned the possibility of lying on the bathroom floor armed with a fork, sneezing, shrieking and swearing with an overexcited fox widdling on the fixtures.

Brack blinked at me and jumped off my leg to go and search for any leftover bits of meat. I sat for a moment longer. The tiled floor was cold and smelled of fox but then, to be honest, so did pretty much everything I owned. I *needed* that stopcock. I *needed* my phone.

And so, with a huge sigh that buckled the MDF of the cupboard, I went back to scrabbling. Eventually, I caught the tines of the fork in the base of the cupboard, which turned out to be slightly loose. By jabbing and dragging, I managed to dislodge the board the phone was on and, muttering 'don't fall off, don't fall off', tow it slightly closer to my fingertips. This enabled me to clutch the very corner of the phone case and rescue it from the back of the immersion tank. I had to drop the fork in order to do so, but that was collateral damage I was prepared to take. I had other forks, but only one phone.

So now I had my phone back in my hand, a bruised elbow, one fewer fork and a fox who was trying to take up the floorboards in the living room. Oh, and a missed call from the estate agency, which I returned in case they were phoning to tell me that they had forgotten that they had sold me a cottage with no stopcock and an immersion tank that was probably going to tiptoe upstairs in the night and try to get into bed with me.

'Sorry, no,' trilled the young man on the other end. 'Just a courtesy call to make sure you got possession and moved in all right!'

I stared around at the magnolia walls from my position on the bathroom floor. 'Well, I'm here,' I said. 'How "all right" it is remains to be seen. Are you *positive* there's no information about the stopcock?'

'Let me check again.' There was a moment of covered phone fumbling, far too short for him to have dug out anything on the cottage and I suspected he was just kicking the underside of the desk to make suitable 'computer' noises. 'No, nothing here, I'm afraid! Why don't you ask the neighbour?'

Because he thinks I'm spying on him through his windows already, I didn't want to say. 'He's out,' was all I could think of. 'Yes, left early this morning.'

'Oh!' The voice went up the register a bit further. 'Oh, well. His name's Euan McGillan, by the way, we sold him that house a couple of years ago. You know, just in case you wanted to know or anything.'

'Is it?' I said, dryly.

'Your place has been a holiday cottage, rented out for... ooh, for *years*. Yes, the elderly couple who owned it died and some cousin has inherited it and needed to sell so we were glad you came along when you did! Not everyone wants to live in the middle of nowhere in a house that hasn't seen a proper clean since Elton John was a lad.'

'Darren!' I heard the voice from his end of the phone. 'What have I said about too much information?'

'That it's a bad thing in an estate agent, Dad.'

'Right. And what are you doing?'

'I'm just... look, I'm going to have to go,' Darren lowered his voice to a whisper. 'Just checking you were in, and you are, so...' He hung up abruptly, leaving me staring at the phone.

I knew the house hadn't been occupied for a while, but I hadn't known it had been a holiday cottage. I looked at the walls again. It would explain the slightly soulless nature of the décor, the lack of fitted carpets and the random, left-behind furniture. At least now I knew the name of my miserable next-door neighbour too. Euan McGillan.

Not that it mattered, because I was going to carry on calling him Mr Misery in my head, and I didn't think I'd ever get close enough to him to use his actual name. I stared at the phone, then

I stared at the airing cupboard. I wavered for a minute. Should I reclaim my fork now or leave it to gather generational dust?

Sod it, what else did I have to do with my time? I inched a bit closer, pressed my bosom against the tank, which I was sure was leering, and stretched my other arm around the far side, fingers wriggling in an attempt to touch the fork handle. My groping fingers found the edge of the loose board first, and then something else, something that jutted upwards as though it had been trapped under the board. It felt springy, flat, and thin and plasticky.

Intrigued, I scissored my fingers until I caught the thing between them, then gently withdrew my arm, trying not to scald myself against the hot water pipe again. It was an oblong of white card, slightly bent, like a little paper bridge. I let it ping onto my lap. It could at least have had the decency to be a roll of fifty-pound notes, or a treasure map or something that warranted me digging like Brack among the floorboards.

Disappointed, I dusted at the card, which sprang up and flipped over, revealing itself to be a photograph, details ghostly and faded from being stuffed under the floor in a hot cupboard. I got up and went into the living room, where Brack had curled up on the newly installed rug and was eyeing me with his usual foxy disdain.

'I found something,' I told him, although he didn't seem interested. 'It's a picture.' Yep, still no reaction, other than a twitch of a tail. Brack was fed up and letting me know it. 'Where,' he seemed to be saying in every line of his smooth russet coat, 'is the large outdoor run I was promised? Where are the digging opportunities? The mice? This is not what I expected when you shut me in the metal box for hours, and I am *not happy*.' An ear twitched in my direction. 'I am, in fact, disconsolate.'

In my head, Brack talked like Oscar Wilde, in a slightly

plummy, upper-class voice and used archaic vocabulary. I had no idea why.

'I'll sort your run out soon, promise.'

If foxes could sniff in a haughty way, Brack would have done so. Instead, he just tucked his nose further under his tail.

I took the photograph closer to the small front window and tilted it to catch a glimmer of the dull grey light that was coming in. Two-foot-thick walls were great for the actual *structure* of the house; nice and solid, good window seat, no noise from next door, but they did mean that the windows were small and overhung. Light got in, but it didn't stream, it trickled.

The photo was very faded. It had white bordered edges like the pictures that my mum and dad had had in their old albums, surrounding a picture of a young woman in a garden, all over-washed with that slightly orange tone that I presumed was the by-product of age and being shoved under the floor. She was standing, looking slightly awkward, in front of a large flowering bush, her hands cupped in front of her in traditional 'I don't know what to do with my arms' style. Her hair was long and loose and slightly curly and she wore an ankle-length skirt in a fabric with huge circles on it. They may have been purple, but the slight sepia tinting made them look like dried blood. Her chin was up in an attitude of pride, but her eyes weren't looking at the photographer. She was focusing somewhere over his shoulder, so whatever was making her smile, it wasn't the person taking the picture.

I turned it over again. With the improved light, I could see a faint pencil impression on the white card of the back. There was not much of the actual lettering left, but the indentation was visible if I tilted it the right way: *Stella, June 1972*.

I flipped it back over again and made a face: 1972. That was practically historical. My mum would have been eight and Dad five in 1972 and any time before I was born existed in my head in a kind of black and white unreality. I knew the world had been there, I'd seen films, TV programmes, my mum's family album and all that, but somehow in my head, everything that happened before my birth hadn't been properly formed. Maybe a family had stayed in the house and left a picture that had gradually been swept into the most inaccessible part of the cottage? I looked at it again. That woman, girl really, she didn't look more than early twenties, would be in her what, seventies now? If the picture had been *that* important, someone would have come back to look for it. Nobody had missed it since 1972, so I was probably free to throw it away. Right now, I had more pressing concerns than an old photograph; there was the absence of a fork, for a start, and then the stopcock mystery needed solving, even if that did mean going next door. Maybe I could push a note through the letter box? With a long stick? From Lancashire?

Behind me, Brack stretched, yawned and got up to saunter towards the door. Then he peed on it.

Yep, I really needed to find that stopcock.

4

Later, I drove cautiously into town.

I had an odd, dislocated feeling driving along roads where the hedges didn't loom over single-track roads from high banks. Here in Yorkshire, the roads, narrow as they were, ran along the edges of big wide fields, feathery green with sprouting barley. The sky wasn't squeezed into glimpses of cloud or blue between hilly horizons, instead it curled overhead and seemed limitless. Even the town, now my nearest shopping centre, was different. No huge sprawling new developments, just tidy little rows of ancient buildings, where the shops looked as though they had once been someone's front room, given a bigger window and a wider door.

There were, reassuringly, no artisans to be seen. Even the shops which sold paint were utterly practical, displaying rows of tins with no recourse to shading or colour-wheels. They looked far more as though they were used to selling to people who wanted to paint over stains and do up the shed, rather than high-light feature walls, and they'd have no truck with anyone who wanted to 'ombre' anything.

I went a bit overboard and started buying things with such

abandon that shopkeepers called people in from the back room to watch. I bought paint, brushes, wood stain, several tins of something I wasn't quite sure about but was told it would make my floor look 'reet loveleh'. I also bought some overalls, industrial-grade rubber gloves and a scraper. I think someone sold me a rubber doorstop and two rolls of electrical tape at one point, but I was beyond caring by then. I loaded up the car, which sagged alarmingly over the back wheels, and drove back to the cottage, ignoring the scary slopping noises from the boot and every indication that my rear suspension was dragging on the ground.

Then I realised, again, that I needed water. I was going to have to bite the bullet and talk to my neighbour.

I unloaded the car very, very slowly, in the hope that he might come out and ask what I'd been buying, or even offer to help me carry some of the more unwieldy items but he didn't, which wasn't really a huge surprise, given his thus far unsociable nature. Once the car was emptied, I hovered about outside my front door for a while, pretending to myself that I was admiring the view of the bare, thorny hedge and the field opposite, then pulled myself together and walked out of my front gate and through next door's. I tapped cautiously just above the 'No Callers' sign and then took several precautionary steps backwards, so I was halfway down the path by the time the door opened.

'It says "No Callers".' The voice came through the gap. Deep, slightly cracked, as though I'd woken him.

'Yes, I know it does, I just—'

'What's so difficult to understand about it? No, the negative. Callers, people knocking. No Callers. The exact opposite of what you are, in fact, doing.'

But he hadn't shut the door. Maybe he was enjoying keeping me out here in the cold. 'I need to know where the stopcock is and I thought you would be able to tell me,' I said quickly, in case he decided to slam the door. 'The estate agent told me to ask you,' I added, in case he thought talking to someone this adversarial through a tiny sliver of part-opened door was my way of enjoying myself. 'Otherwise I wouldn't have disturbed you.'

'Oh.' The door edge wavered.

'My name's Tamzin Jones,' I said, although I had no idea why I either wanted or needed to introduce myself.

'The stopcock is under the manhole, just outside your back door,' he said. The door was beginning to close.

'Thank you. Oh, and would you happen to have the number of a local handyman? Only I need to build a run outside for Brack... for the fox, and I don't have a lot of tools.' It suddenly occurred to me that I should have invested less in internal decoration and more in practical building materials, but it was too late now.

A moment's silence and the edge of the door, which was all I could see, jiggled a bit.

'I'd prefer a female handyman, well, person, but I don't know if there are any out here.' I was gabbling a bit now. 'I don't want just any strange man wandering around in my house when there's only me and it's quite isolated out here. Isn't it?' I finished, although I didn't really need his confirmation of the isolation of the only two houses for miles.

A bit more of a pause, then the gap opened wider, and he stepped into it. Not actually over the threshold, but at least I could see who I was talking to now. 'The cottages weren't always isolated, there used to be a farm up here,' he said. 'There's a bit of the old farmhouse left in your garden.' He pointed to the overgrown bramble thicket which clumped in the middle of the patch of ground at the side of my house. It waved back. 'But I haven't got any phone numbers to hand. Of handymen.' Another pause, then, 'Sorry,' added swiftly and rather breathlessly, as though he'd been poked in the ribs by the Ghost of Good Manners.

Encouraged by this beginning of a conversation, when I hadn't spoken to anyone properly in a while, apart from to say, 'Have you got it in a bigger tin?' I opened my mouth to ask more, but he'd already gone back inside and closed the door. The 'No Callers' sign fluttered with the force of the closing.

'Thank you!' I shouted, in case he was standing just inside the door with his ear to the wood. No answer. Not even a twitch of the curtain.

I wondered what he was doing in there. Euan McGillan couldn't be much older than me, although I'd again seen a trace of a grey streak in the stubble he'd chosen to wear for today's appearance, and he'd been wearing ordinary jeans and a shirt, not pyjamas or anything else that would lead me to believe he'd just got out of bed. Besides, he'd been making a cup of tea in the kitchen earlier. So, was he sitting there watching *Midsomer Murders* DVDs or glued to conspiracy theories on YouTube? When I went back inside my own front door, I leaned against the wall for any sound clues, but there was nothing. For all I could hear, he was propped up in the corner behind the door, waiting with a shotgun for the next person who violated the 'No Callers' sign.

But he was not my problem. What *was* my problem was a bathroom and a front door that a fox had peed all over, and the fact that I hadn't had a shower since Truro. So I went in search of the elusive, but apparently present, stopcock.

Later that day, I made a start on the painting. It was rapidly dawning on me that the rooms had been painted magnolia for a reason – that reason being that, once the sun moved out of them, it was really quite dark indoors. I'd tried the classy grey colour I'd planned on painting the living room on the wall over the log burner, but the lack of light made it look as though I were trying to camouflage a battleship. The forest green I had been going to put on my bedroom walls was going to make waking up an interesting experience, I'd worry a trail of breadcrumbs had lured me into the woods and birds had covered me with leaves. The less said about the pale yellow eggshell paint I'd got for the skirting, the better. Brack had already had a fair go at making them that colour with bodily fluids. Maybe Dom had been right. Maybe I didn't have an eye for colour. Maybe I was doomed to live in a house that resembled a primary school painting competition.

I gave up on the painting and opened my laptop. I'd got the internet up and running, which made me realise how much I relied on it for my contact with the real world. I was sitting in front of half a dozen unopened emails, which I suspected all wanted to sell me exclusive executive houses, when there was a rattle and slide at the front door. The sound sent Brack slithering off under the kitchen table, ears flat and tail lowered, and I had to spend a couple of minutes reassuring him back out again before I could go and investigate.

There was a piece of paper lying just inside the door as though it had come through the letter box weighted with disappointment. It was thick paper, much folded, and on opening I found it held a scrawled series of numbers and a block printed 'HANDYWOMAN'. Euan McGillan must have shoved it through rather than knocking and giving it to me. Maybe he'd seen the paint tins.

I didn't know whether to feel relieved that he didn't want any more contact with me than I wanted with him, or slightly affronted at the peremptory note and delivery system. So I settled for a sort of middle-ground mild annoyance tempered with gratitude, and phoned the number scribbled on the paper. 'Jill' said she could come in the morning for an initial visit where we could decide what needed doing and she could quote me. I felt a bit lighter by the time I hung up.

Things were moving. Things were happening. There was the painting. And my meagre furniture took longer to arrange in the tiny rooms than I'd ever thought possible, mostly because there was so little space it was like an exercise in geometry trying to get sofas out of the way of opening doors and yet not right where you wanted to walk. The bed was circling the bedroom like a caged tiger, first against one wall, then the other, then under the window and back to the first wall again as I tried to find a configuration that wouldn't mean having to climb over the headboard if I needed to go downstairs in the night. I didn't manage to give the rooms any 'accents' other than the broad Yorkshire they'd presumably come with, and left 'pops of colour' as the noise it made when I opened the tins of paint.

Finally, I went outside to properly survey the rest of my purchase. The estate agent's pictures really hadn't done the place any favours. No wonder I'd been able to offer slightly low on it and get my offer accepted. In the pictures, the white-painted stone of the front had looked grey and tired, the cottage and its neighbour had seemed huddled into the landscape. In real life, the two houses rose proudly, gleaming in the sun. The incipient spring had caused bursts of growth to green up the front garden, although I feared that most of the greenery was weeds, and I found that the back garden had a gate concealed among the rose bushes that led out onto the area at the side. The 'paddock' was delineated by a wire fence that sagged like a bad line drawing, containing about half an acre of tussocky grass and, in the centre, the bramble patch around the jutting bricks.

I put Brack in his harness, which he hated, but it at least gave him the freedom to wander and sniff, and we walked out to investigate the brambles. They were just starting to unfurl some leaves, which emerged cautiously from the tangled skein of stems, like tiny green noses protruding to check whether it had stopped snowing. I walked around the clump, while Brack dived in and out, mousing for all he was worth and then rolling around on his back in the sun, his long, black-stockinged legs waving among the uncut grass as he writhed over the cushions of grass and moss.

There were definitely walls in there. I could see the way the bushes had wound their way around the structures, using them as support and shelter from the wind, almost sentient. One wall, maybe a gable end, still stood around eight feet high, but the rest seemed to have fallen into rubble or been pulled by undergrowth down to lesser heights, standing like snaggle teeth in a green grin. In some places, the brambles were so thick that I couldn't see any trace of building, but by pacing around the clump I estimated that they delineated a building that would have been reasonably large. Didn't Mr Misery say that it had been the old farmhouse? Which meant that this stretch of ground that was now pocked and rutted with grass that didn't look to have been mown for years would have been the farmyard, with our cottages forming the western side. I gazed across the wire fencing into the field where the cows had bunched themselves together at the far end, under a tree, lazy tails swishing at early flies. There was no trace of the other side of the farmyard there, and no sign that any buildings had once formed the eastern range. There must, once, have been barns, stables, sheds, even if only to shelter the yard from the east wind. I wondered how long ago it had fallen into ruin.

Brack dug a small hole and ate a worm. It was disgusting, like watching a two-year-old eat spaghetti, but I'd got used to it. He'd found the uneven ground slightly hard going, his remaining hind leg having to do the work of two, and he was clearly tired now, curling himself down in the bleak sunlight to watch me. His stare was disconcerting, unblinking and amber, as though he was summing me up and trying to work out my most vulnerable points for a swift and decisive attack.

'Maybe we could build your pen around these walls,' I said, mostly to hear a voice. 'It looks like it might be the sort of place to attract mice and rats and things.'

Brack just carried on staring. I often had to remind myself that he was a fox, not a dog. He didn't learn words in the way a dog would, or respond to communication. He showed me a degree of affection, but it was the affection of something that knew it relied on me for food and safety, not the enthusiastic affection of a creature born to domestication. I briefly rehearsed the idea of getting a dog but one look at Brack, relaxed at my feet, and I knew it wouldn't be fair. And if I got a cat, he'd either dismember it or the two of them would team up against me in a competition of comparative disdain and vague contempt and I'd had enough of *that* to last me a lifetime.

With a tug on the fox's harness, I turned to go back through the garden into the cottage. The wind was cold and I wanted to light the wood burner to check that it worked, and there was *still* unpacking to do. As I turned, I could once more see into the windows of both cottages. Downstairs, the wide kitchen windows overlooked the gardens, and upstairs the window of what was my spare bedroom had a view that cleared the hedges and gave out onto the fields and presumably, once the low cloud dissipated, the moors.

My eye caught a fleeting movement at the upstairs window of the next-door cottage. Just a flicker of white shirt below a flutter of hair. Euan McGillan had been standing at his window and had moved out of sight as I'd turned round. Had he been watching me? I'd moved to get away from that. The feeling of being watched, of every movement scrutinised and noted and used against me. That was the whole *point* of this tiny cottage on the top of a hill with nothing around but wind-bleached grass, waving tendrils of bramble and a herd of placidly unaware cattle. I hadn't counted on a next-door neighbour, omnipresent and staring at me with an expression of grating resentment, like a particularly miserable minor god.

I straightened my back. Well, sod him. I had every right to be here, this was my house, my garden and my scrubby little patch of land. I drew my shoulders back a bit further, then realised that this looked as though I was showing off my boobs, and slumped them down a little way. Then I looked down at Brack, who had the wind rippling his fur into red-brown surf. 'Shall we go in or have another walk around?' I asked him, loudly enough to have been heard by anyone who might have been listening in and wondering whether they could drive me under cover by lurking behind half-drawn curtains. I knew as I said it that it was utterly pointless. The windows may have been old, but they were double-glazed and I doubted that Mr McGillan could have heard me anyway, even had he been listening, with the way the wind whipped the words from my mouth and sent them wheeling down the valley. But it made *me* feel better. More in control.

Brack's inscrutable eyes told me he had no opinion either way, so I strode across to the garden gate, as much as one can stride when walking over unevenly humped grass, rutted and pitted with years of over and undergrowth. There was no sign of any more movement from that window. I kept half an eye on it until I'd gone inside but the room beyond the window was just a dark square, like a closed eye.

* * *

I was arranging things on a shelf the next day, wondering how far it was to the nearest artisan, when there was a knock on the door. Brack, curled in front of the log burner, just twitched his tail.

'You could at least bark,' I said to him, futilely. 'Or howl.'

Tail twitch again. I sighed and opened the front door, first quickly checking that there wasn't anything unpleasant obviously in view. Brack had pooed between the bathroom and the kitchen earlier, and I didn't want casual callers to get the opinion that I lived in squalor.

'Hi, I'm Jill Ferry, you wanted me to take a look at making a run?'

The lady standing on the doorstep, trying to shield herself from the wind inside an enormous utility jacket, had short black hair that stood up from the coat's collar like a brush and the kind of weathered face that could be any age from thirty to sixty.

'Blimey, it's a bit whiffy, did a beast get in while the place was empty?' She swung her head back so that the fresh air could take away the smell of fox. 'Nobody's been in to clean since Mrs Watson died, and that's been a good six months.' She sniffed, and I couldn't tell if the sniff was disapproving or just trying to rid her lungs of the smell.

'Er, no, that's my fox. Which is why I want a run built.' I stood back and waved her into the gap between the front door and the only place the sofa would fit, which formed a small enclave before the room proper.

'Oh yes, I see.' Jill caught sight of Brack, who stood up and stretched, then settled back down in front of the log burner, a respectful distance from the flames but close enough to feel the benefit. 'Pet, is it?'

'Not really, and he's not used to being in the house quite this much. He needs to be outside.'

She sniffed again. 'You're telling me.' A practical, and obviously experienced, eye took in the wall I'd tried the grey paint on. It had dried to a somewhat streaky finish because I'd begun to doubt myself before putting a second coat on and now had a heavy-duty military hardware look. 'I see you're experimenting with colour.' She said it in the tone of one who'd had to put right a lot of 'experiments with colour' and couldn't see what was wrong with having everywhere magnolia anyway.

I quite liked her. She had the reassuring air of someone who knows what they are doing, who isn't necessarily going to listen to your view of things but is going to do what needs doing and probably more efficiently and effectively if you just stay out of the way and don't say too much.

'Er, yes,' I said and hustled her into the kitchen before she could give me any advice. A tiny surge of obstinacy made me grit my teeth at the grey-washed wall – maybe it wasn't so bad after all? Maybe I could learn to live with it? It was my choice, after all, if I wanted to coordinate with the *Bismarck*.

We walked around the bramble clump and I explained what I needed. Jill stood with her hands on her hips, at least, I think they were her hips, inside that massive coat it was hard to tell, and nodded.

'Yep, I can do that. Fence this lot in securely, leave the walls, it's basically just a big chicken run you want, with thicker wire.' She kicked at the brambles with her work booted toe. 'Shouldn't take too long, you'll be wanting that fox out of the living room pronto, I should think.'

We turned around to go back to the cottage, and found Euan McGillan standing at the end of his garden, silently pruning the greenery that formed the hedge between our houses. He gave no sign that he'd seen us, but the way he was snipping in a desultory way at the privet made me wonder if he'd come out just to earwig our conversation.

Jill surprised me by waving an arm. 'Hey, Euan!'

There was a moment of suspension, where it looked for a second as though he might try to duck down and hide behind the shrubby hedge, and then he nodded back. 'Hello, Jill.'

'I've known Euan since we were at school together,' Jill said, pulling her neck down into her coat, tortoise-like. Then she raised her voice again. 'How's the loft space holding up?'

'It's good,' he replied, clearly torn between wanting to dive back indoors and the fear that Jill conjured in me that, once she'd started a conversation with you, she would follow you around until she'd finished it, even if that meant tracking you to the toilet and sitting outside the closed door talking until you came out.

'Okay, when you need me to come and sort out putting in a window, give me a shout.'

'I will.' And then the staccato, 'Thanks,' tacked on like prosthetic good manners.

He stood at the hedge-line and watched us walk down the garden. I assume he watched us right in through the kitchen door, but I was not going to turn around to see, it was already getting a bit too incipient horror film for me. I closed the back door firmly, which cut off the wind and concentrated the smell of fox, and offered Jill a cup of tea.

'Why the hell not?' She cheerfully pulled out a chair and sat down, elbows on the kitchen table. 'It's not like I'm rushed off my feet and you seem a little bit... worried?' She ended on the question, looking at me directly out of eyes that were as direct as Brack's. 'You don't need to worry about Euan. He's a perfectly nice guy, just a bit...' She waggled a hand in a sign that could have meant anything from, 'He's normal but quiet, keeps himself to himself' to 'He only dismembers people at weekends, once he's got into his cocktail frock and high heels, and you're all right as long as you remember to call him "Mother".'

'I'm not worried about him,' I said a bit stiffly. 'We've hardly even spoken.'

'Ah, well.' That, also, could have meant anything. 'You just moved in, then?'

I hadn't had anyone I could have called a 'friend' for a long time. Too long. And before I knew it, I found myself pouring out my story, heavily edited, of course. I told her everything – about the desire to move from Cornwall, the finding of this little cottage for sale at the other end of the country and buying it without even looking it over first. I may even have mentioned my intention to do something drastic to the dreadful fireplace, but then I had to say something to explain the marks all round it. I'd found a tyre iron in the back of the car and tried to lever the mantel away from the wall, which hadn't gone well.

'It was a long way to come if you didn't like it,' Jill said. Despite her talking like an oncoming juggernaut, she could listen surprisingly well. She sat and drank her tea in silence, even though I was spilling words at her in an increasingly shrill manner, and she only spoke when I stopped to sip at the Earl Grey I'd made to try to counteract the smell of fox. 'But they're nice cottages, these. His place,' she jerked a head at the wall which separated me from Euan McGillan, 'always had young couples in until he bought it. This one was let out as a holiday home. I did a bit of work in it from time to time, heating, electrics, that sort of thing. The owners were friends of my parents, y'see.'

'I found a picture,' I said suddenly, surprising myself. 'Under the boards by the immersion tank.'

'What the hell were you doing taking up the boards in there?' Jill made an astonished face. 'Put that tank in five years ago, no need for you to be poking back there.'

I couldn't even begin to explain the whole 'stopcock, fork, phone' debacle without having Jill make me feel even more incompetent than I already did, so I just fetched the picture of 'Stella' from where I'd left it under the empty fruit bowl, and showed it to her.

'Funny to think that they had colour cameras back then, isn't it?' Jill mused, turning the picture over and reading the back. 'Seems so long ago.'

'Do you know who she might be? Or why her picture might be under my floorboards?'

Brack wandered in, sniffed Jill's trousered leg and scratched behind his ear. I silently willed him not to choose now to pee.

Jill stared at the photograph again. 'Nope. But I can tell you that picture was taken outside here,' she said. 'Up the end of your garden. That bush, that was a big forsythia. Not so big here, but I took that bloody thing out maybe ten years ago, and it took some doing. That's why I remember it.' She handed me the picture back. 'But other than that, nope.' She looked at me with suddenly sharp eyes, over her mug. 'Why do you want to know who she is?'

I laid the photograph down on the table between us. 'I don't, really. Just curious. Not enough else to do at the moment, I suppose. My job, work, is freelance writing, magazine articles. They send me all the raw material and I turn it into the stuff that goes into the magazine. Beauty of it is that I can do it from anywhere.' I sipped. The acrid sweetness of the bergamot tea suddenly made me feel sick and I put it down again. 'All I really need to do is sensationalise it, and that's not too hard to do. Drop in a few exclamation marks, two mentions of improper nudity and the word "absconded", and that's pretty much it.'

Jill looked around meaningfully at the still rather sparse kitchen, with its wooden work surface, tiled wall and enormous window. 'Pays well then, does it, this magazine lark?'

I felt instantly ashamed, as though I'd deliberately misled her. 'Oh no! Quite dreadfully, really. I...' I swallowed. I could say the words now. I really could. Aloud, into a room with people in. 'My grandmother died and left me some money. Oh, not lottery win life-changing amount, but...' I tailed off. It *had* been a life-changing amount. For me, anyway. 'Enough to buy the cottage,' I finished.

'Ah, that's good. Least I won't have to worry about you paying my bill.' Jill put her mug down. 'Can get a bit lairy when I need to keep sending letters. This table, they left it in the house? Thought I recognised it.'

I relaxed with the change of subject. 'Yes. This table and that enormous chair in the living room – all things that wouldn't fit out through the door, I suppose.'

Jill nodded. 'They'd have to take the windows out, or chainsaw them up, I guess. Easier to leave them. And the Watsons hadn't been in much, not in a long while, they'd probably forgotten they were even here. Solicitors hired a firm to clear the place out before it sold when old Mrs Watson finally went. Think some second cousin inherited and they wanted rid as fast as possible. Like I said, it had been a holiday cottage, rented out for years.'

I looked around at the thick walls, bare wooden floors and piles of stuff that I *still* had to unpack. 'It's in very good condition. They must have looked after it well, considering they never came here.'

Jill grinned. 'That's down to me. Well, me and Mum. She was the caretaker for the place, came in and cleaned between guests, turned any maintenance jobs over to me. It's partly why I took your job on, insatiable curiosity about who'd bought it.' The grin was unabashed and bright, and I liked her even more. 'Plus, I really can't leave well alone. And there's Euan, of course.'

I couldn't imagine anyone being interested in my neighbour for any reason other than making sure you knew where the bodies were buried and being able to provide an up-to-date photofit. 'Are you and he...?' I tried not to look as disbelieving as I felt.

'Oh Lord, no!' Jill pushed her chair back and stood up. For a second, I wanted to apologise in case I'd upset her, but her down-to-earth manner soon reassured me. 'I don't think he does relationships. Well, he did, back in the day, quite the heartbreaker was our Euan, when we were at school. Since he's been back, he's been pretty solitary, dunno what happened there, maybe he broke his willy.' A momentary silence resulted, and I really hoped I hadn't smiled at the possibility that Mr Misery's misery had been caused by erectile disfunction. The oil tanker that was Jill's conversational technique took some steering, but it had finally hit the shores of 'having other things to do'. 'Right. I'll be back tomorrow with some gear to get started. Or maybe the day after, there's a lady in Pickering wants some painting done.'

'You get a lot of work?' I walked through with her to the front door. She could just have gone out of the back, but it seemed more friendly, somehow, to show her out of the front. I made sure to rush her past the fireplace, although I saw her notice the marks in the plaster.

'Oh, yes!' Jill gave me an oblique look. 'It's amazing how many people prefer having a woman knocking around their house with paint tins and screwdrivers.' Another quick look. 'Really amazing.' She flashed me another smile and I noticed the way her dark eyes lit up, and there were dimples. She looked suddenly younger, more mischievous. 'See you tomorrow.'

And she was gone, hurrying down the lane to a battered old van with 'J Ferry – Maintenance' painted on the side. I closed the front door and immediately felt limp and purposeless. 'It's lack of practice, that's what it is,' I said to Brack, who jumped up beside me onto the sofa, pressing a hard little pad against my leg as though in encouragement. 'I need to start talking to people again.'

A cold nose edged under my arm and he nudged it aside until he could creep onto my lap. Strangers unsettled him. I stroked the smooth fur of his head and looked into the fathomless golden eyes. 'Yes, I know I talk to you, but you're not people.' The stare continued, absolutely level and unblinking.

But I kept stroking. It might be true, but he was all I had. A lame fox, a cottage so isolated that it made the middle of nowhere seem like a metropolis and a job writing 'My Mother Ran off with my Husband's Transsexual Triplets' pieces for weekly magazines.

But at least it was something.

5

STELLA, MAY 1973

Andy's hiding pictures of me all over the cottage. I found some yesterday, slipped in the gap under the window ledge in the front room. Not the mucky ones, I think he keeps those to himself. These were pictures he'd taken of me out in the garden. I was sitting out on a blanket in the sun, cos it feels nice and when I'm a bit brown you can't see the bruises so much. I didn't realise he'd been putting them there until I found them. I can't say anything, I know that. Can't even say that I found them, so I put them back, tried to get them exactly the same way as they were so he won't realise. I don't know why he does it. I did ask him last time I saw, when he'd got the camera out when I was doing the washing and he kept telling me to turn round and, 'Stop looking so miserable, your face is longer than that wet washing!' and then he laughed so hard. So I asked him why he was taking pictures all the time. He laughed some more and said it was so he had something to keep to remind him. He said it in a really funny way though, not like he wanted snaps of good times to look back on, it was more like – I don't know. I'm tired and I can't think straight. Then I wondered if he's hiding these for me to find? So I might think that he's put his special pictures around the house too, for anyone to come across? But I know he won't do that, he likes to keep those to himself too much.

We had another row last week. I bought some chocolate with the Wednesday shop, just a couple of bars and some sweeties, so I've got something nice to look forward to. I let myself have a couple every day, when I've got the housework done and I can have five minutes' sit-down before I put the dinner on. Just some Spangles or an Opal Fruit, something that tastes nice. Somehow the inside of my mouth always has this funny taste, I've got a broken tooth and it keeps cutting my cheek, but something sweet takes that taste away for a while. I have to hide the wrappers, of course. I can't put them in the bin or he'd see, so I make them all flat and tuck them in with my ladies' things where I know he won't look. Every few weeks or so, I clear them out and put them on the fire, but in summer when we don't have the fire lit every day I have to slide them away right up under the carpet in the top room. Well, on Wednesday he came home early, just as I was putting the shopping away, and he found the chocolate because I'd put it in the bag with the veg instead of in my handbag like I usually do. It started out small, him telling me I'd get fatter than I already was, and did I want to end up like that lady we sometimes see in town, who has her shopping in a little trolley that she pulls along behind her, and has her ankles all swollen over her shoes. And I was so *stupid* because I tried to laugh and tell him that I only had a little bit every day, just something nice to look forward to, and then I'm down on the floor and he's punching at me and shouting and all I can do is just curl up in the corner between the twin tub and the fridge and wait for it to be over.

I shouldn't make him angry, I know that. If I didn't make him angry, he wouldn't need to hit me. So I try, I really do try. I remember to clean the bathroom every single day and to make sure his clothes are laid out every night for him to put on in the morning. I give him a good breakfast before he goes to work and remember not to mind if he's late home, even if the dinner is spoiled. But there just always seems to be something *else*, some other way I let him down without knowing it. Like I say something, or I look at him funny or I ask him for something in the wrong way. Oh, it's not all the time. Often he will laugh it off, just give me a quick squeeze or a smack on the bum and tell me not to be cheeky or not to get too cocky or something. But it's almost better when he does explode. Because then... then it's like the worst has *happened*. I don't have to wait for it any more. And I know there will be this little bit of calm afterwards, sometimes it's days, sometimes it's weeks, when it's like the tension has all gone out of him and he's just back to being my lovely, kind Andy again.

But then I can feel it coming back, what I call 'the other Andy' in my head. The one who doesn't like the way I've drawn the curtains or what I've made for dinner, or who finds dust on the shelves. The one that has to show me how I've let him down or how I've failed him. Then I get the explosion that's like when a boil bursts and it's all mess and horrid and blood and stuff for a while, but it does feel so much nicer when it's done. Until you feel it starting to come back and then you're all on edge until it bursts again.

It was different this time, though. After he'd finished, he didn't throw me in the bathroom and tell me to stop snivelling and make myself presentable. He kind of shoved this paper at me and told me to get my dad to sign it, otherwise he'd show my parents the photographs – *all* the photographs, and he didn't mean the family snaps, and did I want Mum and Dad to see the kind of daughter they'd brought up? And then he went out and he was gone all night. Well, once I'd heard his car go and I knew he wasn't going to think of something else and come back in and carry on, I got up. I got the bleeding stopped and I put some ice on where I knew the bruises would come up worst and then I looked at the paper he'd given me. He must have gone to a solicitor or something, because it was all legal and full of big words, but I remembered some of them from the typing I used to do for Mr Harris. It was a transfer deed to put the cottage into Andy's name. So it wouldn't belong to Dad any more, but it would all be Andy's.

All I could think was what if they'd all been right all along? What if Andy wanted to sell the cottage? My lovely little cottage! So I'm walking around, just touching things, like the curtains I'd sewn myself and the walls I'd painted and papered myself. And my garden, where I'd just got all the veg coming up and the tomatoes ready to plant out. I looked out of the window, out at where the old house used to be, where it's just some crumbling old walls and a bit of chimney now, and I imagined my house being like that, all tumbled down and abandoned. But maybe Andy wouldn't want to sell? Maybe he just wanted the place in his name because he doesn't want Dad to have the final say in anything we do to it? I know Andy wanted to build a garage, like they've got next door, but Dad said no. I think Dad said it because he knows Andy loves his cars and he'd fill a garage with cars and bikes and things and maybe even start his own business fixing things from home, but I've not seen Mum and Dad in a while to ask why we couldn't have one.

Then I thought of Mum and Dad seeing those pictures. The ones Andy makes me pose for. Where I have to hold my dress up and pull down my drawers and... I don't like to think of the things he makes me do. I think he gets his friend, Seth, to develop those ones, because I sometimes hear him laughing to himself upstairs when he's gone to bed early. He says things like, 'Seth must have *really* liked this one!' and I know it's when he's going through those pictures that he's got locked in the wardrobe. But I don't say I know. I pretend I don't know where they are or what he's *really* doing up there.

So what do I do? Ask Dad to sign the papers? Or wait for Andy to bring out the pictures, maybe one day when they've come over for tea? Not that they come much any more, but they would if I asked them.

Now I just don't know what to do.

6

I didn't want Jill to turn up the next day and find me exactly as she'd left me, so I spent the rest of the daylight hours unpacking, hanging pictures, shaking out rugs across the floors – everywhere except where Brack was likely to pee – and generally trying to make the little house look lived in. I hacked a bit more at the fireplace, and then stuck a dust sheet up over it to hide the amateur nature of my assault. It was proving more resistant than I would have thought possible, and several of the surrounding tiles had cracked and split. Plaster was coming away in lumps. I couldn't work out why the plaster came off but the fireplace didn't. I'd get round to doing something about it later, I told myself, then went to try to tidy away some of the spare boxes of stuff that had come with me from Cornwall.

The loft was an almost-bedroom. It had stairs going up to it, which went up from just outside my bedroom door and made negotiating the landing in the middle of the night a bit hair-raising, and the ceiling was so low under the eaves that I had to crouch. But it was a room, somewhere to store all those boxes that just wouldn't fit anywhere else. *Why* had I brought so much stuff?

It wasn't even as if the house had looked big in the estate agent's brochure. How had I ever imagined there would be room for my rattan armchair, my seven bookcases and the assorted collection of lampshades, rugs, spare bedding and all the other stuff that I'd packed onto the lorry in such desperation to get away?

I humped another box that I knew was never going to be unpacked up into the roof space. There were a few things left up here as well, which led me to believe it had been advertised as a third bedroom when the house had been a holiday cottage. A balled-up pair of socks with dinosaurs on had been overlooked and were gathering fluff in a far corner. A bright yellow plastic yo-yo and an unwritten postcard showing Whitby Abbey were sitting on one of the big beams, half-hidden. I picked them up and tucked them away in one of the open boxes, which held a life-time's worth of tea towels and pillowcases.

From downstairs, Brack, who'd been confined to the bath-room while I moved stuff, started yipping, so I pushed the pile of boxes deep under the eaves. As I slid the pile, the carpet rucked up where it had come loose and I had to move all the boxes back out to get it to lie flat again. Then I stopped. Under the carpet, perfectly flat as though they'd lain there unnoticed all this time, were sweet wrappers. At least, I thought that's what they were. I crawled into the space and pulled them out, tucking the carpet back as I went, and pushing the boxes back in after me.

Yes, now I could see them properly, they *were* sweet wrappers. Old sweets, things I'd never heard of like Ice Breaker and Span-gles, and an orange packet of something called Bar Six. I made a face at them. They'd obviously been there for years, tucked down under the carpet underlay, which was fragmenting with age. Someone who'd slept up here and couldn't be bothered to make the long trek downstairs to the bin, probably. A child, eating sweets in bed, illicitly, whilst on holiday, maybe.

But these were *old* old. How long had the place been a holiday cottage? I'd never seen these sweets anywhere in a shop. What the hell was a Bar Six, anyway? The back of the wrapper told me it was a delicious hazelnut cream in crunchy wafer, covered in chocolate. And was, apparently, 4p. I couldn't remember the last time 4p had even been a thing, let alone when you'd been able to get an entire bar of chocolate for it.

The thought of hazelnut cream and chocolate made me hungry. A look at my phone told me that it was the middle of the afternoon, which would account for the way the sun had moved away from the front of the cottage and was now sliding in through the windows at the back. I went down from the loft, easing my back, and looked out of the landing window, over the gardens. Euan McGillan was standing, facing away from the houses, halfway down his own garden path. Just standing. I mean, at least he wasn't staring *in*, which would have been uncomfortable, but there was something about his back view, facing out across the field of cattle, that was worse than disconcerting. Because I couldn't see his face, and therefore expression, I had no way of judging his mood or intention. There was nothing that gave away any hint of how he was feeling or what he was doing. No rigidity of shoulder or tension of arm, but equally he didn't look as though he was about to spread a picnic blanket and stretch out to relax.

He was wearing only a shirt and jeans. No jumper, no jacket. Although the sun was gaining in warmth every day, there was a wind that came from nowhere, swirled around us on our little hill so its direction seemed always indeterminate, and it held the memory of winter on its edges. Why hadn't he at least put on a jacket? He was barefoot, too, I noticed, feet spread in the grass of his lawn. He looked as though he had grown there. There was something elemental in his half-clad, shoeless form, as though he was deriving nourishment from the air. Either that, or he lived on Pot Noodles and toast, because there was definitely a lanky vibe about him.

What the hell was he *looking* at? The tiny fenced and hedged block of land that was our gardens? Or further out, into the field, where the brown and white cattle grazed, some rooks swirled aimlessly overhead, and a large tree was beginning to show the very faintest wash of green against the pale blue sky? Maybe he had his eyes shut? Maybe this was some branch of Oriental mysticism or meditation, requiring standing very still and fighting off hypothermia with nothing but the power of the mind and inadequate clothing?

From his bathroom prison, Brack yipped again. He needed exercise, he needed stimulation. I was going to have to put him in his harness and take him out down the lane. I would have taken him for another exploration of his new intended home, but I couldn't face the thought of having to walk past the stationary figure in the garden. I had no idea whether I should ignore Euan, call a cheery greeting or ask him what he was doing, and the thought of any of those things made my hair prickle. So I opted for the coward's way out and we crept out of the front door and, with Brack tugging at the extent of his lead and flying into hedges, we walked away from the cottages, away from the road and out into the open countryside that lay beyond.

That was when I finally found the view of the moors that I'd been promised. The rise of the hill beyond the cottages meant that I hadn't been able to see it. It would only be visible from my house if I'd either stood on the roof or drilled a hole through the side wall. But it was there. Slow, lumbering shapes against the skyline, which made me feel slightly claustrophobic, as though the land was trying to rise up and take over the sky.

I turned around so I didn't have to look, and there were the cottages, there was the muddy, unpaved lane and, further down the hill, the grey line of the road into town. And there, still standing motionless as though someone had removed his battery, was Euan McGillan. Sideways on now that I'd walked up here, I could see that he had something in his hands, held at chest level, like he was making notes. What on earth was he *doing*?

Now I was torn. Between the unholy bulk of the moorland on the horizon and the man doing God only knew what in his garden, I felt trapped. As though nothing was safe, not outdoors, not my house. As though this was nature's way of telling me to pack up and go back to Cornwall. Back to the house on the hill in Truro with traffic and seagulls and tourists and shops that sold more than one kind of cheese.

Brack sat down and scratched his ear vigorously with his remaining hind leg. The sight of his stump, where he should have had an elegant black limb, brought me back from the cycle of thoughts. I'd left Cornwall behind for a reason. Well, several reasons, really, but home was here now. And if my neighbour was a loner who actively courted frostbite and the scenery was openly hostile, well, I'd just have to put up with it, wouldn't I? Going back was not an option.

No. Going back was *never* an option.

* * *

Jill arrived cheerfully early the next morning. And while she may have been cheerful, I was still half asleep and hunched over the kitchen table with a mug of hot tea and my dressing gown, providing Brack with edges to chew.

'Thought I'd make a good start today in case I can't come over for a while,' Jill announced, as I watched her pull materials from her van. 'It's fine, I can go around the side, no need for me to disturb you.'

She was wearing overalls that looked so robust that they would never wear out and were probably handed down from generation to generation, and enormous gloves. She looked – I couldn't quite put my finger on it, but something about her made me feel inadequate. I caught myself thinking this and laughed into my mug in a hollow kind of way. *Everything* made me feel inadequate these days. A three-legged fox made me feel inade-quate. The way the tap dripped after being turned off made me feel inadequate.

I watched Jill make her way over the uneven grass to the bramble-strewn hump that was going to be Brack's new home. Safely enclosed, so he couldn't dig his way out and starve to death in the hills or be shot. Brack had never shown any desire to become a free fox. His only hope for continued survival was, basi-cally, me, but I didn't underestimate the power of the mating urge should a vixen with an alluring smile and a wanton walk come by, and Brack in the wild would have all the survival ability of a sugar lump in a rainstorm.

He was domesticated by default, so it was my job to look after him. Which meant paying Jill to eliminate brambles and turn those ruins into a serviceable enclosure. I sipped at my tea and felt inadequate again. I *could* have cleared the ground myself. I *could* have bought in the wood and wire and concrete and nails. But I hadn't bought any equipment for eliminating undergrowth; no shears or wire cutters or hammers or saws. Nothing useful. Just a lot of paint I wasn't sure about now. I *could* go back into town and stock up on tin snips and pliers and all that. I'd spent so much last time that the local shopkeepers would probably throw a party next time I drove in. I was single-handedly keeping several DIY shops in business down there. But I didn't know what to ask for, or what I'd need. Jill was here, she was capable. I'd just sit here with my mug and my houseful of tea towels and rubbish, I thought, as my eye settled on the historic chocolate wrappers that I'd brought down from the loft and had yet to hurl into the bin. Why did I find it so hard to discard rubbish? Because it meant the past was *really* the past, and I couldn't come to terms with that yet?

Too philosophical for this time in the morning. Even the DJ, when I turned the radio on, hadn't got cheerful yet. The sun, which dawned at the front of the cottage and then crept its way overhead to plummet at sunset behind the gardens, was barely even illuminating the dust on the window ledge in the living room. On the plus side, this gave me hours to get on with straightening the house and maybe to fire up my laptop and do some work. But the minus side held a lot more appeal, so I stayed sitting at the table and just made myself another cup of tea. I made one for Jill too.

'Wow, you've got so much done!' I gave my inadequacy a voice when I went outside. 'I haven't even got dressed yet.'

Jill took the mug. 'Like I said, I never know when a really urgent job is going to crop up that means I'd have to down tools here and go to Thornton or Appleton to deal with an old lady's leaky boiler.' She sipped rapidly, like one of those drinking bird toys. 'So I like to get a lot done, when I can.'

I looked at the site, where the walls were clearly visible now. A smouldering pile of thorny branches was refusing to burn with any alacrity at the edge of the enclosure, and there was lots of turned earth and alarming looking equipment scattered about. 'You can see the outline of the old house now.'

'Mmmm.' Jill pulled a face. 'It's been a ruin for over half a century. Farm went out of business, no one to take over. They sold off the land, let the house fall down and converted the cottages into proper houses. You know, put in a bathroom and took out the pigsty.' She grinned at me over the mug. 'We took a while to grasp that civilisation wasn't a flash in the pan up here.'

'And my house was a holiday cottage for about forty years. Doesn't leave a lot of time for it to have been a family home.' I looked back over my shoulder at the cottage. There was no sign of my robotic neighbour.

'I'll have to ask Mum who used to live there.' Jill drained her mug and handed it to me. 'She's lived round here all her life, she'll know.'

I thought about that photograph. Those old sweet wrappers. 'It would be nice to know. The deeds just say Mr and Mrs Watson, who owned it while it was a holiday cottage. They don't give any names further back.'

'I'll ask her, but you'll have to remind me.' Jill took a deep breath. 'Right. Better get on. You don't want that fox in your house longer than you have to, shouldn't think.'

I thought of Brack, whom I'd left happily eating something under the kitchen table. 'No,' I agreed with her, although the thought of being completely alone in the cottage made me feel a little ambivalent. He might be smelly, and look at me as though he was trying to work out the best method of going for my throat, but he was company. And then, with more certainty. 'No. He needs to be outside.'

I went in to get dressed, because I was starting to feel rather exposed in my flannelette pyjamas and fleecy dressing gown. And lazy. I should *do* something. So I showered and dressed, flicked through my laptop and wrote a few notes. I peered under the dust sheet, in case the scars I'd put in the fireplace wall had mysteriously healed up overnight, and stared at the streaky grey paint. It didn't look a lot better in full sunlight. Then I tidied the kitchen in a desultory way, with no real commitment, and stared into the fridge. I needed to order a food delivery, so that took me another hour, by which time the pile of burning undergrowth in the garden was sending a plume of sullen smoke skywards, as though signalling to the gods. Jill was perched on the resident brickwork with a packet of sandwiches when I looked out of the kitchen window, and she had her head up as though she was watching something a long way away. Then, when I looked to my left, I saw that she was talking to Euan McGillan, who was pressed against the furthest extent of his garden, earnestly discussing something with Jill. I could see his mouth moving and his hands waving as though he were laying out an imaginary banquet, and Jill nodding and occasionally checking on the progress of the burning heap.

I felt like an absolute outsider. Which I was, of course. But, hells, this was *my* garden, *my* patch of burning bramble. I longed to stop feeling like an onlooker, an observer of my own life. I closed the laptop and, seizing a packet of biscuits to give myself an excuse I knew I didn't really need, I went outside.

They stopped talking at once. Well, Euan did. He went instantly silent as though my presence was the blanket over the budgie cage of his existence. Jill stood up and began to pack the remnants of her lunch into the Tupperware box on the top of the now completely exposed wall. 'Getting there,' she said cheerfully. 'Should be able to start putting the run together tomorrow.'

'Little old ladies' boilers permitting,' I said, carefully taking no notice of my neighbour at his garden fence.

She laughed and my breath caught for a second. It was so long since I'd made someone laugh that I had to do a quick mental check to make sure she was laughing because I'd said something amusing, rather than laughing *at* me. 'Well, nobody's rung me yet. So tomorrow's looking good.' She raised her head and threw a meaningful glance across at my frozen neighbour. 'Tomorrow, Euan?'

He made a noise that could have been anything from assent to an impersonation of someone trying to start a lawn mower, and then turned to walk off indoors again. When his back door closed, I said, 'Is he always like that?'

Jill laughed again. 'He's having trouble adjusting to someone being next door on a permanent basis. Holiday makers came and went, and your place was often empty for weeks at a time. He's just not used to you yet.'

'I'm not going to have to sit outside very quietly for hours holding out a bar of chocolate, am I?'

She laughed again, a proper, amused laugh. 'Well, there's a thought!' She packed her lunchbox away into the robust bag she'd arrived with. 'How did you get the fox used to you being around?'

I opened the biscuit packet and held it out. 'I didn't need to. When I got to him, he was so badly injured that he couldn't object, and then, when the vet had finished with him, I was the one with the food. It wasn't really difficult, he was so young.'

Jill took a biscuit and looked across at the other cottage. 'Yeah, Euan's a bit harder than that. Although I know a local vet who'll do you a great deal on tranquillisers, if you need them.'

'For Euan or the fox?'

I'd forgotten I could be funny. Forgotten what it was like to say whatever was uppermost in my head without second guessing and editing myself. But it was coming back. It gave me hope that the inadequacy wasn't going to last forever, too. 'Either. Both.' Jill dunked a biscuit in the coffee she'd poured from a flask. 'Although I shouldn't say either of them are given to uproarious parties or all-night drumming sessions.'

'Well. Brack is shut in the bathroom. Euan is – actually, he's completely and suspiciously silent at night.'

Jill refused to be drawn into speculation, which made me like her even more. She ate her biscuit, then stood up and arched her back. 'Right. Just got to clear this end here...' She waved a gloved hand at the tall wall, where the internal brickwork flickered flags of torn wallpaper and dusty traces of paintwork. There seemed something 'wrong' in seeing the inner parts of a house exposed to the elements, like a person walking around with their internal organs on show.

I took the biscuits and went back inside. Brack needed exercise and I wanted to walk up to the top of the hill again, to check that the moors weren't creeping incrementally closer, like a giant geographical game of Grandmother's Footsteps. I'd just got my boots on and was searching for Brack's harness when Jill came to the back door and tapped.

'I've just found something,' she said. 'And as it's on your land, you ought to decide what to do with it.'

'Is it treasure?'

'No. Cos if it was, it wouldn't be you that gets to decide. I know all about treasure trove and all that, never fear.' Jill stayed on the doorstep while I put my coat on. Her work boots were coated in mud and her dark hair had fallen from its spiked-up style to lie flat on her head. She looked like a depressed hedgehog.

'It's not an old fireplace, is it?' I asked cautiously. I was beginning to get a complex about the state of my wall, in which the dust sheet was flapping in the breeze down the chimney, like a tiny haunting.

'No. And don't think I haven't seen what you're up to in that living room.' There was a tone of amused pity in Jill's voice now. The tone of someone who is very, very good at doing something, watching an amateur trying to copy them with no tools and an insufficient understanding of the mechanics. A bit like the judges on *Strictly*.

'So, what is it?' I followed her along the garden and then out into the paddock, where the bramble heap smelled like autumn; a mound of fire-blackened stems and detritus, still giving off a greenish smoke.

'Here.' Jill reached over the low wall into what had been the building. 'Found it when I cleared the last patch, shoved into what would have been the old bread oven.' She pulled a small plastic suitcase onto the top of the wall. It had once been brown, an imitation of a leather case, but now the plastic covering was peeling off, showing the cardboard underneath. 'It's full of clothes.'

I thought of the pile of old sweet wrappers from my loft. 'Does nobody throw things away around here? It's like Yorkshire is entirely occupied by pack rats and hoarders.'

'Ah, you've met my mother,' Jill said cheerfully, tipping the contents of the case onto the grass. 'No idea what they were doing there. But some of them are still good.' She held up a faded yellow thing that had sleeves and was, presumably, a blouse. It was otherwise shapeless, and the material had rotted into tatters, so it looked as though the wearer had been the victim of a particularly vicious slasher. 'Looks handmade.'

I bent down and poked the heap of fabric with my finger. Fold marks and mildew and the general damp from being hidden in the wall of a house had made a lot of it unrecognisable, but one or two of the garments had maintained their structural integrity. There was, mixed in with the clothing, a small shoulder bag of suede squares stitched together in a patchwork, and a floppy brimmed hat in lurid pink.

'I'm not surprised someone hid them, though,' Jill went on. 'They're a bit garish. I'd have burned them and then buried the ashes, although some of the colours are probably seared onto my retina for good now. What is it?'

I'd seen something. Underneath the pile, a scrap of... I pulled it free. 'This. This looks like the skirt that the girl in that photo is wearing.' Filthy, tattered in places almost into lace, but those unmistakeable brown circles were still visible.

'The one you showed me yesterday, taken in your garden?' Jill looked dubious. 'Well, it could be, I suppose. But you can't tell whether that's a skirt or not, it could just be left over fabric from *making* a skirt. Or curtains. Or cushion covers. Although, if anyone tried to bring that into my house, I'd have to shoot them.'

'Why would anyone hide their clothes?' I straightened up, bringing the circle-patterned stuff with me. It smelled of earth and mould. 'There isn't a body in there, is there?'

Jill pulled a face. 'No. No room, the bread oven's pretty small. Probably someone whose mother, very sensibly, wouldn't let her wear anything like this, so she'd hide it and change for an evening out. It's making my eyeballs wobble. You wouldn't need disco lights if everyone was wearing stuff like this, you'd bring your own strobe effect.' She put a hand on my shoulder. 'It's all right, Tamzin. There's nothing sinister about it. She probably either forgot they were there or grew out of them and didn't know what to do with them, so she just left them there.'

'I think her name was Stella,' I said. 'If it was the girl in the photograph.'

'Everyone was wearing this kind of thing back then, though.' Jill began putting all the scrappy bits back into the mildewy confines of the suitcase. 'Clothes like this were ubiquitous. It's a wonder the human race didn't die out. Or go blind.'

'True.' Then I looked over my shoulder at the two cottages. There was no sign of Euan for a change, although there was a light on upstairs. 'But it's not exactly densely populated around here, is it?'

'My mum was one of eight, in a three-room cottage like this.' Jill handed me the case by its peeling plastic handle. I felt oddly reluctant to take it. 'Two families living up here, there could have been loads of people.'

'It was only the 1970s, not the 1500s,' I pointed out. 'I'm fairly sure that even North Yorkshire had contraception back then.'

'Maybe.' Jill knocked mud off her boots against the wall. 'I don't think Grandma would have had any truck with nonsense like that, though. Hence Mum being one of eight. But then, she was born in 1960, so they were still washing at the pump and ploughing the fields with their teeth.'

Another grin flashed my way. She was teasing me, I realised, with a sudden hot flash of not knowing what to say. I *knew* she was joking, nobody grew up in the sixties like that. Or did they? I was afraid to smile back, just in case she would then round on me and ask me what I was grinning at, didn't I *know* how hard times had been for people? Then I took a deep breath. That was then. This was now. Jill wasn't... Jill wasn't like that.

I smiled back.

The world didn't end. Jill just bent back to the wall, pulling away stems of ivy that had clambered up the brickwork like adventurous stevedores, her gloves making squeaky, slipping noises against the sappy stalks. The air smelled suddenly bitter, the scent of broken ivy branches mingling with the sweetness of the burning brambles. There was nothing to be gained by staying, and Brack still needed to go out, so I picked up the sagging cardboard case and went back inside.

The fox was skulking through the rooms, looking for something else to eat, but he came over happily enough to have his harness strapped on, and then took off out of the front door to sniff extravagantly down the front path and along the lane. He pressed his little burned raisin of a nose to the ground, ears flickering, coming up with a vole and then something indeterminate but crunchy, while I just wandered along slowly behind him, admiring the way the sun gleamed along his red back, highlighted his white cheeks and gave his black socks a golden auburn tinge. His half-hop, half stride method of locomotion was so familiar to me that I hardly even noticed it was unnatural now. Brack was a red streak, an astringent smell and a truncated lope, which was why it was sometimes nice to get him outside and really look at the way his rough waterproof guard coat feathered at the edges or how small his paws were.

He needed to go to an animal rescue centre. One where he could meet other foxes, form a pair bond. He'd never live wild, he was too damaged and too domesticated, but he should be somewhere he could have a proper range, a space to call his own. A mate. Kits. The unnaturalness of the way he lived now was my constant dichotomy – keeping him safe meant keeping him pet-like.

The path up to the top of the hill wasn't familiar enough for me to walk it without thinking yet. Brack had to stop and scent mark every few metres too, zigzagging his way across the grass that edged the muddy lane as though on a mission. We wound up, over the gritty surface pocked with shallow puddles out of which Brack would lap occasionally, then on to where the lane ended in a gate to a tractor-etched path across open fields, hedged on one side but rough grazing on the other. I leaned on the gate and looked over the valley at that threatening blue ridge of moorland humped on the horizon like a dead whale.

'We're all right here, aren't we?' I asked the fox. 'Lots of space.'

He sat at my feet in the sun, flicking his ears, eyes narrowed against the light so it looked as though he were smiling, his white markings seemed newly painted on in the brightness.

'Nicer than the city, anyway,' I continued my monologue. 'More space for you.' The fox maintained his enigmatic silence and I sighed. 'You're not much of a conversationalist, are you?'

'He's a fox.' The voice came from behind the hedge and made me jump. Brack whipped around, grekking his warning aggressive sound, and then hid behind me, as Euan McGillan stretched himself up from where he'd been hidden, crouched under the hedge in the field alongside the track.

'It was a rhetorical question!' The words held the snap of adrenaline. 'Are you hiding?'

A couple of dark blinks. He was wearing an old green coat that was battered into shape around him, hair awry in the wind, and stubble that looked as though he'd thought about having a shave but got bored halfway through. 'Yes,' he said, and then ducked back down behind the hedge again. I could just see, between the blackthorn buds and the close entwined branches, his coated shoulder, long legs in sturdy dark trousers and underneath it all mud-encrusted walking boots, as they moved off further up the hill, still crouched.

'That's weird, you know,' I half-called after him, not sure if I wanted him to hear or not. Brack emerged from the shelter of my legs, still in his defensive stance. Now he was a fully grown adult fox, he'd lost the cute, friendly-to-everyone behaviour and gone full on 'I am terrified but will defend you to the death, although it may be from several miles away' mix of aggression and fearfulness that I was still getting used to.

We headed back down the lane. I didn't want to go any further and run the risk of walking into my peculiarly postured neighbour and his inadequate concealment techniques. Why the hell was he running around field boundaries crouched double?

The thought that he'd been stalking me crossed my mind briefly. Had he been behind us all the way up the track? Watching? But then I remembered Brack. If an unknown person had been moving anywhere near us, he wouldn't have hunted voles in such a relaxed way. He couldn't scent as well as a dog, but he'd have noticed movement, or picked up on Euan's presence in his uniquely foxy way, and he would at least have stopped to look and listen. Sometimes fearfulness was useful. Sometimes being afraid was what kept you safe.

So, no, Euan McGillan hadn't followed us. He must have been up there already, then. Hiding. In a hedge. I wasn't sure if it was weirder to imagine that he had just been lurking aimlessly around in the undergrowth or that he had been hiding from me. Either alternative was peculiar behaviour, and if you added it to his penchant for standing motionless in his garden, or lurking around behind windows, he was giving off vibes of someone who might need to be given a very wide berth. Possibly Cornwall wouldn't be far enough.

Jill had packed up and gone when I got back. There was a note shoved under the back door that said: *Should be over tomorrow. Gone to get wood.* I stood and looked at the smoking remains of the bramble bonfire, then glanced up the hill to where I'd had my encounter with the Incredible Crouching Man.

Then I double locked both doors and went to do some work.

7

STELLA, JANUARY 1973

I don't know what happened. I mean, I know it was my fault, of course it was, and I must have said something, but I don't know what. And now it's so hard to make sense of what I'm thinking and my head hurts but I *need* to know what I did so I don't do it again, because... because I was afraid today. Afraid of Andy. Afraid of my own *husband*, and that's not right, is it?

My monthly was late. Not very late, but I'm always regular, 'like that old clock, you are,' my mum used to say, and I'd get all embarrassed that she knew, but she always did. And I knew it should be on Tuesday because I'd been counting on the calendar. And nothing happened. Or on Wednesday, when I had to be careful because it's the day I go in on the bus and get the shopping and I wanted to get something nice to put in the ice box. Andy bought this new refrigerator, and it's got this little bit at the top you can put a block of ice cream or something in, and he likes his ice creams, does Andy. I thought, well, I know it's winter but it might be nice for his dessert one day, to surprise him. Cos he likes it when I do something nice for him, and then he's all kind to me and we snuggle up and watch TV like we used to and he doesn't go down the pub with the lads. But then, I didn't want him getting *too* snuggly and wanting to do... *that thing* again, not if I'm expecting. Until the doctor says, then I have to think of the baby. And I didn't want my monthly to come when I was on the bus or anything, but it didn't, so that was all right.

But all the worrying about whether it would come got mixed up with the excitement of what if it *didn't* and I was going to have a baby, and I forgot to get quite a lot of stuff, even though Andy made me a list. I forgot to get that marge he likes in his sandwiches – even though I think butter is better and the marge tastes all greasy and it's like pretend butter – he says it's what he's always had and he's not going to change because I want to be all 'posh'. So I forgot that, and I forgot to ask the butcher for some suet, which I said I'd do because Andy fancied some dumplings in his stew. I was just walking back to the bus stop when who should come along but Dawn, and her with that Michael that got a walloping off his dad that time he tried to look up my dress when I was on the swings. I said hello and she said hello and I was so happy to talk to someone that I just started chatting and chatting and she was dead friendly, which I wasn't expecting. She said that she and the girls had missed seeing me around and why didn't I come down to her mum's next Wednesday week, cos she was having a Tupperware party and it would be a right laugh! So I said I'd ask Andy and see what he said, and she and that Michael sort of looked at one another, like I'd done something wrong by saying that. She started to ask me what it was like up at the cottage when I heard a car pull up beside us. I looked, and they looked, and it was Andy!

He told me to get in the car. And he had that face on again. I saw Dawn look a bit worried then, and I wanted to show that I wasn't worried, even though I was, a bit, because I knew she's a terrible gossip and she'd have it all round Kirkby before breakfast that my marriage was in trouble. I didn't want Mum and Dad getting to hear that, not from her who's going with a lad who likes looking at girls' knickers. So I just pretended that we'd already agreed to meet and I said something like, 'Oh yes, I forgot you were giving me a lift home, I'm all scatter-brained today,' and I got in the car with my parcels and my bag. And *then* I remembered that I'd forgotten the marge and the suet, but by then it was too late, and we were driving.

Andy was really quiet all the way back. All I could think was that he was going to be really cross when he found out I'd forgotten the marge and the suet, and I was trying to work out how I could get the bus back to town and buy them without him finding out. So neither of us spoke until we got back. There's nobody living next door now, since old Mrs Dawson died. I suppose someone must have inherited it, but I don't see anyone to ask, so it's really quiet and I knew I had to get in and light the fire and get the dinner on. I went to get out of the car and Andy just said, 'How long have you been seeing him?' And I was feeling a bit guilty about planning to sneak back into town to get the suet and so I wasn't really listening and my mind went all blank. So I just said, 'Seeing who?'

I don't really remember what happened next. It's all a blur. I saw him pull his arm back and then my face was numb and I could see my nose was bleeding all over the dashboard. That's when Andy dragged me out of the car, and he was shouting about me meeting up with other men and he'd seen the way I was looking at Michael and did I think he was stupid? And I was trying to stop my nose bleeding and my parcels were falling all over the garden and he's dragging me, pulling me into the house by my clothes and my hair, and then he sort of threw me on the floor just inside the front door.

I know it got dark and he was still going on. When I tried to get up, he'd half-push and half-punch me back down. The floor was really cold, the whole cottage was really cold, I needed to light the fire and I kept trying to tell him that I just wanted to cook dinner and get the place warm. I was worried about getting blood on the new settee cover cos I knew I'd never get it out properly. So I curled up, to try to keep warm, and he was going on and on and about all these lads he thought I was seeing when his back was turned and how I was such a bad wife and the place was never clean because I was too busy – well, doing things with all these other people. He was swearing and shouting and using language like I only ever heard from the local boys when they were drunk and they knew their dads couldn't hear. Some stuff I didn't even *understand*. I got colder and colder, but my nose stopped bleeding, and it was like I didn't know him any more. He was like another person, some stranger just walking around and shouting and sometimes he'd bend down and shout right in my ear, like he thought I couldn't hear him. Every time I started to say something, to try to tell him he'd got it wrong, Michael was with Dawn and I never saw *anyone*, let alone other lads, and that I did my best in the house... he'd start shouting louder and hitting the walls.

Then he just – stopped. I heard his feet walk away and he was gone a couple of minutes. Then he came back and threw something at me and it was cold and wet and he told me to get up and clean myself up, I was a disgrace lying there all filthy. He'd given me a tea towel, one of the good ones. So I sat up a bit, but I wasn't sure he wasn't going to push me back down so I did it slowly, and wiped at my face. Andy just sat down on the sofa, he put the telly on and then he asked me, in his usual voice, what's for dinner?

Like I'm not lying on the floor all bloody and freezing, like I'm already in the kitchen. I didn't know what to do. I'd been crying, and my head was aching, and there's blood all on my good blouse that I'd put on specially to go shopping, and in my hair. But he's talking to me again, not shouting, and he sounds – normal again.

So I just got up and went into the kitchen and turned on the stove. I cleaned my face up as well as I could while I fried him up some bacon and eggs and went back to pick up all the shopping that was dropped and spread all over the living room floor. Andy was just sitting there, watching *Screen Test* and shouting out the answers with his feet up on the settee, even though I've asked him not to put his boots on the new covers. But I'm not going to say anything now, am I? The ice cream had melted into a big sticky patch, and I had to scrub it up. I was crying while I was doing it because I'd wanted it to be a surprise and it was all spoiled now, so I'm scrubbing and trying to keep an eye on his dinner and he's sitting there laughing at Michael Rodd on the telly like any other Wednesday night.

Then Andy saw what I was doing. He came over and I pulled away a bit cos I thought he was going to hit me again. But he was so *nice*! He lifted me up and he laid me down on the sofa and he said not to worry about the cleaning up, it could wait until the morning. He dished up his own dinner and he sat and ate it while he stroked my hair and said I didn't have to worry about anything, it would all be all right.

And now... now I don't know. Am I really such a bad wife? I mean, he had it all wrong about me and Michael, of course, but maybe I *did* chat to him for too long. Maybe I *was* looking at him too much. I didn't mean to, but I can see how Andy might think there was something funny going on. And I know I don't always keep the house as clean as I could, spiders just seem to come from nowhere and even though I seem to be dusting all the time, there's always more dust!

Worst thing of all, my monthly arrived. Late that night, when we were in bed, I felt the cramps start. I went downstairs and sorted myself out, and all the time it felt like a little disappointment, just one more way I'm not being a good wife. I can't even give Andy that son he wants.

8

I was more prepared the next morning. When Jill turned up, I'd already boiled the kettle and dug out some more biscuits. I was dressed in outdoor work clothes and I'd tied my hair back. I had printed off a basic run design too, to give us something to work from and I'd raked the ashy remains of the bramble bonfire off into the grass.

I thought, watching Jill park her van in the lane and wave a cheery greeting at me through the window, today was a good day. There would be more todays in the future.

Brack peed against the door, and my feelings of control collapsed a little under the weight of the mop bucket. Once he was outside, I could start to decorate properly and make the little house more mine, I thought, spraying the door frame with disinfectant and hoping that I'd got there before the wee had soaked into the wood. No point in painting anything else yet, whilst I still had an animal with urine like hydrochloric acid scented with cesspit. But it was nice to be planning and having ideas. Maybe I could have a rethink about colours, paint over the grey wall and hire Jill to decorate? No point in trying to do it myself, when I had all the manual dexterity of a hippo with its feet tied together and the colour sense of someone who's read one too many interior decoration magazines.

Cautiously, I opened the back door to let Brack out. Hopefully he'd peed enough around the garden that he'd know it as his territory now and wouldn't decide to use the new freedom to go streaking off over the hills. He hadn't had his breakfast yet and knew very well where I kept his food, so he was unlikely to make a break for freedom. He was rolling on his back in the sun when I followed him out.

'I thought I could give you a hand today.' I indicated my unflattering but practical clothing. 'Here's a rough idea of how I want the run to look.'

Jill gave me an appraising sideways glance as she carried another armful of wood around the side of the cottage and up towards the old walls. 'That's good,' she said. There was a weight behind her words, and I wasn't sure what it meant. 'It'll be easier with two. If you were working, I was going to give my ex-husband a ring and get him out to be a spare pair of hands.'

This unlooked for and unasked confidence startled me and I wasn't sure why. Because I hadn't even thought about Jill having a life outside her availability for me? The realisation of my selfishness made my neck prickle. 'You've got an ex-husband?' I asked, rather feebly.

'Oh, yes. Sy.' Jill stood long pieces of wood on end up against the brickwork. 'Been divorced, what, ten years now? Can't live with him, not allowed to kill him, besides, he's my girls' dad and he might be an idiot, but he comes in useful.'

'How old are your girls?' I'd got this now. Got into the swing of the question-and-answer format. As long as she didn't turn it round on me, I'd be all right.

'Fifteen and seventeen. Ariadne and Seph.' She puffed a bit, swinging more wood across the paddock. 'Persephone. Sy's idea. Luckily, the girls take after me.' The planks clattered down. 'Never written poetry in their lives.' Then she straightened up and squinted off behind me. 'And there's Euan.'

'Oh, what's he doing?' I didn't turn round. 'He's not just – standing there again, is he? He was creeping around in the hedge yesterday. He's very strange.'

'Goes with the territory,' came the voice over my shoulder.

'I actually meant he's literally *here*.' Jill sounded amused. 'Come to give a hand, Euan?'

'Yesterday you said I should come over and talk to—' he stopped.

'Tamzin,' supplied Jill.

'Yes. About the fox.' Euan stopped being behind me and slunk around into my field of vision, like Brack tracking a mouse. He had the shapeless green coat on again but he looked a bit less muddy than yesterday and his feet were, again, bare. I wondered if he was under supervised release or something. He sat down on a bit of newly uncovered wall, not seeming to notice his under-shod feet, even though both Jill and I were wearing boots.

'You ask then, I'm off to the van for another load.'

I widened my eyes at Jill, asking her, without daring to put it into words, not to leave me alone with this incredibly strange man. I'd already backed up a few steps to put some distance between me and him.

'I'll be two seconds,' she said. 'It's all right.'

I didn't know who she was supposed to be reassuring.

Euan leaned back and picked at the ivy that remained on the lowest level of the wall. I looked out over the field. I didn't want to meet his eye, I was scared that my feelings would show. *Never let them know you are afraid.*

'I'd like to borrow the fox.' It came out on one breath, as

though he were nervous. The nervousness was oddly reassuring, as though there was only room for one person to be anxious in any given conversational exchange, and if it were him then I was excused anxiety.

'What for?' My eyes swivelled around to look at him properly now. 'Not something bad.'

He blinked again, that odd, slow blink that I'd noticed yesterday. As though he was processing my words and could only do it with his eyes closed. *Robot*, I thought again. 'No, nothing bad. I'd like to draw him.'

'Um,' I said, and glanced over to where Brack was standing, perched in a wobbly way on his remaining hind leg with his front paws half in a newly leafed bush in the garden. He was sniffing the leaves. 'In what way?'

'Euan's a wildlife artist.' Jill was dragging another length of timber along the grass. 'He's quite well known, too. Been on *Countryfile* a few times anyway, and that's all you need for fame around here.' She grinned at both of us. 'He would like to use your Brack to model for a picture he's been commissioned to paint for a local hotel.' The grin widened. 'I thought I'd better just cut to the chase,' she said to Euan. 'The way you two communicate, it would take you until next year to get to the important bit.' Then back to me. 'He asked me yesterday if I thought you'd agree. I told him to ask you today.'

'And this is me, asking,' Euan said.

Well, everything made a *bit* more sense now. When I'd seen him standing staring into space or creeping about in the hedgerow, presumably he'd been watching creatures, birds doing whatever they did? Or maybe he was a peculiar man who just happened to draw animals.

'I don't know,' I said, genuinely. 'He's not a pet. He's afraid of strangers and he doesn't like sitting still.'

Euan smiled at me now. It took away some of the 'fixed' nature of his expression, made his dark eyes crinkle and showed white teeth amongst the grey-flecked stubble. There was no grey in his hair, I noticed. His beard made him look older, but his uneven, windswept hairstyle made him look a bit like a child whose mum has set about him with her sewing scissors. I dropped my eyes. The habit of not looking at men directly was still with me. 'Same as most animals,' he said. 'I'm used to it.'

'Can't you just video him and draw from that?' Brack was digging a small hole in the lawn, chasing worms or beetles, his golden eyes focused down so tightly that he didn't even look up to see if anything was watching him.

Euan shook his head. 'Needs to be in front of me. I watch films with different eyes. Need to *see* them to draw.' Blink blink.

Inside, my brain flapped around. I didn't want Euan in my house and, anyway, with a stranger in the house, Brack would just get into his cage and hide. 'Can you sketch him out here?'

A nod.

'Well, you'd better get on with it, then.'

A pause and then another short nod and Euan got up from the wall. 'I'll get my stuff.' He wandered, barefoot with coat and hair flopping about, back to his own garden, climbing over the wall at the end rather than going round to go in by the gate.

I stared at Jill, who was looking at my run drawing, obviously trying not to laugh. 'Did you two cook this plan up between you?'

'Nope.' She turned the paper around and held it up against the brickwork. 'He asked me to ask you, but I thought you might as well have a conversation. You're next-door neighbours, for heaven's sake. You're going to have to talk to each other sometimes, even if it's only about the septic tank. I just offered to referee.'

'I've talked to him. I asked about the stopcock.'

'And of such things are great friendships made,' Jill replied, slightly tartly. 'Right. I reckon I've just about got the wood for most of this, we can get the tall part done today. You hold that up here and I'll measure.'

I did as I was told and followed instructions. I held things and measured things and cut the odd narrow plank with Jill's big saw, while she screwed and hammered and clambered about on the remaining farmhouse structure. Out of the corner of my eye, I could see Euan McGillan watching Brack, who had explored the garden for a bit and then settled down, head pillowed on his flanks, to sleep in the watery sunshine. Euan had a set of pencils in his pocket and a board with paper on and he seemed fully occupied, keeping well away from the fox but watching his every move.

'He's all right, really,' Jill said. 'He's a bit – well, he wasn't like that when we were at school, he was always a bit dreamy and hob-led, but always great at art. Now he spends too much time on his own out here, I guess.'

'What the hell is "hob-led"?' I propped a very long piece of timber up on end.

'Oh, you know, away with the fairies, pixielated, a bit fey.'

'Not quite all there,' I supplied, trying to stop the wood from falling down onto my head.

'Oh, don't get me wrong.' Jill looked quickly over at Euan. 'He's not daft or anything. He just wasn't academic at school, only ever wanted to draw things. His maths book was beautiful...' she trailed off for a moment to put some screws in her mouth and begin fixing two planks to an outer framework. 'He was a bit of a stunner, all the girls were after him, but he only ever noticed the animals. He'd only go out with girls who had a dog or a cat or something; he got really good at drawing horses too. But then we left, and I don't know where he went after that. Some art school somewhere, I think, we lost touch. Then Mum said he was back, moving out here and he needed someone to do out his loft, so I came out and we got friendly again.'

She stood back and rocked the elaborate woodwork to check for stability. 'Oh,' I said.

'He keeps himself to himself.' Jill gave me another of those direct looks. 'You don't need to worry about Euan.'

'I'm not—'

'There's usually only one reason that women want another woman to come and fix their sink or put their windows in,' Jill said, half under her breath. 'It's fine. You don't have to tell me anything, but just know that Euan isn't like that. He's a good, quiet man who only really thinks about things as they relate to his art.' Her eyes were so sharp they almost felt as though they'd punctured right through to my soul and I couldn't think of anything to say.

'Right. Lunchtime,' Jill announced, switching the mood of the conversation so abruptly that I nearly let go of my two-by-four. 'Get that kettle on, Tamzin, you can drop that timber down, I'm not going to get round to that bit for a while.'

I wasn't really sorry to be heading indoors. Not because of the work, that had been fine; fun even, matching up wood and doing practical things outside in the sunshine, feeling capable and using muscles that were usually only employed to keep me from falling through the sofa cushions. But as I walked through my garden gate and Brack bounded up to join me in case there were any snacks going, I felt the cold sweaty wash of shame go over my shoulders and cascade down my back. Was it *that* obvious? If Jill could pick up on it, could everyone? Anyone? Did I have a big sign on my forehead that said 'victim'?

Euan had gone, I noticed, when I looked out of the kitchen window. 'I hope you posed nicely,' I said to Brack, who was sitting with his paws precisely placed and his tail curled around them. People didn't usually notice his lack of a limb until he walked, and sometimes not even then. He moved with the sinuous grace of all vulpines and only a slight limp. He yawned pinkly and licked his nose.

I took our tea mugs out and the rest of the biscuits and then realised that Euan hadn't gone indoors. He'd gone to talk to Jill. The people-pleaser in me wobbled a bit about going back in and making another mug of tea, but I managed to fight it off. He only lived next door. If he wanted a cup of tea, he could make it in his own kitchen.

But I held the biscuits out to him first, a gesture of appeasement, and then hated myself. Euan was sitting on the grass with his back against one of the low, half-tumbled walls, while Jill sat on the ivied edge of one of the others, plastic box of sandwiches resting alongside her. There was something about the comfortable way he sat and the casual way his coat was unfastened to let the wind tweak at the edges that made him look as though he'd grown there. They were conversing in what seemed to be a light, general way. I wondered if Jill had told Euan the conclusions she had come to about me, but decided that she probably hadn't. His attitude towards me was still that of an eccentric elderly person meeting RuPaul, an acknowledgement that here was another human being but with a gulf as wide as this entire valley between experiences.

That was fine by me. I didn't *want* him to think about me.

'I drew your fox,' Euan said. 'Look.'

From behind his back, he pulled out a sheaf of thick paper and handed them to me. On each one was a separate sketch of Brack. Unmistakably Brack. Euan had captured the way Brack would glance up from his curled sleep, slit-eyed against the sun. The curve of his back as he trotted, placing each paw delicately.

The raise of his head, the way his mouth tipped slightly up at each side as though he were smiling.

'Wow,' I said, astonished that this odd man actually could draw well. 'These are amazing.'

A shift of shoulder, acknowledging my praise but without any real pride. 'I can paint him from these. Might need to check colours sometimes.'

The attention to detail was astonishing. Euan hadn't just drawn Brack, he'd drawn his surroundings as they interacted with him; the grass stems that bent around his sleeping form, the stones in the wall behind him. The tiny winged insect that had attracted Brack's attention and made him get up and wander along the budding roses. Beautiful, intricate snapshots of moments in a fox's life.

'Told you. He can draw a bit, this one,' Jill said, looking down on us from her perch.

'Pretty much all I can do,' Euan said, but he smiled as he said it. 'Didn't exactly cover myself in glory at school.'

'At least you didn't get kicked out like Elspeth James,' Jill said tartly. 'And Ryan Thomson's still in prison.'

Euan shrugged under the green coat.

'Where did you study art?' I asked, tilting the sketches so that the sun showed the very finest of lines, the ones that gave character to the pictures.

'Newcastle.' He blinked, but only briefly. 'Only place that would take me. They have me back now for open days, because I'm on TV, and London want me to go and study down there now. Weren't interested when I left school, though, not enough qualifications.' He blew out through his nose, sounding like Brack encountering an unpleasant smell. 'UCAS points. Bloody well not going there now, when they wouldn't have me before.'

A flight of rooks swirled briefly above us, calling and arguing in a drift of dark feathers against the blue sky. Euan tipped his head back to watch them and Jill and I exchanged a grin. 'Artistic temperament,' Jill said, folding the paper her sandwiches had been in back into the plastic box, neatly sealing the lid on afterwards. 'You know about that, being a writer.'

I wasn't, I thought to myself as I washed up later that evening, really a writer. I'd *wanted* to be, of course I had. I'd taken my degree in journalism to give me a start into the world of publishing. But I'd got trapped into writing sensationalist stories for the women's magazines that now seemed to make up most of the content. And I certainly didn't have artistic temperament, whatever that may be. I wasn't even sure I had any temperament at all now. It had been shuffled aside to make room for tea drinking and worrying about colour schemes.

I dried my hands and then noticed the split suitcase of fabric remnants that Jill had unearthed from the old building, sitting on the floor shedding remnants of leather-look coating, like an elderly snake. I got the photograph of 'Stella' out from under the fruit bowl and tugged the material from the case, laying them side by side on the big pine table that I'd inherited with the house. It certainly looked very much like this was the skirt she'd been wearing, long swathes of the fabric, printed with those huge concentric circles in a colour which might once have been blue or purple but was now faded and dirtied down to a muddy colour.

'Who the hell are you?' I asked the picture. Stella smiled back, a slightly guarded face surrounded by that flicky hairstyle. When I looked out of the kitchen window and compared it to the photograph, I could see a vague similarity in the lines of the garden path, although the area that was now all laid to lawn had been mostly vegetable patch, judging from the photo. Lines of canes formed rows just behind Stella's shoulder, leading down to a blurry area which was my garden wall but looked as though it had been higher back then. In addition to the long skirt, Stella was wearing a dark, long-sleeved top, either blouse or shirt, buttoned to the collar. I couldn't see her feet, the skirt and the angle of the picture cut those off.

Why did I care? What did it matter to me that a young girl had stood in my garden nearly fifty years ago and had her picture taken? I pulled a face and put the photo down again. I went back to stacking plates and ignoring Brack's snuffling for food for a minute, but then found myself picking up the skirt material again. Why had this been hidden away in the old ruins? Were the sweet wrappers anything to do with her? I'd looked online, the wrappers had seemed very typical of the early seventies, with their just-post-decimal prices and the lurid colours and font. This picture had been taken in 1972.

Still ignoring Brack, I flipped open my laptop and looked up my cottage. Nothing of note, the estate agent's details were still there on RightMove, there were some old adverts for the place as holiday accommodation; the photographs showed the beams, the old table, the loft room made up with twin beds, and were angled to make the living room look much bigger than it was. The only other bits I could find were planning notices, showing that next door had an application for a loft window current, and a few older ones for replacements of doors and windows. Nothing else. I typed in 'Stella' and the address, but nothing came up. It was annoying. Like an itch in the back of my brain. I'd got so used to being able to just type in a few random lines and getting back all the information I wanted that this historical black hole was a puzzle I found myself wanting to solve.

I fastened the photograph to the fridge with a magnet that had previously held the water bill up, and went for a shower.

9

The weeks passed. Jill's visits became more sporadic as people started wanting external jobs around the house done, and Brack's run was held in stasis for a while as the buds popped and the grass grew around it. New bramble shoots began to rise from the hacked ground and wind their way through the wire, and inside the ruins of the old farmhouse it became mossily green. A small sapling that I'd asked Jill to leave was thrusting apart some of the brickwork, a slender silver trunk inserting itself like a finger and picking at the stones, crumbling rock to dust, like an illustration of the power of nature.

I summoned all my courage and went back into town. Clearly, word had spread of my financial profligacy because I was greeted with small cries of joy from the local shopkeepers. Samples of wallpaper were pressed into my hands, and I was treated to tea and cake and lengthy discussions of the latest decorating trends. They'd obviously heard from Jill that I worked for magazines, got something of the wrong end of the stick, and were all eager to be 'noted suppliers'. I didn't like to spoil their illusions, so I entered many a spirited chat about maximalism versus Scandi simplicity, and the latest lighting effects. All that money that I'd spent on the reading material before I'd moved hadn't been entirely wasted, at least, I managed to hold my own, even though I did come home with fourteen rolls of paper featuring embossed flamingos and a stippling brush – neither of which I was ever going to use.

I occasionally saw Euan out and about at a distance. Sometimes he'd be standing very still in the big field, often under the tree with the cows snuffling and sidling around him as they kicked the sandy soil up to dust. Every so often, Brack and I would encounter him creeping the hedgerows as we took our evening walks. I'd stopped being surprised at finding a fully grown man bent double in a ditch staring at cowslips, or thrusting his way through the flowering hawthorn bushes. Now I just said, 'Evening, Euan,' and sometimes he would reply. Often, though, he didn't seem to hear me, or would answer only with a jerk of the chin and a half-smile, pencil between his teeth and a small slip of paper in his hands. I wasn't so worried now that the oddness had an explanation. Well, sort of. Other artists, I was sure, sat in their studios and created art without having to have constant visual prompts. But Euan was – well, different.

'If we build a kind of house attachment on the back here,' Jill said one morning, stretching wire between wooden supports, 'you could use this as a chicken run. Once Brack's not around, I mean, I'm presuming you aren't going to move serially from fox to fox.'

I looked down at Brack, who was currently in his partly erected run, lying under the shade of the now-leafed sapling. The sun had some heat in it and the shadows were short and intense, as though they'd been concentrated down to stubby black lines. 'One is more than enough,' I said. 'I should ask about to see if there are any wildlife sanctuaries around that could take him. He's fully mature now, it's not fair to keep him on his own.'

'You should ask Euan.' Jill drove another staple into the wood. 'He visits places like that to draw the animals when he can't find them in the wild. He must know all the animal shelters and centres within a fifty-mile radius.'

'Because when he's been to one, he's not allowed back again?'

'He's not that bad!' Jill stood back and admired her work. 'How's that?'

'It's looking good. And yes, I see what you mean about the chickens. I could have them free range and just shut them in here at night.' I imagined my own little flock of hens, fresh eggs. But that would mean no Brack. No more of that red streak that greeted me in the morning, wowing for food, no more warm, redolent body curled beside me on the sofa. He *had* to go, to live somewhere as near wild as he could, with company. But not yet.

'How did you come by him, then?' Jill looked at the fox. He was a bit less cautious in her presence now, but wouldn't approach her, even if she held out a sandwich. 'You didn't buy him as a pet, I presume?'

I began tidying up some of the odds and ends of wood that we'd dropped. Over beyond the fence, I could see Euan, big green coat discarded now to leave him in a T-shirt and jeans, but still barefoot, standing staring at the hedge. It was practically normal now. 'He was a tiny cub. I was out walking one day. There were some men with dogs, they'd been setting them on foxes, I think. They ran when they saw me coming, but there was this tiny cub with his ears all torn and one leg... Well, it wasn't looking good. I think the dogs had been dragging him by it. I picked him up and took him to a vet, and once they'd amputated the leg and treated the other wounds, they gave him back to me to rear.'

Brack, as though he knew I was talking about him, raised his head. Yellow eyes met mine, his curiously intelligent long-slitted pupils very narrow in this bright light. Did he remember being wild? Probably not, he'd been less than six weeks old, according to the vet. Still in the den, still fed by his mother, still sleeping bundled up with the rest of the litter. I didn't know what had happened to them, I didn't like to think about it.

'Too much of a pet to let go, too wild to keep, eh?' Jill put some more staples in her mouth and started on the other edge of the wire.

'I'll keep him until I find the right place for him to go.' I sounded a bit fierce. 'Just because he's smelly and destructive, I'm not going to release him into a field somewhere.'

Euan crossed the field and came towards us at an oblique angle. He reached the wire fence that delineated my patch of land from the field, hesitated, and then climbed over it. Brack raised his head, saw Euan's approach, and scuttled himself under the reviving patch of bramble growth inside the run.

'What is it today?' I asked.

'Skylarks.' Euan leaned his head back and his eyes followed something I couldn't see, up, up into the shining blue. 'They fly like leaves.'

I couldn't tell a skylark from a sparrow, so I didn't comment.

'There were deer this morning,' Euan went on. 'Four roe, up at the copse.'

'I've never seen a deer,' I said, leaning against the brickwork. It was more for something to say than anything else. Euan had a way of making announcements like this. 'I mean, I have, in zoos and parks and things like that, but not in the wild.' I looked out across the field, at the little dots high in the sky that I now knew were skylarks. 'I feel like I've missed out.'

'You make Truro sound like downtown Manhattan.' Jill spat out the last staple. 'Do they not have wildlife in Cornwall?'

'I didn't really go outside the city much,' I said. 'Only to the beach. Not many deer on the beach.'

'They can swim,' Euan said, again, very definitively.

'But they can't surf.'

'No.' He stood looking at us for a moment. 'Would you like to see them?'

My mind had been elsewhere for a moment. 'See what?'

'The deer.'

'Well, yes, I...'

'I'll fetch you. Tomorrow morning. Show you.' This startling suggestion was followed by the slow blink. 'I mean, if you want.'

I was supposed to be starting again, wasn't I? This, here, the little cottage, these two people who were, probably, close to being my friends. Starting again. But it didn't have to be the same. 'Can we make it the morning after?' I had to bite my lips together not to burst out with sudden excuses, explanations, *justifications*. But I did it. He didn't need to know, I just had to see how he reacted to having to change his plans.

'Probably even better,' was his response. 'Supposed to rain tomorrow.'

Something inside me uncoiled. A little plastic knot of tension that wound itself up when I knew I had to contradict or gainsay, winding itself like a little scroll of all the words that I knew needed to come out.

'What sort of time?' I asked. 'So I can set my alarm.'

Long blink. 'I'll bang on the wall.'

Jill watched this exchange with her head tipped to one side and I saw a smile grow from the bud of a lightening around the mouth into a full-flowering grin. She didn't say anything, but I saw her look from me to Euan and back. Then, pragmatic as ever, she just said. 'Right. One of you hold this end here for me. I need to attach it to the back of the run.' And just as easily as that, we'd moved away from the deer and the birds and back to planks and screws.

* * *

It was dark. I'd been dreaming about the streets of Truro, the crowds of tourists that poured in away from the beaches and holiday resorts when the weather turned inclement. It had been a foggy day outside the cathedral... something huge, flying overhead through the fog... a threat, sensed but not seen...

Thump thump thump.

I was thrown from sleep, heart hammering. It came again. Thump thump thump, a heavy booming from the wall next to the bed and I sat up, trying to locate the origin. The room was so small that it was ninety per cent bed, and the noise echoed around and came from everywhere.

Then I remembered. I thumped back with my fist, which hurt. Then I got up, put on warm clothes and let Brack out for a wee, then put him back in the bathroom with a whispered instruction to go back to sleep. I had no idea why I was whispering, there was only me and Brack there and the only other person within hearing distance was, demonstrably, up and awake, but something about the pre-dawn silence, broken only by an early rook gusting overhead when I opened the door for the fox, made anything louder feel profane.

I stood about in my front garden for a few moments. Should I go and knock on Euan's door? The 'No Callers' sign still fluttered there, corners torn to jagged teeth where it had blown away from its drawing pins and been reattached, so I decided to just wait.

'You can't wear that.' He'd come out of the back door and around the cottages and was behind my left shoulder. 'That coat.' His voice was quiet.

I spun round. 'I didn't realise there was a dress code,' I hissed back.

'It's too rustly. They'll hear us coming. Wait there.'

As opposed to what, I thought. Going back indoors and slamming the door, getting back into bed and muttering under the covers about what was so unsuitable about my nice waterproof jacket? I was very, very tempted.

But then Euan appeared again, out of the front door this time, carrying a green coat which looked ominously like the one he wore to creep around in. 'Here.'

'But I...'

'Quickly. The sun will be up soon.' He held the coat out at arm's length, as though I were a nervous wild animal.

'And you'll crumble to dust?' But I took it. I unzipped my jacket and put on Euan's. It hung to my thighs. I hadn't realised he was that much taller than me, but now, as we set off up the muddy lane through the crepuscular grey light, it was obvious. I tried not to feel nervous. *Never let them know you are afraid.*

But Euan kept a distance between us. At first, he strode on ahead, chin tucked down into his own jacket collar, but when he'd had to stop and wait for me for the second time, he slowed down a bit and only walked a metre or so in front. I struggled on, the uneven surface was difficult in the dark, but as the grey of pre-dawn started to become the long shadows of a rising sun we couldn't see yet, it got easier.

'How far is the copse?' I puffed, more to say something than because I wanted to know.

'Half a mile or so.' He stopped suddenly and I almost walked into him. He didn't react, but put a hand on my arm, fingers up, a warning or just calling a halt, and I was about to ask what the matter was when a great white shape floated down the lane from behind us. It came within half a metre of crashing into us, then tipped its wings to change course and flew off over the hedge, dotting along the field edge ahead of us as though cruising.

'Owl?' I asked.

Euan smiled, his eyes still tracing the bird's flight away down the hillside. 'Barn owl. They're nesting in the old stone barn up at the top. That's the male.'

I stared at him. 'You can tell from *here*?'

He looked away from the owl and down to me, and his expression was almost pitying. 'The female is incubating,' he said. 'Won't see her for a bit, he's taking food to her.'

'Oh.'

'Besides, she's bigger and darker. You'll know her when you see her.'

The way he spoke about the owls, almost as though they were people he'd met at a dinner party recently, made me realise how differently he saw things through his artist's eyes. What was just a big white bird to me was an individual creature to him; he knew where it nested, what it was doing, he could probably have sketched it for me if I'd asked. I didn't like to tell him that the female would just be another bird to me. Truro wasn't exactly inner-city, but it was dawning on me with the rising sun how little I'd got out and explored. How estranged I'd become from the world around me.

That recent estrangement must be the reason that I was noticing everything so clearly this morning – I'd been shut away from it for so long. Late spring in the city was just when the delivery lorries came at dawn instead of in the dark, when you could turn your heating off. When you got annoyed with the noise your neighbours made out in their gardens, instead of inside. Our garden had been a yard, always overshadowed, always slippery with moss. All tall-rising brickwork in the shade of redundant chimneys. You could smell the sea, hear the gulls, but... it had always had the whiff of the prison yard about it.

Euan turned off the track before we reached the top, clambering over a grey-with-age field gate channelled and fringed with missing and broken wood, and waiting for me to follow. Then we walked around the edge of the field, which rose and dipped like a roller-coaster ride, until we could see the small stand of trees above us. Euan put a finger to his lips, crouched below the line of the hedge and we advanced upwards, hustling along with one shoulder against the thorny whips of new growth. Just as we were about to slide under the trees of the copse, he pulled on my sleeve to stop me and made a 'down' motion with both hands, as he sank into the shelter of the hedge. I copied him but with rather less grace.

There was a slight ditch at the base of the hedge, where the grass was boggy. First my knees were wet, then my thighs, but the green coat of Euan's stopped the rest of me getting damp as we lay, prone, in the depression. I opened my mouth to say something, but Euan shook his head. He did the 'wait' signal with his hand again.

Why had I agreed to this? I thought 'seeing deer' meant a slow ramble in the sunshine, a glimpse of creatures at a distance that I couldn't have distinguished from cows even with binoculars, and home in time for a cooked breakfast. Not lying in a damp gulley with wet trousers, next to a man whose single-mindedness looked set to break records. I sniffed and shifted my weight.

Suddenly, from behind us, came a rustle and through the hedge to our right, a deer tiptoed, forcing its body through the undergrowth. I'd always thought deer were small and elegant, but from down here at ground level, this one looked bloody enormous. It stopped, so close I could see its nostrils twitching as it scented the air, ears flickering for a second, and then it moved on. It seemed to be following a well-worn path, hooves scrabbling up the slight incline of the dyke, and then on into the field. Another came behind it, smaller and finer boned, both of them dark in their russet coats against the new blue of the sky. Then another, this one raggy with winter fur still clinging in clumps to its neck and flanks. The group of three stood as if undecided for a moment on the edge of the channel. They were so close that I could almost have stroked them, had I not been horizontal and holding my breath; narrow faces with huge brown eyes and a sense of coiled tension, etched against the horizon. Nostrils flared, one nuzzled at the grass that grew especially lush here in the damp, its face almost level with mine for a second.

A bright eye looked into mine, full of the madness of the wild for a tiny moment, then heads came up and they were gone, white rumps bouncing away off down the field and the sun gleaming along those red-brown flanks. I let out my breath.

'Deer,' said Euan, unnecessarily.

'Wow.' It was the only word I had.

'They come through here almost every morning.' He straightened up and then got to his feet. 'That's the path they make, just there.'

Now I could see the gap in the hedge, the narrow trail sliced by slotted hooves like a little muddy tightrope along the edge of the ditch.

'They came so close!' I was still half-gasping.

'They're fairly used to me now. I can get reasonably close, as long as they haven't got young with them.'

'And you draw them?'

He did that half-shrug again, that acknowledgement of a talent that was, presumably, so natural to him that it was like being complimented for having a nose, or being able to smile. 'Sometimes. Sometimes I just watch.'

'Oh, that didn't sound creepy at all,' I said without thinking. Without stopping to curate the words before they came out. And that coiled plastic thing that lay in my chest dug a sharp edge of warning under my ribs.

But Euan just smiled. It made him look more approachable, looser and more friendly. 'Drawing wildlife is only fifty per cent actual drawing,' he said, helping me to my feet with a hand under my elbow. 'The rest is observation.'

He led the way upwards now and I realised we were close to where the track I walked Brack along turned into tractor path. 'I'm not sure that's true,' I said. 'I could observe all day and I still wouldn't be able to draw like you.'

I waited for the presumed reply, 'You could if you just tried, you just need to put the hours in, practice, keep at it,' but he didn't say that. Instead, he said, 'I nearly lost it, you know.'

The sun hit our backs as we came out onto the dust of the trackway that led down to our houses. 'Sorry? Nearly lost what?'

'The drawing. Being able to draw. I had a stroke.'

Oh. *Oh*. A sudden memory of my grandmother, groping for words. Knowing what she wanted to say but not being able to frame the sentence. That explained, a little bit, his habit of the slow blink. 'That must have been horrible,' I said, knowing it was inadequate, but what else could I say?

'Tough, yes.' He didn't smile this time. He looked at me and frowned a little bit. 'You know about strokes?'

'My grandmother.' Well, I didn't really have to hide this, did I? Didn't have to keep this part of my life to myself. 'She brought me up after my parents died when I was ten. She had a stroke, just over five years ago.' It sounded such a simple sentence, but it encompassed so much. My having to move back to help her in the house, the sudden end to the internship I'd had on a huge-selling magazine that had been my supposed entry to the world of publishing. 'She improved, but she found life very frustrating afterwards.'

Part of that frustration had been having to rely on me. Having to have me there, when she knew I could have been out in the world, starting my life. But we'd only got each other.

'Frustrating. Yes. That's one word for it.' Euan made a noise that sounded like a sigh, but with more weight behind it. Then he started walking again, kicking up dust under his big army-style boots, as though he was punishing the ground for being there.

'Oh, Jill's here,' I said, after we'd walked almost to the cottages without speaking again. I wanted to break the silence, and banality was all I had to hand. 'Thank you for showing me the deer, Euan.'

He turned and smiled again, and I noticed how the sun had already darkened his skin a touch. He had very dark hair and eyes, the incipient tan with that darkness made him look as if he were a part of the country. Dark as the shadows we'd skulked in. The unexpected observation took me by surprise.

'It was my pleasure, Tamzin.'

I half-hoped then that he might say something about Jill, stretch this moment further, but he just raised a hand in farewell and went in through his front door, closing it firmly behind him. The 'No Callers' sign fluttered like a flag.

10

A week went by. A late Easter meant that Jill had her girls home from school, and they came to take over my job of holding wood and sawing, while I stayed indoors. Under cover of supposedly knocking 'Ten Ways to Tell It's Love' into shape – a filler for a monthly magazine that probably wouldn't even get used – I was secretly working out a way to remove the fireplace without bringing down the dividing wall or alerting Jill to what I was up to. I'd got as far as chipping off the old tiles, but whenever I tried to lever off the surround there was an ominous cracking sound and big bits of plaster came away. I had the awful feeling that one really hard push would mean Euan and I sharing a living room and a lot of rubble. It was probably unwise, and it was almost certainly unsafe, but it made me feel I was working. Doing *something*.

Once I'd given up on the fireplace, I decided to paper the loft with the flamingo wallpaper. Some of it went up crooked, some of it had bubbles in that made the wall look as though it were growing nipples. The whole effect when I went into the room now was of being plunged into a fever dream after eating too much cheese, but that didn't matter. I'd done it. By myself. And I need never go up there again, unless it was to retrieve spare tea towels, so I could ignore the 'walking into a zoo whilst on heavy-duty drugs' appearance. Maybe I'd give stippling a try, one day.

But today, what I found myself mostly doing was sitting at the kitchen table, drinking tea, looking out of the window at Jill and her daughters, laughing and building Brack's run. The back door was open to let the chilly sun in and Brack, and his smell, out and I could hear them cheerfully chatting and arguing from across the garden. Ariadne was tall like Jill, rangily built with long dark hair. Seph had excitable blonde curls, very fair skin and was usually covered in Factor 50 sun cream because of it.

Behind me in the living room, another lump of plaster fell off the wall. Luckily, the dust sheet was covering the worst of it. I had gone back to my article writing to try to distract myself from the fact that my cottage was probably going to fall into fire surround-shaped ruin and 'Ten Ways' was not going well. I'd only got about three and none of those were really convincing. I hit a few keys in the hope that random letters would suddenly form words that made sense, and sipped at the tea.

There was a tap at the front door. Because the house was so small, I could see right through, out of the kitchen, down through the living room and out through the front window from where I sat. I saw the shadow of a figure darken the window briefly for a second and then vanish. By the time I got to the front door, tininess of house notwithstanding, there was no one to be seen, just a manila envelope on the doorstep. I stared at it for a moment with my heart hammering.

Is this it? Has he found me?

But outside my door was nothing but birds arguing in the hedge across the track, the smell of recent rain and the illusory warmth from the sun. It was just an envelope. I picked it up.

Back in the safety of the kitchen, I opened it. It wasn't sealed and a sheet of thick paper slid out when I tapped it on the table, still slightly cautious in case of severed fingers or explosives, even though I knew there was no such thing in an envelope this thin. At first, I thought the paper was blank, but when I turned it over there was an exquisite pencil sketch of a deer taking up most of the surface. Captured in the act of stepping over the ditch we'd lain in, delicate as a debutante exiting her carriage, the deer had its head up, eyes bright and ears cocked warily. It was so lifelike that my knees felt damp again, remembering, and I looked over at where I'd hung Euan's green coat up on the rack next to my rustling waterproof. He hadn't asked for it back. I hadn't, in fact, seen him at all since that morning of the deer-watching.

I laid the sketch out on the table and found I was stroking the pencil lines as though I was smoothing the winter-roughened fur of the deer itself. I looked from the picture to the green coat and back again and then thought, what the hell. I should, at least, say thank you.

The 'No Callers' sign was drooping from one drawing pin, curled forward across itself like a forgotten scroll when I knocked. There was a very long pause, before I saw a figure appear behind the door. 'What is it?'

'It's me, Tamzin. I brought your coat back. And I wanted to say thank you for the drawing.'

'Oh.' I could imagine him standing there, giving a long blink while he thought. 'Oh. All right.'

The door opened a crack. Euan was barefoot, in jeans dotted with paint and a T-shirt bearing a washed-out advertising slogan in French.

'I don't want to disturb you,' I said, reassuringly. 'I just wanted – well. The picture. It's beautiful.' I held out the coat. 'And I thought you might need this.'

More of Euan became visible as he stepped into the gap. His hair looked wild, even though he was indoors it seemed to have a breeze blowing through it, and he obviously hadn't shaved in a while either because that grey streak was even more noticeable. He looked like a student woken up on the sofa from an afternoon nap in front of *Doctors*. 'It's just a working sketch.' He rubbed his hand over his face, and I saw that his fingers were stained with white paint. 'I thought you'd like it. After the deer.'

'Would you like to come over for a meal? Tomorrow night?' The words had escaped me before I had time to even think about them and I tried to bite them back but it was too late. *You've got to stop this, Tamzin. Feeling sorry for men doesn't do you any good. Just because he looks as though he hasn't eaten anything but Pot Noodle for a week is no reason to cook for him.*

'Oh.' The fingers tugged at the half-beard. 'I'm not sure. I...'

'You're working, no, that's absolutely fine. I just wanted to thank you for the sketch and I was going to ask Jill to come too but, no, you carry on painting.' I was backing my way down the path as I spoke, trying to find a conversational opportunity to turn round and run out of the gate. It was a *stupid* idea. He was fine. He'd managed to feed himself up until now, and I was beginning to realise that I really and truly didn't want a man in my house. Outside, yes, outside it was fine, where there was space, but *inside*? No, no, no.

'What time?' Euan called through the slice of darkness that wasn't door. 'Tomorrow?'

'I'll bang on the wall,' I said, trying to work out how I was going to get out of this. A sudden emergency, perhaps? I could pretend to take Brack to the vet – but no, the way everyone knew everyone else around here, the vet would probably turn out to be his second cousin and he'd find out I'd never gone. Maybe I could have a fireplace-related emergency? *Shit*. Why did I do this? I'd thought I'd got better.

* * *

'You *have* to come!' I was practically on my knees to Jill. 'I don't know why I invited him and I can't... not on my own. *Please*, Jill.'

Jill, who had her overalls tied round her waist by the sleeves and was sweating in her shirt, looked at me sternly. 'It's Euan. He's fine.'

You don't know, my treacherous brain whispered. *You never know someone. Not really.*

'On the other hand,' she went on, 'it's Seph's turn to cook tomorrow night and I am mightily sick of pasta. Don't tell her I said that.'

The girls were sitting in the sun, side by side on the far edge of the nearly built run, watching Brack, who had crept his way over to lie cautiously near them. He was pretending to be asleep, but his eyes were open, darting from one to the other as though he suspected they were hiding a knife. You could take the fox out of the wild, but you couldn't take the wild out of the fox.

I just wished he wouldn't assume everyone was an axe-murderer.

'Thank you.' The words were limp with relief. 'I don't think he would have come if you didn't, either.'

Jill looked over to Euan's cottage, shading her eyes from the sun with a work-gloved hand. 'Yup. He's as bad as you are.' Then she seemed to realise what she'd said. 'Sorry.'

'No, it's fine. I know I'm over-cautious.'

She raised an eyebrow and met my eye. 'I'm sure you have your reasons,' she said calmly. 'Like I said, you're not the only lass around here who prefers to have a woman about the place. I've heard some stories, I can tell you.' Then she straightened, retied her overalls and called to the girls. 'Right. Let's get this frame in place, then we're done for the day.'

'Thank you.'

'About seven?' Jill started moving towards the reel of wire. 'Tomorrow? Only I won't be over to do the run, I've got a washing machine in Pickering that's refusing to spin.'

I smiled. 'That's fine.' The relief that Jill would be there to mitigate the effects of Euan meant I'd agree to almost anything. Then I turned to head back into the cottage and Brack got up to come with me, padding silently along beside me with his muzzle tipped up so he could see my face. 'What?' I asked him.

I just got an enigmatic nose against my leg.

Just before I went in through the back door, I heard Ariadne's voice. 'Are you picking up lame ducks again, Mum?'

'She needs a friend,' Jill replied, her voice low but carrying across to me on the breeze that was stirring down the valley. 'Plus, the money she's paying me for this job is keeping you two in hour-long showers and Xbox games.'

'Why does she need a friend?' That was Seph, whose teenage tones were a little more strident. 'Can't she get her own?'

I couldn't hear Jill's reply. I slid indoors and shut the door. I didn't *want* to hear the reply. Jill was right, I did need a friend. I didn't have any here. I didn't have any left in Cornwall. I'd thought I didn't mind. I was starting a new life, I didn't need or want anything anchoring me to the old one; I had my work, my cottage, Brack. I'd lost the knack of making friends somewhere along the way and I wasn't overly concerned about getting it back, but Jill's words had made me sound so... so *pathetic*.

Then I saw that sketch on the table. The deer so well-observed, alert for danger. It must be tiring to be that on edge all the time, I thought, and then laughed, feeling stupid. It was that high-level alertness, that on-edge feeling that was stopping me from making friends, wasn't it? Apart from elegance, big brown eyes and a delicacy of movement, weren't the deer and I very alike? And if I wanted to stop it, then I had to start somewhere, and that somewhere might as well be dinner with Euan and Jill.

I closed down 'Ten Ways' and started looking up recipes.

11

The slow cooker was simmering obediently and I'd got bread ready to go in the oven. Home-made apple tart was safely in the fridge, after an emergency run for ingredients to the supermarket in Pickering, during which I had been slightly distracted by a shop which sold cushions, and now I just needed to change into something that looked as though I hadn't made any effort. It was time to brave the Clothes Cupboard of Doom.

This was the cupboard on the upstairs landing, where I had hung all my old party clothes. Dresses that I couldn't bear to be parted from, despite the fact that opportunities to wear beaded satin or layers of chiffon were decidedly remote out here. They were my dresses of memory. Dresses from the way I had been before, when there had been parties and dinners; when I'd been to film premieres – right at the back and not meeting any of the stars, of course, but the magazine had sent me with my official lanyard to write up the occasion and I'd had to dress for it. I briefly stroked a green velvet twenties-style top. I'd almost met Orlando Bloom in that top. And here was the blue dress that I'd been wearing when someone had walked into me whilst they had been trying to avoid stepping on Anne Hathaway.

That was then. I shuffled through the hangers. What did I have that said 'relaxed, informal dinner with a woman who nails planks to other planks and a man who hardly speaks'? Wide-legged black trousers, I thought, said all that. And the green velvet top. Which called for the black beaded collar, costume jewellery that I'd hidden away in a box on the top shelf, shoved thoughtlessly high up out of the way because I never thought I'd need to wear any of it again. I had to fetch a chair from the kitchen to get it down, I'd pushed the box so far to the back of the shelf, and there was a fine film of dust forming already over the lid. I groped it down, and then ran a hand over the shelf to check on the filth levels. I'd kept on top of the general housework, but dusting *inside cupboards* was too close to madness for me.

And there, at the back, pushed down where the shelf was attached to the wall, were more photographs. I could feel the thin cardboard edges flickering under my fingers and had to fetch a box from the living room to pile onto the chair to reach right to the back of the shelf and pull them out.

Old pictures again. I didn't look at them. Not yet. I had the curious feeling of expectation, the same feeling I used to get when I'd look at a new copy of the magazine, leafing through to find my byline under a tiny article about teenage make-up, or when I got out of the taxi at one of the publicity events. A prickle low in my stomach. A feeling of standing on the very edge of something that could be huge. The feeling that had been so close a cousin to insecurity and fear that those two emotions had managed to creep up on me unrecognised, until it was too late.

I tucked the photos under the fruit bowl, which seemed to have become the natural resting place of things waiting to be dealt with – the Council Tax bill was under there too, and a letter from the electricity company warning me about impending alterations to the supply. I reattached the dust sheet to the wall in the living room, swept up the worst of the plaster dust and stared at the unsuitable grey paint for a while. I'd distributed the recently bought cushions around the room, trying to go for an unstructured, layered look, but I'd actually got something closer to 'bouncy castle', so I piled them up on the sofa instead. Then I shut myself in the bathroom to change, away from Brack who was following me around the house looking pathetically hungry because of the smell of cooking. After that, I took him out to his newly secure run and shut him in with his dinner of rabbit scattered around the burgeoning undergrowth, checked the clock, took some deep breaths, and banged on the living room wall.

There was an answering short knock, a thud of falling plaster, and then silence.

Jill arrived and parked the van on the verge. She'd dressed up too, I was glad to see. I would have felt really daft in my elegant yet practical outfit if she'd turned up in jeans.

'You look smart,' I said, opening the door for her.

'It's nice to wear something that doesn't smell of creosote.' She stepped past me into the house. 'Blimey, that's a lot of cushions.'

I looked, slightly sadly, at the huge pile. 'I know.'

'If you sit down, you'll be suffocated.' Jill poked at the sofa. 'You'll just disappear into a mass and never be seen again.'

'I think I may have a problem.' I picked up a couple and rearranged them, which consisted mostly of turning them through ninety degrees. 'If I ever get hold of a John Lewis catalogue, you may have to stage an intervention.'

'They're very... um... well, most of them are lovely.' Jill stopped in the kitchen doorway. 'Plus they distract the attention nicely from that fireplace. Euan here yet?'

'Not yet.'

Jill fixed me with a look of mascara'd intensity. 'I'm not trying to matchmake, Tamzin, honestly, just letting you know that Euan's always been a decent guy. I've known him since we were five – apart from when he went off to Newcastle. I mean, I know I can't know all the ins and outs about him, but I know his family, I've been on Duke of Edinburgh expeditions with him and, God, those are enough to bring out anyone's internal monster; he's okay.'

'I've invited him to dinner, Jill, not to move in.'

'He couldn't. With all those cushions, there isn't room for another adult in here.' We heard a diffident tap at the front door. 'Anyway,' she said, and put down a bottle of elderflower cordial. 'Driving,' she added shortly and slightly miserably.

I opened the door and Euan was smiling at me from the step. He'd shaved since yesterday and the new smoothness of his cheeks made him look younger, almost boyish. His hair was combed and smoothed down and he'd clearly made quite an effort. He held out a bubble-wrapped package.

'I didn't have any drink. But there's this. Why have you got all those cushions?'

With dignity, and a careful ignoring of both the cushions and the now ominously bulging dust sheet, I led him through to the kitchen, and Euan and Jill started enthusing about the mouth-watering smell while I opened the package he'd given me.

'Oh. Oh, Euan.'

It was a watercolour painting of Brack. Identifiably, absolutely, Brack, from the white-cheeked grin to the neatly curled tip of his tail, sitting in his precise paws-together pose, amber-eyed and gazing intensely at me from the picture.

'That's nice,' Jill understated.

'It's so lifelike.' I tipped the picture to catch the light, and Brack's auburn coat glistened in response.

'I thought, you know, if you ever had to – if you found a wildlife place to take him. Something to remember him by.' Euan looked very big in my kitchen. He wasn't burly, or even rugged, just tall in his white shirt and grey chinos, but there was something about him tonight that seemed... broader. As though he'd expanded. And I realised it was because he was standing up straight, not dipping his head in the diffident stance where his hair dropped across his face and his chin met his collar. Tonight, he was straight-backed and assured.

I looked from him to the picture. Yes. There was pride in him. He was proud of his work, for all he delivered it with a tiptoe and a shyness. He *knew* he was good. A quiet confidence that I wasn't going to make a disappointed face and criticise the colouring or the line of the muzzle, because he *knew* it was right.

It was an attitude that was oddly attractive.

I served the meal and it was all very relaxed and even convivial. Jill told amusing stories about some of her clients and Euan, rather haltingly, as though he didn't want to be thought to be showing off, talked about filming for various TV programmes which had featured his work. When I went to fetch the apple tart from the fridge, I looked back over my shoulder at the scrubbed pine table around which they sat, lit by a low-level lamp on the window ledge which threw a puddle of light into the middle of the room. The tiles on the walls gleamed – they bloody well should do, I'd been scrubbing them most of yesterday – and the scene looked blissfully natural. Just friends, having dinner. No excuses, no having to apologise. No storming out, no punishing silences. Just a calm, chatty meal in my own little house. Where I could drink alcohol and my only worry was that they'd wander into the living room and look under the dust sheet.

I probably had a glass more than I should have done, because when the meal was over and I'd piled the plates in the sink and we were all sitting over coffee, I brought out the sheaf of photographs I'd found in the cupboard.

'That's the same girl, isn't it?' Jill squinted at the muted colours. 'The one in that other photograph you found?'

'Could be.' I fetched 'Stella, 1972' and we compared the pictures. In these, the most recent, Stella looked thinner and her clothes were more what I'd describe as on the 'housewife' scale. Neat little dresses or skirts, and her hair was cropped to an unflattering length. She also didn't seem to be posing for these pictures, they were 'snaps' of the kind that you'd quickly take of someone to tease them about later. In one she was leaning over, her back to the camera, cleaning the bath that I recognised as being the one in this bathroom, although with new side panels now. A couple showed her cooking, smiling a tight sort of smile, as though she'd been instructed to 'look at the camera' in the middle of trying to assimilate the ingredients in a tricky dish.

Among this collection of pictures was a strip of black and white photo-booth pictures, curled with age and dryness into a tube. We flattened them out.

'That must be the boyfriend,' Jill said. 'I wonder if that's who took the rest of the pictures?'

'The boyfriend' was a narrow-faced man, shoulder-length bouncy hair and wire-framed glasses, wearing a wide-collared patterned shirt. These were dated 1971 and it was the younger Stella, the one who'd stood happily by the forsythia bush in the garden, in a pink tank-top over a white blouse, obviously sitting on the lap of the man. They were both beaming at the camera, squeezed into the booth, arms around one another.

'He looks a bit like a weasel,' I observed. I'd been looking up wildlife in order to be able to hold my own in conversation in case Euan started talking about things I'd never heard of, and it was nice to be able to use some of my new knowledge.

'He does, a bit.' Jill held the strip of pictures up to the light. 'Eyes are very close together. I wonder what kind of a boyfriend he was.'

'Husband,' Euan said. He'd got a picture which blurrily showed the happy couple. The narrow-faced man and Stella in what looked like a hotel hallway, surrounded by garishly dressed people, most of them moving out of the shot. The couple were hand in hand, Stella wearing a white dress with more layers than a mille-feuille pastry and holding a bouquet decorously in front of her.

She looked – proud. And a little defiant, with her chin in the air, curls of hair escaping from her tiara-style headdress with the veil pinned back above it. Her new husband wore a fancy patterned shirt again, no tie and very tight trousers. He also looked a bit smug.

'Where were these?' Jill shuffled through them and laid them out on the table as though she were dealing cards.

'Pushed right to the back of the cupboard on the landing.'

'Well.' She gave the pictures another look over. 'I shouldn't think anyone ever used that cupboard, no wonder stuff's been left. Bit odd that they didn't clear it right out when they moved, though.' She flicked at the couple in the pictures. 'I should ask Mum about it, she'll know who lived here back then, I should think.'

'We could try looking it up,' Euan said. 'Use the computer.'

I felt something lift under my ribcage. I was interested in this girl, who looked so young and happy, getting married, living in my cottage. I wanted to know about her. Where she'd moved to. Maybe even get to meet her and show her what I was doing to her old home and how it suited me and Brack. Plus, there was a look in her eyes in those pictures, something that spoke to a hidden part of me. I wanted to know how it all turned out.

'You can, I've got to get home and make sure that Seph hasn't poisoned her sister.' Jill stood up and stretched. 'Thanks for dinner, Tamzin, all round to mine next time? I'll be here tomorrow, might be able to get that run finished off, if the weather holds.'

'It'll rain,' Euan said confidently. 'Look at the moon.'

We looked. The moon was blamelessly shining, nearly full, out of a clear sky.

'Yeah, okay.' Jill sighed. 'I'll take your word for it, Euan, but I'll still be here. And, Tamzin, no more cushions for the love of God. It's like a padded cell in there.'

She left, and Euan and I looked at one another. I wasn't nervous of him, not really, but he looked bigger. I could feel myself recoiling, drawing back into myself with the fear pricking away behind my eyes.

'I'll go too. You look up the cottage.' Euan got up and moved to the door, behind which we could hear Jill's van grumbling into life. 'Let me know.'

I opened the door for him, grateful that he was going and trying not to show it. 'I did have a bit of a go, but very superficially. I'll try again.'

He blinked, slow and deliberate. 'She looks sad,' he said, and nodded towards the photographs still covering the table. 'Even though she's smiling, she looks sad.' He bent slightly forwards, and I thought for one moment that he was going to kiss my cheek, but he just nodded across me. 'Hang the picture on that wall,' he said. 'The fox will look good against that light.' Then he pointed at the dust sheet. 'He'll look better over there, but you're going to have to sort out the plaster first. Oh, and I quite like the cushions.'

And then he was gone, moving as quietly and deliberately as he did when he was watching animals, down the path and in through his own front door, closing it behind him without turning to see if I was still watching, which I was, but from behind the curtain. I heard the soft thud of his door, and then the customary silence. He either tiptoed around his own house, or he genuinely made no sound at all.

And he'd noticed the fireplace. Bugger.

12

Andy's right, I'm not a good wife. I *try*, I really do! I clean every day, and cook so his dinner is on the table when he gets in, even if he's been to the pub first. I borrowed Mum's sewing machine and made some new curtains – they look so pretty, all flowers in orange and brown because the magazines say that's really fashionable at the moment and I want our little house to be all up-to-date and everything. I put Grandma's tablecloth on the big table for when we have dinner and I get the carpet sweeper out every morning to keep the bits down.

But I'm bored. I told Andy that I wanted to go to town and see my friends but he said they wouldn't talk to me anyway. The lads at the garage have been saying that Jeanette has been spreading all these lies about me, saying my wedding cost so much that it put my dad in debt and he had to borrow against the company for it. Which is stupid, cos even Jeanette knows that Dad has been putting money aside to pay for my wedding ever since I was born! I don't want to go now and have people looking at me and pointing. I have to go in on market day to get our food and stuff, but I go in early, before they all get off work and do Market Wednesday, going round the pubs. So I'm here, on my own, every day. And when Andy comes in, I just want to talk to him, I want to show him what I've done in the house and the garden, but he says he just wants to sit and watch TV cos he's had a hard day. I'm to be quiet until he's had a bit of a rest and a beer, and he'll tell me when he wants to talk to me.

He shouted at me today. He's never really shouted like that before. He gets cross, of course he does, and he's still angry that Dad won't put the house in his name, but he's never really shouted *at* me like that. I was only trying to show him the material I'd got to make some covers for the settee – it's quite old and it came from Mum and Dad's and Andy thinks they should have bought us a new one, so he was quite 'off' when they brought it up. He got a bit cross when I laughed when he got it stuck in the doorway trying to get it in, and he went back down to town and didn't come home until the pubs shut. But the sofa is comfy, and we can snuggle up together and watch TV of an evening, and so I thought I'd re-cover it to make it a bit smarter and match it with the curtains. I got the material out of the bag and I was spreading it out on the table to show Andy while he had his dinner. And that's when he shouted. I can't even remember what he said, not really. He threw his plate on the floor and said something about not even being able to enjoy his dinner in peace and quiet, and he had that look on his face again. So I tried to make it up to him but he didn't want to look at me, he said, didn't I know that he wanted quiet to eat? He said lots of other stuff, but I was crying by then and I couldn't really hear, and he pulled me out of the kitchen and out onto the stairs and he shut the door. It was dark and I'd hurt myself on the stairs and I didn't know if I could come back out or not, so I went up to our bedroom and I looked at the beautiful new curtains and that made me cry even harder.

I think I went to sleep, because it was proper dark when Andy came in and my eyes were all sore and my side hurt where I'd fallen on the stairs. I didn't know if I should say something to him or not, I didn't know what he'd be like, and I couldn't see his face because it was dark. But he was really sweet and he said that I had to stop making him cross and then everything would be all right. I was so happy that he was back to normal that I let him do – well, some things that the lads had told him about and he wanted to try. It wasn't very nice and I didn't enjoy it very much, but it made Andy love me again, and he cuddled me all night and said that we were the perfect couple and how much everyone wanted to be like us. Then, in the morning, he told me my face was all blotchy and ugly and to go and wash before I kissed him off to work. And he took some pictures of me with that camera, even though I said it was odd to take pictures of someone who looks ugly, but he said that he wanted to show me when they were developed, so I'd know and remember not to look like that again. But I never see those pictures he takes. Oh, I've seen some, ones he's taken around the house and stuff, but the other ones, the *secret* ones, I think he puts those in his suitcase in the bottom of the wardrobe and he locks the door. I know he's got something in there that he likes to look at, when I'm downstairs watching the television and he comes up to go to bed because he's got an early start or something, and then he always calls me up a bit later and he's got the wardrobe door open and he wants to do stuff then.

My side still hurts a bit. I don't remember Mum having to be quiet until after Dad ate his dinner when he came in from work. They used to sit in the kitchen together for ages in the evening, while I did my puzzles or read my books. Dad would read bits from the newspaper out to her and I could hear them laughing. Dad didn't go out again, either. He'd always say, 'I'm back to my girls!' when he came in and not go to the pub or to meet his friends; sometimes we'd all go out for a walk somewhere if the weather was nice, but that's all. But then, I know the lads go round the pubs on Market Wednesdays when they have a half day at work – even though Andy says that's because we're stuck in the Old Days when market was a big thing and when everyone met their friends and it's like we've never heard of the telephone up here. So maybe Dad was just different. Which means Andy's right and all the girls let their husbands do what Andy wants to do to me. They must all have dinner on the table and then go and sit in the other room, and they must keep the house really clean and like a show home all the time.

And that means I really am a bad wife. I just need to try harder. Keep the house better and not talk to him when he gets in and not want more than I have. Cos I've got everything I ever wanted, haven't I? A handsome husband who works hard and a lovely house. Now we're just waiting for the kiddies to come along and everything will be perfect.

13

When I woke up the next morning, I'd been going to fire up the laptop and do a more in-depth search for any information on the cottage, but I got distracted by having gone to bed and left the washing-up. Morning me was a bit cross at night-time me, because stuff was stuck on the plates and I'd left the apple tart out of the fridge so the pastry had gone soft and floppy. Night-time me, I decided, was a slattern, who didn't deserve morning me, and I crashed the crockery around in the soapy water, with Brack giving me little worried looks from under the table where he'd settled with an old bone he'd dug up from somewhere.

Outside, Euan had been right, damn him, and it was raining. A slow gauze of drizzle, blocking the view and bringing the sky down across the fields until it nearly touched the end of the garden and putting a sheen of wetness across all the surfaces. I saw Euan, green coated and wearing a hat that looked like a camping toilet, carefully closing his front door and setting out up the lane, stopping every now and then to stare into the mist, like a still shot from a magazine.

That reminded me again of the photographs. Of Stella, so

happy in 1971 but thinner and with that look in her eye by 1973. It was the expression that I recognised. I'd seen it on my own face often enough, caught in mirrors or in pictures that I'd had to stand and pose for. That look that said, 'What went wrong?' That look of having lost oneself somewhere underneath someone else's idea of who I should be.

I took a mug of tea out to Jill when she arrived. 'Thanks. Girls didn't want to come in the rain.' She took the tea from me and wrapped her hands around it. 'Nice to have the choice.'

'You didn't have to. The rest of it will wait.' I looked at the nearly finished wiring. 'It's secure and useable for now.'

'Never leave a job unfinished,' she said, with a meaningful look. 'It's twice as bad if you've got to go back to it.'

I thought of those caked-on plates and had to agree.

'Did you do a search yet? On the cottage?'

We huddled down in the shelter of the high brick wall. The rain was coming from all directions at once in a grey, seeping mass. Jill didn't really seem to notice, but I was getting damp. 'Not yet. I'm going to have another try, the last search I did I only found planning information.'

Jill took a last swig and handed me back the mug. 'Like I said, I'll ask Mum. But she spends winters over in Crete with my sister, who lives there.' A deep sigh. 'Lucky bugger. All our conversations tend to revolve around why *I* don't get myself a nice winter place and give up work. Honestly, it's like she never had children or had to work herself. Just because Jenny married rich and old and ended up a widow with a house in Greece and a toy boy – well.' Another sigh. 'Mum usually comes back around the end of May. Once she's back over here, she gets a bit more invested. I can ask about the cottages then.'

I took the mugs back into the kitchen. Euan was coming down the lane. I saw him stop at the fence to talk to Jill, leaning his arms against the sturdy post and rail that stopped the cattle from escaping, the rain decorating his green coat with water sequins, like a relic from the seventies. That reminded me of the pictures again. Scenes from a life that was probably still being lived, somewhere else. I picked one out at random, Stella in this kitchen only with an old cooker with electric rings and an eye-level grill and a white enamel sink. She had her back to the worktop and a pair of laundry tongs in her hand as though the photograph captured her midway through washing day. She was smiling, but it was the smile of someone told, 'For Christ's sake, smile, will you! You've got a face like a market trader's elbow.' That stretched mouth. Trying, trying to look happy enough.

But the eyes of someone who has died a little more inside at the insult. The eyes of someone who knows they can never get it right, however hard they try.

I tried the computer again, running through all the search terms I could think of. I managed to find some old photographs of the farm from the 1920s, when a passing local photographer had captured horse-drawn hay wagons coming into the yard, and I could see my cottage, with a lady in a flowered overall standing at the front. It had had the old style sliding sash windows back then, and a wooden front door that didn't look as though it was ever used. But that was all. It was as though life went on in the rest of Yorkshire, but didn't touch these little houses out here on the track in the hills.

On impulse, I picked up the photographs and fastened them to the fridge with one of the Cornwall fridge magnets that I'd brought with me. The comic-style map, with the piskies and the cream tea stuck over the outline of the county, looked at odds with the strained smile in the photograph on the top, but I didn't change it. It was important, that juxtaposition of frolicking fairies and clotted cream with the expression in Stella's eyes.

'Did you get out?' I asked the photo. 'Or did you learn to live with it?'

There was no answer other than Brack crunching up his bone under the table.

* * *

A few days later, I found I'd started waking in the night. I thought I'd got over the shock of the silence of the nights but it seemed that my brain had decided again to realise that it was very, very quiet once it got dark. It seemed to like to worry me by prodding me awake at around 3 a.m. for a couple of hours' fretting and wandering around the house, carrying a mug of tea and peering out of windows.

I'd rarely woken in the middle of the night in Truro. Well, not without cause, anyway. Here, every sound was magnified by the silence that surrounded it. An owl shrieking at the bottom of the valley would sound as though it was outside my window, the wind coming from the east caught at my windows and made them boom and the letter box rattle. Back in Cornwall, I'd been protected by the city around me. All night, traffic had drowned out the sounds of nature, and the twenty-four-hour shop at the end of the road had meant that there was a near continual stream of people dodging in and out for emergency booze top-ups or a sudden rush on nappies.

Here, the nothingness was both reassuring and a threat. I'd leap awake from a dream of being younger, looking after Gran or trying to get to work and failing to find a bus stop, and there would be nothing to distract my thoughts. Nothing outside my window but blank, whistling dark. This night was no different, except I thought I'd heard a noise.

First port of call was, as always, to check on Brack. He

overnighted in his run now and I woke to a kind of distant and irrational fear that someone was trying to snatch him. I pulled a jacket over my pyjamas and, with my mobile phone torch held out like a beacon, I went out across the paddock. The run was, as ever, secure, and Brack was sleeping curled up with his nose under his tail, pushed into the shelter of the small tree. He raised his head at the sound of my approach, and then went back to sleep again. Clearly, I didn't look as though I was about to either feed him or let him out, in my peculiar clothing combination.

I turned off the torch and looked around. I could hear the wind in the distant trees of the copse, but this far down the hill it was only a passing breeze. The faint glow in the sky off to the east that was Pickering was muted, and I could see the stars arching above me in the navy sky.

'You're out early.' The voice came from the lane and made me jump so hard I dropped my phone.

'What the...? Who's there?'

The voice had been hushed, half-toned.

'It's me.' Euan climbed over the post and rail fence that lined the track and then the wire strand that divided my paddock from the field. 'You aren't dressed.'

'No, I was checking Brack. Why are you up and out?' I tried to cover my confusion by searching the grass at my feet for the phone. I didn't want to step on it and ruin any kind of air of confidence.

'Dawn is the best time for wildlife.' Euan shrugged himself deeper into the ubiquitous green coat.

'But it isn't dawn.' I stared at the horizon, which was as black and star-strewn as the rest of the sky.

'They would see me coming if it was.' He bent down and picked up my phone, then handed it to me. 'Want to come along?'

I thought about my warm bed. The mug of tea I'd left on

the worktop. Then I thought about spending the time until it got light lying in the dark thinking about my mistakes. 'All right.'

We stood for a moment or two. 'You'd better get dressed,' Euan said eventually. 'You can't come in your pyjamas. It's cold.'

'Oh.'

'But you'd better hurry. It's only an hour until dawn.'

I looked back at him over my shoulder. 'An hour? How far are we going – Sheffield?'

'And not the noisy coat.' He leaned against the tall wall that formed the end of Brack's run, easy and relaxed despite the dark.

I dashed in and hauled on some warm clothes. I was tying up my boots when I stopped suddenly, struck by the thought that I was going along with this without any fear.

Was *this* how it was meant to feel? Just a minor annoyance about having to hurry? The thought rocked me. But then Euan tapped on the kitchen window and I had to hasten myself into a big woollen jacket that made, as far as I was aware, no noise at all, and out of the back door to where he stood, carelessly resting against my patio furniture.

He nodded slowly when he saw me. 'You'll be too warm, but that's all right.'

'I don't think I will.' The night air was teetering on the edge of frost. I'd been horrified when the plant nursery had said that they weren't selling tender plants yet because of the frosts. In Cornwall, they would have overwintered outside, and I'd had a jab of culture shock.

Euan didn't say anything else. He just set off, over the fence, heading down the track this time. We followed the path until it met the metalled road which we followed for a while, then broke off to walk through damp woodland at the bottom of the valley. We crossed a small stream and then began to climb back up, but before we left the woodland completely, Euan put a hand on my arm and, with a finger to his lips, he pointed.

I couldn't see anything. I scanned the edge of the wood. About ten metres beyond where we stood, the trees broke, there was an earth bank and then fields, and I couldn't see anything more of note than trees gradually unfolding leaves where the early May sun got to them. I raised my eyebrows at him.

Euan nodded sideways, off to his left. I looked again. Two very small badger cubs had just emerged from the side of the earth bank and were sniffing at the ground, half-in and half-out of the hole. 'Oh!' I couldn't help myself, caught by surprise at the sight. They instantly whisked away back underground, and I could have bitten my tongue.

'You have to stay quiet,' Euan observed. 'Or they know you're here.'

'Sorry.' I pulled a face. 'Really. It was stupid of me.'

He looked at me; we were very close together with the trees pressing in all around us, so I could see his eyes reflecting starlight and the green of the burgeoning leaves. 'They'll be back,' he whispered. 'Don't worry.'

'It was just so stupid,' I whispered back. 'I know I need to be quiet.'

He didn't reply to that, but I felt my face flaming with the idiocy. A hand on my sleeve tugged me on and we emerged through the trees into the edge of a field where the grass grew thick and lush, pocked with bog cotton and tadpoled stretches of dark water.

'Here. Sit down.' He pulled at me again and we sank down onto a dry patch of ground, our backs to a hedge which ticked with a hidden electric fence, and the field running uphill in front of us. Dawn was beginning to glimmer, the light lifting to pale grey.

From a pocket, Euan pulled a flask, unscrewed the lid and poured. The smell of coffee, bitter and sharp against the scent of lightly crushed grass and damp, made my mouth water. He held the cup out to me. 'We could be a while, so I always bring refreshments.'

'Thank you.' Yes, it was bitter, but hot and welcome. The warmth of the plastic mug in my fingers, the smell of the morning and the occasional brush of Euan's coated shoulder against mine as we crouched in the hedge bottom almost made me want to laugh. 'What are we waiting for?'

'Anything that comes along.' He took the cup from me and poured another dose of coffee.

'There's a rabbit over there.' I pointed. The rabbit had probably been there all along and just become visible in the rising light, but, after my badger faux pas, I felt I had to contribute something useful.

'Uh-huh,' he said into the cup, and I had the feeling he was trying not to laugh. 'I think we'll just wait a *bit* longer.'

'Sorry,' I whispered again.

'Tamzin.' He looked at me now, dropping the cup to the grass and blinking that slow, delayed blink. 'This is my job.' His voice was only a little bit above a whisper so I found myself having to concentrate on the words to hear them above the sound of birdsong, which had risen noticeably. 'You're not supposed to know.'

'What, I'm not supposed to know it's your job?' I hunched myself further down into my woollen coat. 'Is it a secret?'

He laughed then, his whole face seemed to open up and lose the guarded expression that he usually wore, under the sideways hair and above the incipient beard. 'No. I don't expect you to know how to be around the animals. I've been doing this all my life.'

'Creeping through hedges in the dark.' I picked up the cup

and handed it to him. 'I bet the girls were just queueing up for you.'

I spoke without thinking. Again. Almost as though I'd forgotten how to watch my words and police my tone; almost as though none of that was important any more. I waited for his response.

It wasn't what I expected or what I'd been half-bracing myself for. All he did was give a small smile which didn't touch his eyes, a motion of his head that could have meant anything, and then he started pouring another cup of the fragrant coffee. My heartbeat settled back down again, and I realised how braced I'd been.

'What's that?' I caught a movement out of the corner of my eye. 'Over there. Deer?'

He glanced up. 'Ah. That's more like it.' The cup went down again. 'Hare.'

'Are you sure?' The hazel-coloured creature was walking across the grass, coming towards us. It looked huge.

'Yep.' There was that note of humour again. 'Adult male, by the look of it.'

He was drawing the hare in his mind, I could see it. The way his eyes fixed and only flickered to watch the movement of the animal as it loped slowly down the slope, still heading towards us, stopping now and then to sit, ears erect, or to drop its head to graze.

The light was lifting almost imperceptibly, moving from the grey to the white light of proper dawn. Further down the field, a red-brown bird descended from a tree and then rose away again to flutter stationary over the rim of the field.

'Kestrel,' Euan said to my unasked question, but he kept watching the hare's advance. At a point about midway between us and the boggy patch of ground, the hare stopped and reared up. A lump on the ground that I had taken to be a clump of muddy grass suddenly got up and shot away, hotly pursued by the hare, until I could see they were *two* hares, sprinting their way across the field until they vanished into the opposite hedge-line. It had happened so fast that I'd hardly had time to register that I'd actually been staring at another hare all the time.

'Did you know that one was there?' I asked Euan, who'd picked up his coffee again.

'I saw it go down.' He sipped. 'They go so still you forget they're there. But I was watching the way the light looked on its fur as the sun came up.' He waved a hand at the sky. Cautious beams of sunlight were creeping over the tops of the trees, giving half of the wood a wash of pale green.

'Your drawings are incredible.' I looked out over the field. He wasn't seeing what I was seeing, I was fairly sure of that. Where I saw patchy grass growing and a hedge, he was seeing light and shade and all of the colours I was unaware of.

'Thank you.' Blink. 'I can't do anything else.' A swallow of coffee. 'Not quite true. I can play the guitar. But not very well.'

'I never hear you. Through the wall, I mean.'

The cup went down and he was staring at the scenery again. 'I don't play any more,' he said quietly.

'Did the stroke affect that too?' The steam from the coffee was spiralling upwards, dissipating slowly into the morning air. I watched it, because I didn't want to look at his face.

'I had a brain injury,' he said, after I'd watched the coffee cool for a while. 'The injury gave rise to the stroke.' He stood up then, and held out a hand to help me to my feet. I realised how cold my hands were when I felt his grasp, his fingers were warm and damp from holding the coffee.

He hadn't answered my question either, I noticed. Almost as though he was trying to give rise to a different conversation. 'That sounds bad,' I said, not wanting to lead him anywhere he didn't want to go.

But he stayed there, back to the hawthorn, gradually letting go of my hand. 'My wife hit me with a frying pan,' he said. 'On the head. The stroke came later.' Now he was shaking out the coffee cup, screwing it back onto the flask and putting it away in his pocket, prosaic actions amid all the green beauty.

A bird began to sing. A warbled rise and fall of notes, so pure into the air that I almost didn't want to say anything to interrupt it. But I had to say something to acknowledge his words. But what? He had a wife? That, given his appearance, wasn't totally unlikely. That she'd hit him? But I didn't know what part *he* had played, he could have been going for her with a knife.

So I picked the part that sounded oddest. 'A frying pan? Those are heavy.'

'This one was. Actually, I think it might have been a wok.' He turned around, scanning the valley. I couldn't tell if he was blinking, processing the words. 'It didn't seem important to ask.'

And now I *had* to know. 'Was it a violent relationship?'

A shrug. Just a rise and fall of shoulders in that green coat, but it said more than his words. All he said was, 'She hit me,' but the shrug spoke of shame, of being thought a liar. It spoke of the cognitive dissonance of being with someone who said they loved you whilst treating you in a way you would never have treated them – a way that you wouldn't have treated your worst enemy. It was a shrug of defeat and hopelessness and almost disbelief.

Then he started to walk, with me following, squelching through the boggy bottom of the valley with the suck and tug of boots in mud, the high metallic whistle of birdsong and no more words until we came back to the edge of the woods again. 'Don't tell anyone,' Euan said. 'Please.'

'What, that your wife beat you?' I was breathing hard and, yes, I was too warm in my coat.

'It makes me feel...' he tailed off. 'I couldn't fight back,' the words burst out suddenly. 'How could I? I couldn't make her stop by hurting her back, that would make me as bad as her, and she was five foot nothing – who would believe that she could do any harm? But she'd wait until I was asleep and then wake me up pouring water on my face and she'd shout and scream when I wanted to go to bed; hours and hours of shouting until I'd say anything to get her to let me sleep...' Another trailing off of the words.

'Do you still see her?'

He shook his head. 'Moved back home to get away. She's an ex-wife now. We're divorced. She emails, sometimes. I ignore them.'

'Euan.' I had nothing to follow up with and not enough breath for what I needed to say.

He stopped and turned. Gazed down the length of this little valley bottom, which looked to be full of nothing but trees and wet grass but the cacophony of small birds gave the lie to the appearance. 'You've got the "No Callers" thing too,' he said slowly. 'I can see it.'

Again, he wasn't looking at me. Those artist's eyes were raking the bark of a silver-trunked tree where branches as fine as hair bore tiny leaves, uncurling slowly like a baby's fingers. 'What do you mean?'

He sighed and turned, and now I had his full attention, and it was disconcerting. As though he were taking in every detail of me like a laser scanner. 'You hunch, you scuttle. You don't ask. You make sure it's all right before you laugh.' Another sigh. 'Survivor knows survivor, Tamzin.'

Then he was off again, crossing the little stream and back out onto the road, busy now with people heading to early-start jobs, tyres against tarmac drowning out the sound of the birds. We didn't speak again, until we turned up the dusty lane with the cottages bathed in the newly risen sun at the top.

'I have to draw now,' Euan said. 'While I remember.'

And then he was gone, heading off inside his house.

'Thank you,' I half-called after him. I wasn't sure what for. The walk? The coffee? The confidences?

His hand made a dismissive gesture, but his mind was clearly already on composition, on the play of light on brown fur; working on capturing the movement of hares as they tore across a boggy field. At least, I presumed that was what was behind his abrupt leaving. He might just have been contemplating what to have for breakfast, it was very hard to tell with Euan. He'd practically turned enigmatic into performance art.

I fed Brack in his run and then sat down to talk to him through the wire while he ate. Well, it wasn't so much 'eating' as 'growling and gobbling'. Brack treated me as a competitive sibling when he had food and I felt the pang of keeping a wild animal in a human environment again. He *needed* more freedom and foxy company. Somewhere he and his inadequate number of limbs would be safe and protected, but not be *too* safe. He needed to fight and spat with other foxes, to mate and to raise litters of cubs. I wanted him to have territory, not live in a comfortable prison.

'That's it,' I told him firmly, as he buried the remnants of his meal in a patch of earth near the house part of the run. 'I'm going to look for a sanctuary to take you.'

I got a sharply focused look for that. Harsh, bright eyes that looked as though they could see into my soul, whilst really he was just looking to see if I'd got any more food. Then he growled and went back to digging. The earth on his paws and nose made me more resolute. 'You need to live somewhere with more space. And other foxes.'

I got up stiffly from where I'd been sitting at the base of the run. This morning's early excursion up and down dale had tugged at muscles in my legs that weren't used to that sort of thing, and the ache reminded me of Euan. I looked over at his cottage. There was a light on in an upstairs window, the backs of the houses were still in shadow as the sun wouldn't climb over the rooftops until nearer midday.

A little worm of loneliness nibbled at my heart. There was a lot of day to get through yet. Work was solitary – although I knew there were more editors and writers at the other end of the computer, they weren't *here*. Jill had no reason to come up to the cottage now the run was finished, and she was probably welding pipes down in town, or whatever she did. Euan was painting. It was just me.

So I opened the door to Brack's run and took him back into the house with me, so I could make some furtive attempts to patch up the continually falling plaster in the fireplace wall.

14

'There's a place up on the moors,' Jill said, handing me a much-folded leaflet. 'It's an old farm. Lady whose garden I was doing took some tiny hedgehogs over there last autumn, apparently. She gave me this.' She put her mug down and helped herself to another biscuit.

I looked at the crumpled, brightly coloured paper. 'Wood Farm Wildlife Rescue and Rehabilitation. That's a bit of a mouthful.' The pictures showed gulls trotting around a yard like chickens, a grumpy-looking badger in straw, and hands holding young rabbits.

'They're very good.' Jill looked at me sternly. 'Not far away, so you could visit. And it's run by my second cousin, although I've not seen much of her since we were kids, so that's not much of a recommendation, but better than nothing.'

It had taken me a couple of weeks to build up to this, but now the sun was high in the sky for most of the day and Brack wasn't keen to go out. He either hung around in his run or he lay in a corner in the house. He needed company. He needed outdoors and space and shelter. He needed *more than me.*

'She's said you can visit whenever, just give her a ring first.' Jill drained her mug. 'Any more tea?'

'Thank you. No, honestly, thanks for finding this.' I got up to boil the kettle again. 'I know it's time to let him go.'

'The place does smell nicer without him.' Jill nodded across at the run. 'Foxes aren't great houseguests. You could get a dog. Or a cat.'

'You get used to them,' I said aimlessly. 'You stop noticing the smell. And the biting. And never having a cushion that doesn't have holes in.'

'There you go, then. You can redecorate and pay me to replace the skirting. Or repair that fireplace.' She gave me a wide grin. 'That dust sheet's fooling no one, you realise that?' Then she looked up. 'Sounds like a car coming up the track.'

This happened so rarely that it was a spectator sport. We both went to the front window and stared out, down towards the road, where a cloud of dust showed that something was, indeed, heading in our direction.

'Euan been shopping, maybe?' I strained my eyes but could only see dust.

'Come on. Euan goes out once a year. He gets his shopping delivered, the same as you. You're as bad as each other for never going into town. Have you seen him lately?' She gave me a sharp look.

'No.' It was true, I hadn't really seen much of Euan since our early-morning walk down the valley. 'Just to say hello to out in the garden now and again.' And I didn't dare go back into town. The local paint shops might hold a parade.

'Ah.' She nodded wisely. 'He'll be on a big commission then, probably. Shuts himself away when he's working. Well, no, he shuts himself away all the time, but when he's working he makes hermits look sociable and outgoing.'

'I think he probably has to concentrate quite hard,' I said. 'And maybe the brain injury has made it harder.'

'Brain injury?' Jill sounded curious and that was when I realised I'd said too much.

'It's definitely a car.' I tried to change the subject. 'Who on earth would come up here? The farmer always comes in a tractor, or sometimes a jeep thing when he's got a trailer.'

I kept my eyes on the window. Out of the corner of my eye, I saw Jill turn towards me as though she was about to ask something, but the car came inching its way closer and diverted our attention again.

'Someone who's never been up here before then,' Jill said. 'We all know to come carefully over that bit with the potholes.'

The car had slowed now, as though the driver was looking for an address, which was ridiculous because the two cottages were the only buildings up here. It inched its way towards the verge, put two wheels up onto the grass and then stopped. Nothing more happened.

'Who is it?'

'I can't see. Sun's reflecting off the windows.'

I went to the front door. 'Someone must be lost. They'll be needing directions, I should think.'

I opened the front door at exactly the same time as the car door opened. A woman got out, looking uncertainly at the cottages, catching sight of Euan's fluttering 'No Callers' sign. She was beautifully dressed in a figure-hugging sundress and sandals, Ray-Bans covering much of her face. Her long blonde hair, damp with sweat from the heat inside the car, was caught back under an ornate clip and her nails were varnished a bright red. She looked like some kind of Vision of Metropolitan Life.

'She looks well lost,' Jill observed over my shoulder. 'Nobody dresses like that out here if they want to live to see sixty. She looks like she's off one of those reality TV programmes.'

But I knew who she was. I'd known, but not wanted to acknowledge it, since I saw the car nosing its cautious way up the track.

'Hello, Katie,' I said, opening the door and stepping out. 'So you came.'

She turned, taking off the sunglasses as she did so, a slow move. She was, I guessed, giving herself thinking time. A lipsticked smile spread across her face. 'Yeah, well. I needed... a little break and I thought, "Who do I know who lives somewhere nice that I can go and visit for a few days?" And I found your address and I thought I'd pop up and see you!'

So we were playing that game, were we? Or was it just because Jill was here, hovering behind my shoulder in a little self-produced cloud of anticipatory enquiry?

We stood on the verge while I introduced them. 'Katie, this is Jill, she helps build things. Jill, Katie and I – we knew each other down in Cornwall.'

'It's KT, just the initials.' Katie wafted a hand to Jill. 'Like...'

'Mister T?' Jill supplied.

Katie gave her a look that indicated they probably weren't going to ever be bosom buddies, and opened the boot of her car to reveal one tiny weekend case. I blew out a sigh of relief; I'd been a bit worried that Katie would have brought her entire wardrobe. This meant she wasn't, at least, going to try to move in.

'Shall I put the kettle on again?' Jill asked brightly.

'I think I need to talk to Katie,' I half-whispered. 'Do you mind?'

'Course not.' Jill raised her eyebrows and then lowered her voice to match mine. 'Are you sure you'll be all right? You don't need me to referee or anything?'

I grinned and patted her shoulder. 'I'll give you a call about the wildlife place. You can introduce me to your second cousin and we can look it over together. Maybe tomorrow?' I looked meaningfully at Katie's back, where she was standing scanning the valley, Ray-Bans firmly back in place. 'I'll tell you everything then. Promise.'

Jill's face was suddenly serious. 'You don't have to, Tamzin. Seriously. It's none of my business, if you'd rather forget...'

'I'll need to, I think.'

The bright smile was back now. 'If you're sure. I'll give Nicola a ring tonight. About the wildlife place.' She grinned at me. 'One less thing for you to worry about.' And then she headed off to her van, leaving me with Katie on the doorstep, who was looking up at my tiny cottage, slightly dubiously.

'It's not very big.'

'Doesn't need to be.' I held the door open in invitation. 'Come on.'

As I closed the door behind us, I thought I saw a flick of sleeve at the next-door window, as though Euan had looked out for a moment.

15

STELLA, DECEMBER 1971

Well, it wasn't quite the wedding day I'd expected! But everyone said I looked gorgeous and beautiful – I suppose they always say that to brides, though, don't they? But I felt so proud there walking up the aisle to Andy, and he was so *handsome* in his suit. I cried a bit when I saw Mum in tears when we did the vows. Dad was a bit funny in the car on the way there, though. He was very quiet, and then, just before we got to the church, he asked the driver to wait a minute and then he just turned to me with this really strange look on his face. He said, 'Are you really sure, Stella? I won't be angry if you don't want to do this,' which was quite peculiar because I'd got all my dress and my veil and everything on. So I said, 'Yes,' and that I loved Andy and Dad said that love wasn't always enough but he wasn't going to try to talk me out of it. Then he told me the best thing – he's bought a house! For me and Andy! One of the little cottages up on the old Bracken Ridge Farm, up where Kathleen used to live when I was a baby! Our own house! Dad said he'd keep it all in his name so that if anything happened to Andy I could still live there, only when he said it, his voice was all heavy. A bit like he was trying to say something to me without saying the words?

And then we had the wedding and it was beautiful. We had it up at St Hilda's because Mum says All Saints is common, and besides, we couldn't do a car convoy to All Saints because it's just round the corner and we could walk. So we had all these cars laid on and everyone got driven up to Ellerburn, with the trees all frosty and a little bit of snow lying on the ground, and it was lovely. Then we had the Hall for the reception, which wasn't quite so beautiful cos Dad and Andy had a bit of a falling out. I'd told Andy that Dad had bought a house for us, and Andy wanted Dad to make it over to him. 'For security,' he said, but Dad wasn't having any of it and there were words. But luckily Mum was there and she hustled the two of them into a corner so that everyone wouldn't see and hear, and I know that Dad didn't back down because Andy was really cross about it later on. He told me that I had to tell my dad that a man ought to live in his own house. I'd never seen Andy like that before. He went really red in the face and he kept walking up and down the room and saying things like he never would have married me if he'd known my dad would be like that, which is a really horrible thing to say when you're still in your wedding clothes!

But anyway, Andy soon calmed down. Someone, I *think* it was Mum's friend, Alice, because she's always been a bit flash, had bought us a camera as a wedding present. Andy was really happy about that because he said he'd always wanted a camera and he was taking pictures of me in my dress, even though I told him we'd got a proper photographer cos Dad was paying Mr Bentley to do all the pictures of the wedding and make us up a proper album. But Andy said he wanted his *own* photos. He got me to lie on the bed in my dress and pose for him and it was a bit weird, because he wanted me to – well, some of those pictures were what Mum would have called 'a bit saucy'. I felt a bit silly. But Andy was doing all this David Bailey stuff and he was having such fun and he'd stopped shouting about Dad, so I let him take those pictures. I didn't want to even *think* about what the men down at the chemist's were going to say when they processed them. I'm going to have to get Andy to take the film into York or somewhere to get them done, cos I don't want Mr Williams to tell my dad about the pictures.

So, that was last week. We had our wedding night in the Hall, which was – well, it was lovely, really. Andy was very kind, even though it hurt a bit, but he said I'd soon get used to it. And then we moved up to the cottage and Mum and Dad bought us some new furniture. We had the twin tub and some other bits that we'd got for presents, and it's so beautiful. Just me and Andy and our own little house. I'm going to make it all pretty – I've got the material to make the curtains already, and I'm going to do the garden just like Grandad used to have his, with vegetables so we can eat all our own stuff and not have to buy it. Andy will have to do the digging and the heavy lifting, but I'm sure he won't mind. It's a shame that the bus into town only goes on Wednesdays and Fridays, but now I've given up work I only need to go in to go to the shops, like Andy says.

Jeanette and Jackie aren't talking to me now. Jeanette got me round the back of the school one night, back in, oh, September, I think. Just after Mum and Dad had put the engagement announcement in the *Post*, anyway. She asked me why they hadn't got an invitation to the wedding yet and were they allowed to come, and it was *horrible*. I didn't want to say that Mum and Andy said they'd be jealous, so I just said that we were only having family and she said that she knew that wasn't true because Dean said that Kenneth said that some of the lads from the garage were going, so why couldn't she and Jackie go too? Then she called me stuck-up and a snob and a few other things too, and did I think I was better than them just because I was the first to get married and I was probably... well, going to have a baby anyway, and that was why I was getting married so quickly.

Well, I quite lost my temper! I told her that I'd invite who I wanted to my wedding and I didn't want her and Jackie there if she was going to call me names. And then *she* shouted at *me* and told me I was a stupid cow and Andy was only marrying me because he wanted to get his hands on my dad's money and, well. That was that. Turns out Mum and Andy had been right all along and they weren't my friends at all. So I was glad they hadn't come to my wedding, but a little bit sad too because we'd all been friends since our mums used to meet up and chat while we played in the beck before we all went to school. When I told Andy all this, he was really nice about it and told me that I didn't need them anyway.

I'd got him.

16

Katie and I sat at the kitchen table, in silence. She looked for all the world as though she really *had* just popped up on a visit, remarking on the cosiness of the place, the décor, the number of cushions. She'd not mentioned the now-sagging sheet covering most of the wall. I didn't know if she was being tactful or whether randomly fabric covered walls were something she expected from me.

She looked at the photos of Stella I'd stuck to the fridge and asked if they were old pictures of the cottage, and made all the right noises, as though this was just two mates having a coffee, talking about old times.

Only we weren't. Once we'd skated over the superficials, we just sat. Eventually, though, I had to say something.

'Have you left him?'

Then all the confidence, all the gloss and the glamour dropped away, and Katie looked tired and older. She shrugged. 'It's not that bad,' she said, averting her eyes. 'Not like it was with you. He's different with me. Better.'

I stayed quiet, lifting my cup again.

'He just...' Katie stood up and started circling the room like a nervous horse. 'He's just a bit weird about me having friends. And he doesn't like my mum and dad or my brother. And I just don't seem to have any money left at the end of the month and I don't know what's happening and he – he says it's because I'm a bit stupid and I'm spending more because there's two of us there, but I don't think that's...'

She stopped. Took a deep breath and refilled the kettle without asking if I wanted another cup. 'Anyway.' Her tone was brighter now. 'You said – remember? Just before you left Cornwall, you said... you gave me your address, and you said...'

'I said if it all got too much and you needed someone to talk to, to come and find me.' I'd thought I meant it, at the time. But now, with her here, it was stirring up memories that I didn't want. The mysteriously vanishing money. The 'your friends aren't really your friends, they're all laughing at you behind your back'. The slow, slow ostracism of anyone who wasn't him.

'Yes. And I thought – I dunno. It gets a bit confused in my head sometimes, you know? When everyone is telling me how great he is, and then I come home and...' Katie trailed off. 'I want to talk to someone who knows him,' she said quietly. 'Perspective, you know?'

I wasn't quite sure I could offer much in the way of perspective, other than, 'He's much better seen from a very, very long way away.' I stood up. I was awash with tea by now and needed some fresh air. 'Let's go for a quick walk,' I said. 'Stretch your legs after driving all that way.'

There was so much unsaid. We both understood the gaps, we didn't need to fill them in, and Katie was right, I probably was the only other person she knew who could talk about this. About *him*. Dominic.

We walked up the garden and leaned on the wall looking out

over the fields. 'You own this place?' Katie asked, with a tone that implied it was like owning my own island.

'Yes. My grandmother died and left me everything. It was enough to move and to live on for a bit.'

'Dom said you ran off owing him thousands.' This was the first time she'd slid into mentioning what he must have told her about us. 'And he's going to sue you.'

'Is he?' We stared, jointly, off into the blue of the haze that hung between the sky and the land. 'Well, good luck with that.'

Yes, I could imagine how he'd rationalise that. He'd been mentally spending my grandmother's money well before she died, badgering me for details on how much I thought her house would be worth, did she have investments. All done in a tone that implied it was about building for *our* future, that he knew how to secure the money, where to put it so it would return the best interest. But I'd seen the muscle car magazines, furtively read the letters and emails. He knew *exactly* how he was going to spend my inheritance.

'Who's that?' Katie suddenly turned and I saw Euan, in a paint-splattered T-shirt and jeans, feet bare, walking along the edge of the field towards the cottages. 'He looks – oh my God, it's that bloke!'

'*A* bloke, certainly,' I observed dryly.

'The one that did that picture! Off of...' She clicked her fingers. 'Oh, you know. With the celebs and all that. They filmed him while he painted it and the mouse had all these little whiskers and stuff and then they sold it for charity.'

'His name's Euan.' I feared we'd be here all night if she had to run through his entire list of achievements in an attempt to remember. 'He lives next door.'

'What, there?' She pointed to the cottage. 'Why doesn't he live in some big house? Is he married?' Katie tossed her hair and smoothed down the front of her dress.

'So Dom hasn't trained you out of noticing other men yet?' It was cruel and I shouldn't have said it. But the history between Katie and me and Dom still rankled. I felt sorry for her, yes, but I couldn't bear the thought of her and her designer clothes moving in on Euan's outdoor innocence. I felt, it suddenly dawned on me, slightly proprietorial towards him, slow speech, odd habits and all. Unleashing Katie in his direction would be like putting a kitten in the path of a hurricane. A hurricane with Dominic in the middle of it.

Katie looked at me with eyes wide with alarm. 'You wouldn't say anything though, would you, Tamzin? You know how he gets.'

'Irrationally angry?' My tone was still dry. The thought of Dom leached any moisture from anything.

'He's sensitive. Insecure.' But she didn't really sound as though she believed it and I wondered how deeply entrenched she was. Katie had always had a wider streak of pragmatism than me; I thought she'd be safer from Dominic than I had been.

'Is he coming over here? He *is*.' Katie did a little shimmy. 'Hello. You're Euan McGillan, aren't you? I'm Katie Davidson. KT, just the letters.' It really did tell you everything you needed to know about Katie upfront, I had to give her that.

Euan smiled a slightly distant sort of smile. I'd bet his mind was somewhere up with the skylarks that rose in weird, jerky little flights from the grassland, as though they were suspended from the sky on elastic. 'Can I look at Brack again?' he said to me over the wall. 'I'm finishing the picture off, but I want some detail.'

'Of course,' I said. Katie's widening astonishment at my being on chatting terms with a man she knew from the telly was mildly amusing. 'He's in his run. But he might hide if you get too close.'

'It's fine. Just need to check the positioning of his eyes.' Euan climbed over the wire fence and crept towards Brack's run like David Attenborough through the bush in Africa.

'You've still got that stinky fox?' Katie glanced over at Euan again. 'No wonder Dom left. He said you'd always got it in the house, when you should have just taken it back and left it where you found it.'

'Where he would have died,' I said, still without real rancour in my voice. It was just Katie. She'd swallowed most of what Dominic had told her, unquestioning. But then, so had I, at first, so I couldn't judge her for that. I was judging her like hell for trying to put the moves on Euan, though.

Katie slumped suddenly, as though all the brashness had suddenly syphoned away into the earth of the garden. 'Tamzin,' she said quietly, 'what am I going to do?'

I looked across at Euan again, lying full length on the damp grass within watching distance of Brack, who was up on his hind leg in the run, sniffing something. 'First, you're going to have another cup of tea and maybe a glass of wine if I can find a bottle.'

'I can't leave him,' she continued sadly. 'He loves me.' A deep breath. 'And I love him.' Her voice was a little stronger now. 'In fact, I don't know why I came. I just… it was…'

I took her elbow and steered her back across the garden towards the door. 'Several glasses of wine, then,' I said firmly, and trying not to let any emotion crawl into my voice. 'You're just visiting a friend for now, all right?'

The breath she took was even deeper than before and shuddered slightly as though she were pushing a huge weight back inside her chest. 'Wine sounds fab. I'll only stay a couple of days, Tam, just thought I'd come and – well, I love the new place!'

After a couple of days of Katie staying, I thought grimly, I might well be doing a Euan and heading off solo around the countryside. Or sleeping in Brack's run, however smelly. But right now, she was here and, actually, it was quite nice to have some company to make it worth opening the wine for.

* * *

Early next morning, Euan tapped lightly on the kitchen window while I was boiling the kettle in a wine-addled and sleep-deprived muzzy headedness.

'Is she still here?' he whispered when I opened the back door.

'Yes. She's staying for a day or so.' I thought of Dom. 'Until he feels he's given her enough rope to hang herself,' I added under my breath.

Euan shifted from foot to foot. 'Oh. Okay, I'll leave you to it, then.'

'What is it today?'

'Stoats. There's a family living and breeding in the old stone wall over the other side of the valley. They're wary, but they're getting used to me.' He stuck both hands in the pockets of his coat. 'I wondered if you wanted to come and see.'

I looked upwards. 'I'd better not leave Katie alone,' I said.

'No, of course. Sorry.' He shuffled a bit more. 'Is she a friend of yours? Only, she doesn't *seem* like the sort of friend you'd have. Wee bit predatory. A bit like the stoats.'

He'd not shaved for a couple of days again. The grey streak was back in his stubble and I found myself idly wondering if it felt different to the touch than the dark of the rest of his hair. 'It's a long story.'

Euan looked over his shoulder for a moment, then seemed to make a decision. 'The stoats can wait,' he said. 'Make me tea and tell me?' My expression must have changed because he added quickly, 'Only if you want to, of course. I just thought – you looked as though talking might help.'

Would it? I hadn't talked to anyone about any of this. Not even Jill. And before I came here – well, who would I have talked *to*? And now, now I was feeling lighter and freer and here, in my cosy kitchen, it all seemed to have happened to someone else.

'It's a bit complicated.' I stood back at the door to let him in. 'Katie and I were, not friends exactly, but friendly acquaintances. My boyfriend left me for her.'

Euan did the slow blink again. 'Well, then, I'm amazed you let her through the door.'

'It's not like that. I was grateful. I was too much of a coward to leave *him*, you see. I knew I needed to, I knew that he was...' I tried to frame the words, but they wouldn't come. They were just a blur of movement and colour in my head and the feeling of shame. 'That he wasn't always very nice.' The word hung. It needed to be faced. To be said. 'That he was abusive,' I finished, in a rush.

Euan reacted to the word and, at that point, I thought instantly about what he'd told me about his wife and I knew. Knew that, of all people, Euan would understand. He wouldn't look at me in wide-eyed amazement when I told him about the level of control; of what I wore, who I met, where I went. How I sat, stood, spoke. *Survivor knows survivor.* So maybe I didn't need to say any of it.

'We met when my grandmother had her stroke. Dominic was a doctor on the ward, and when Gran was discharged, we stayed in touch. We started going out, he moved in with me. Gran had bought me a little house, you see. Nearby, so I could help her...' Memories of the narrow house with the mossy yard. The towering walls. 'When Gran got really ill, he sort of *changed*.' I couldn't look Euan in the face. The shame still followed me around, a gloomy shadow just out of my range of vision. 'It was never physical, he never hit me, so I sort of rationalised it all in my head. But when Gran died and he wanted to take control of her money, that was when I found myself a little bit and then he... with Brack... well. But I couldn't leave. I just *couldn't*.'

I turned around now. Euan was still standing just inside the door, silent and absolutely motionless. Only his eyes were moving, sharp and bright, watching my every movement, like Brack. 'So, he left me and moved in with Katie to teach me a lesson, I think. But I was relieved. Upset, yes, because I relied on him a lot. I thought I loved him. But him leaving me meant I didn't have to be brave, you see. I never had to face up to things and leave him. But, when I bought this place, I gave my address to Katie, told her not to let him know where I was but to keep it in case she needed somewhere to get away.'

The shame coalesced at my shoulder. Became a solid thing that weighed me down. 'I should have warned her,' I whispered through its swirling weight. 'I should have told her what he was like, but I didn't. I just ran.'

Euan twitched. I wondered what he'd been about to do. Behind me, the kettle boiled again and I made a big fuss over making us both another mug of tea. I'd never drunk so much of the stuff before I moved here. In Cornwall, tea had been a ritual that had punctuated the day, here it was like the stuff of life and it was hard to get through any kind of social engagement without perpetual cups of it.

'She wouldn't have listened,' Euan said at last. 'Your friend. If you'd tried to tell her, she wouldn't have listened.'

I thought back. Those bright, brittle parties that we'd thrown, Dom chatting to Katie in corners, scenes carefully designed for me to catch them together. His way of showing me that I was waning in his affections, that I should try harder, be better, to keep him. Using clever, fun Katie as a threat. 'I could have tried, though.' I swung round and plopped the tea onto the table. 'Please sit down. You look as though you're trying to keep that wall up.'

Euan smiled. It was a smile that had caution built in around the edges and I reminded myself again that he *knew*. Not all of it, every case was different, but we had enough in common for me to be able to leave out a lot of the petty detail.

'They tried to warn *me*,' he said, pulling out a chair. I winced at the noise it made against the tiled floor and hoped that it didn't wake Katie, still sleeping the morning away in the bedroom above. What I was beginning to feel about Euan might not stand up well to Katie appearing in one of her floaty outfits and full make-up. 'They – friends, told me that Sarah was – that she could be...' He stopped on a shrug. 'But love blots it all out. You think they'll be different with you, because of love.'

'But you got out. You were better than me. If Dom hadn't moved out, moved on to Katie, I'm afraid I'd still be with him, trying to squirrel money away where he couldn't get at it, still having to have my hair long, keep being blonde.' I touched my hair, almost without meaning to. It had been one of the first things I'd done when he'd moved out, cut my hair short.

'Everyone has their limit.' Euan stretched his legs out under the table, his boots dropping mud onto the tiles. 'You would have found yours.'

The shame became part of the hard thing inside me. I remembered Dom discovering that Brack had peed on our sofa. Up until then, he had used being the owner of a three-legged fox cub to build the illusion of his being a kind, accepting, benefactor of the natural world. He'd taken the cub out, tucked him in his coat, to show the children in the hospital. But quietly, at home, he'd made me suffer for taking in the tiny, smelly scrap of fur.

And his reaction to finding that damp patch had been the first time he'd really let the mask drop, and that had been when I had realised. When I had started to see through the act, realised that his 'we'd better get your gran's money put away into investments, take advantage of the higher rate of interest in these special accounts' was him taking over my finances. Putting money where I couldn't get at it and taking control, just as he'd taken over my life. But it took him threatening to throw both Brack and I out of a house *that I owned* to make me realise how bad it really was. The humiliation of that realisation had been the turning point for me.

And yet I *still* hadn't been able to leave him. So I just shrugged and slid Euan's mug towards him.

'Jill's taking you out to visit the sanctuary today, so she said.' He sipped his tea, hands wrapped around the mug. I noticed there was blue paint under his nails and there was something very reassuring about the sight. He was so completely and utterly opposite to the perfect grooming of Dominic, whose insistence that we never left the house unless we were both perfectly dressed and I was wearing make-up got very wearing when you only wanted to pop to Sainsburys for a loaf and a packet of crisps.

'Yes.' Although I didn't want to think about losing Brack, moving away from the subject of my former life was a relief. 'Do you know it?'

Another smile. Euan's face seemed to have relaxed a little, lost some of the wariness in his eyes. 'Nicola lets me go over there to draw,' he said. 'She sells some of my pictures to raise money for the place, and I get to practise on badgers and hedgehogs. They're a bit scary in the wild.'

'What, hedgehogs?' All the ones I had ever met had been tiny, inoffensive snuffly things. Did Yorkshire produce six-foot muscular hedgehogs, with claws and teeth like Dracula?

'Badgers.'

'But you took me to that sett in the woods, where we saw the cubs coming out.'

'They don't attack on sight.' Euan was more than smiling now, he was practically laughing. 'You were perfectly safe. They just get a bit tetchy if you try to get too close, in the wild. So I go to the sanctuary to draw them, and in return I give Nicola some of the pictures. She sells them, makes money.' He sipped his tea again. 'It's a kind of symbiotic relationship.'

He had definitely relaxed now. As though me telling him about Dom had let out some tension he'd been carrying, like releasing air from an overfilled balloon. It made me brave. 'Do you miss her?' I spilled the words quickly, before I could change my mind. 'Your ex-wife? Do you?'

The laughter stopped and he blinked slowly again, as though putting his thoughts into order. 'Sarah? Yes, sometimes.' Now he met my eye, his eyes were almost black. 'Is that bad? I miss who she was at the beginning. Who I thought she was.'

His words took away some of the shame. 'Someone told me that we grieve for the relationship we thought we were in,' I said. 'Well, when I say *someone*, I think I mean I heard it on the TV. I don't really talk to anyone about it. That's why having Katie here is – not good, but it at least means I've got someone who knows what it's like.'

Across the table from me, Euan's eyes were still fixed on mine. 'Tamzin,' he said, very, very quietly. '*I* know what it's like.'

Everything went very still for a moment. Even the fridge motor went quiet.

'Ooh, is there breakfast?' Katie's voice arrived before she did, muscling its way into the kitchen and rifling through the cupboards. Half a second later, she appeared in the doorway, wearing a cute and very sexy nightdress, completely unabashed at the presence of Euan. I gave the nightdress a side-eye. Dom had bought me exactly the same one for Christmas a couple of years into our relationship, and sulked whenever I didn't wear it. Katie's boobs were very front-and-centre in it, as though presented for display on a doily.

'Toast. There's toast.' I waved a hand at the bread on the worktop.

'I don't really eat carbs.' Katie sounded cautious. That caution had been installed by Dom, I'd had it myself. *Don't get fat, don't go grey, don't get complacent.*

'Go on, spoil yourself. You're on holiday.' I handed her the loaf. 'Do you want to come to the wildlife sanctuary with me today?'

Katie threw the quickest of looks at Euan. 'Are you going?'

Euan was trying not to smile and was firmly looking at his boots. Katie was totally transparent, but then so was the nightie. I didn't quite know which was making him smile like that. 'I may tag along,' he said, talking to the floor. 'See how the place is doing.'

'I'll probably come then. Might be fun.' Katie put a slice of bread into the toaster. Then she stopped and seemed almost to shake herself and put another two slices in.

'What about the stoats?'

'They'll keep. I've finished the hotel commission, by the way. I want to show it to you before I deliver it.' Euan put his mug down on the table. 'It's sitting in my hallway. You could come now.'

'But I've got my pyjamas on.'

He gave me a strange look, which I couldn't decode. And then it clicked into place; Euan was hoping that I trusted him enough to be in his house in my pyjamas without worrying.

I wavered, but only a little. 'Of course I'll come now,' I said. 'Help yourself to jam, Katie.'

Euan and I went out of the back door, over the low stretch of wall that separated my patio and his rather weed-strewn patch of concrete, and into his kitchen. This was the first time I'd ever been inside next door and, at first, I was disconcerted. The size and shape of his kitchen was exactly the same as mine, but the layout was different, and his door through to the living room was in the opposite corner. I felt a little bit like Alice falling through into a mirror world.

'Here.' Euan led me into his living room, which was sparse to the point of having one chair and a table, although all the walls were lined with paintings, gallery-style. His front door opened into a small hall rather than directly into the living room, and the hall had a several frames stacked sideways in it in a rack, like a giant book.

I was looking around without trying to look as though I were looking around. The pegs of outdoor coats and hats near the door with a range of boots underneath. The well-worn chair and its saggy cushion, right by the front window, and the table smeared with so many different colours of paint that I couldn't tell if it was wood or plastic. The place smelled of oil and detergent and dust, and closely resembled the cell of a particularly artistically inclined monk.

'What do you think?' Euan had pulled a picture out of the stack, which I could see now wasn't loose but held so you could flip through the selection.

'Oh, Euan.' It was all I could say. This was orders of magnitude better even than the picture he had given me, this was Brack. Totally and utterly my fox, from his little pointed ears to his neat, black-socked paws. He was sitting with his head slightly cocked and an expression that was midway between benign interest and focused hunter.

'The hotel is called the Fox and Rabbit,' Euan said, tilting the picture slightly so the light caught it differently and Brack's fur seemed to ripple in response. 'Brack's the fox. Obviously.'

I wanted to touch the picture. To rest my fingertip on the end of the little black-button snout as I sometimes did with Brack when he was curled beside me, sleeping. Just to say, 'I'm here and I will look after you, whatever.' But I didn't dare. 'It's beautiful. Amazing.'

Euan did the sideways movement of his head that he seemed to do every time I complimented him on his art. A twitch that encompassed everything from an agreement with my pleasure to a slight feeling that he could have done better given another twenty-four hours and a more stable model. 'Glad you like it.'

'Did you do the rabbit too?'

'Rabbit?' He was lost, looking into the canvas as though he was already marking out faults and corrections.

'For the hotel. Fox and Rabbit, you said. Where's the rabbit?'

'Oh. Yes. That's upstairs. I paint in the back bedroom, you see, where the light's best. Down here is where I do my sketching out and the finishing off. Would you like to see? I'll fetch it down. It's not quite finished yet, mind.' He opened the door that led, opposite way round to mine, to the staircase. The walls lining the stairs were also covered in pictures. It was no wonder I couldn't hear anything from this house, it was soundproofed with canvas and oil. 'I'll just be a second.'

He closed the door behind him, and I could hear the muffled soft tread of his feet up the stairs. Now I could check the room out properly without appearing like an estate agent, and I scanned the pictures. Woodland scenes, so vivid that the trees seemed to sway in a painted breeze. Animals, painted and sketched in charcoal; dogs, horses, cows. Above the log burner, which didn't look as though it had been lit since it had been installed, hung a huge canvas view of distant hills and meadows, like a window opening onto a scene of midsummer, although any window just there would have looked right into my living room and been a whole lot less bucolic. Although, if I kept trying to get that fireplace out, it might well become a reality. I made a mental note to get my act together and sort that wall out.

Idly I flipped through the frame holding the pictures in the porch. Brack, a view of moorland with sheep, a sketch of a tree, and then a much smaller picture that hung much lower in the frame. I had to bend down to see it and turn my head sideways.

It was a charcoal sketch, just a few economic lines. Of a woman. Of *me*.

When Euan came back, holding a large frame, I was looking at my portrait. 'Ah,' he said. 'Yes. Sorry.'

'Why are you sorry?' I held the little sketch. The way the lines flowed it looked as though he had captured me moving, hair caught by the breeze, mouth slightly open. I looked animated, fun.

'Because it's a violation.' Gently Euan laid the rabbit picture down and took the sketch from me. 'I drew this because I wanted to see if I could catch the way you looked to me. With that look in your eye. To see if I could draw it.'

'I look happy,' I said.

'Yes. I couldn't draw the emptiness,' he said simply and opened the front door. 'Katie will be waiting. I'll come over when Jill arrives.'

And almost as though he'd let me into a shameful family secret and then regretted it, I found I'd been hustled outside and was standing in Euan's front garden, looking at my own home from an unfamiliar angle.

17

Andy was a bit strange today. I think it's pre-wedding nerves, actually. I mean, I've had the jitters myself, what with Mum getting so carried away with having to make sure that everyone sits in the right place at the reception and that Auntie Doris doesn't sit near Dad's mum's friend Gladys because they don't get on or something. Andy doesn't have anyone to invite, which is really sad, so he's asking a couple of his mates from the garage to come, which will be nice for him. I don't really know them, but that doesn't matter cos I don't know Gladys either, but Dad says Grandma says she's bought a hat specially and she'll probably give us spoons for a present.

I wanted to invite Jeanette and Jackie and Dawn. Dad said they could come, and I even wrote out the invitations, even though Mum said I shouldn't because they might try to upstage me or something. She's never really liked Jackie, I know, because she thinks she's common just because Jackie said 'bugger' that one time we were all out in town. So I asked Andy and he said not to invite them, because they'd spoil the day being jealous and all. I said that they wouldn't, and I just wanted them to see me in my

dress and everything, but he got all quiet and then said he wasn't
sure if this whole 'wedding' thing was really what he wanted. All I
could think of then was Mum's face if we had to call it off and
how angry Dad would be about the money. So I told Mum that
they'd said they couldn't come anyway. She got a face on her for a
bit and then she said that she wasn't surprised, because their
dads wouldn't be able to give them the kind of wedding that Andy
and I were getting and they were probably jealous. So I reckon
they would be, and Andy was right in the first place!

Dad asked where we were going to live once we were married.
Mum said we could live at home with her and Dad, but Andy said
he'd heard of a little flat going up near the garage. He said it's a bit
damp and not very big, and he said it in a really funny way, and
Dad gave him a look, which means he's not happy about it. But
Andy said the flat would be fine and he could afford it on his
wages and Dad didn't want us to get into trouble with money, us
just being married and all, did he? Dad was cross, I could tell, but
Andy didn't notice, he just went on telling me how I could make
the flat smart and we could put the twin tub that the boys at the
garage were buying as a wedding present in the bathroom if it
wouldn't go in the kitchen. Mum gave Dad one of her looks too,
and it was all a bit nervy. So I made Andy take me out for a drive
to let everyone calm down. He was really happy then, which was
a bit strange. He kept saying things like 'let's see if they take the
bait' and stuff like that. I did ask him what he was talking about,
but he got a bit short with me and said 'never you mind' like he
was really angry, and I had to do 'special kissing' when we parked
up on the moors to cheer him up again. But I reckon even Mum
would be fine with that, now we're getting married. And anyway,
you can't get a baby like that, whatever Carol and Marilyn say, I'm
not stupid.

I've told Mr Harris that I'm getting married and I'll be leaving my job in November. It was a bit sad, really. He looked at me for a long time without saying anything, and I felt a bit scared. I mean, I'd only ever been in his office once before, for my interview, and it's dead posh with a big desk and a telephone and one of those things he can press and talk to Muriel in the other office. So I'm there, and he's just staring at me and I didn't know what to say. My mouth went all dry! Then he asks me if I'm really sure this is what I want – well, what does he expect me to say to that? So I just nodded and he sighed a really big sigh. Then he said that he was very sorry, because I'd got all the makings of a very good secretary and he'd hoped that one day I could take Muriel's place, not that he expected Muriel to be leaving to get married any day soon! We both laughed then, because Muriel is about forty and not married and she's much too old now and anyway I don't think her mum would let her. So then he sent me back to the typing pool and I knew the girls had been talking about me because they all went very quiet. Even Miss Foster, who doesn't usually let us talk while we're typing, gave me a funny look.

Everyone keeps asking me if I'm 'sure'. I don't know why – I mean, does any girl know for sure? I love Andy. He's handsome and he's sweet and he'll take care of me. He won't let me work once I'm married and I know he brings in a good wage, I've seen the roll of money he keeps in his pocket. And we'll have loads of babies and he'll be senior mechanic up at the garage, and Dad did say that he'd keep an eye open for a position in his firm that might suit Andy, even though Andy does cars and Dad is all farm machines and stuff. Anyway, Mum's nearly finished making my dress and I tried it on last night, even though it was all over pins still and I felt... I felt like a real grown-up in it. It has layers and layers of all this lace and a sweetheart neckline and what Mum calls a 'high waist'. Mum keeps looking at me when she says it, and then she mutters about it 'hiding a multitude of sins'. I want

to ask her what she means but I know she'd tell me off for
'backchat' if I did and she's really enjoying all the sewing and the
stitching and everything and I don't want to spoil it for her.

And I'm sure. Yes. I am sure I want to marry Andy. He loves
me. He told me. He says I'm his future. And I really do love him.

18

The wildlife sanctuary was wonderful. Acres of farmland had been given over to animals that were either being slowly returned to the wild or that never would be. Nicola had two foxes already, sisters, found starving as cubs and hiding in an old cow byre. 'Mum probably got killed by a car and so never came back for them,' Nicola said. She had the Yorkshire pragmatism that seemed to be fitted as standard, very like Jill. Any sentiment she did carry was well buried. 'I'm sure they'd love a boyfriend, even if he has only got three legs.'

I watched for a while. The foxes had a huge paddock, carefully fenced for safety both for and from the foxes, because there were chickens in the yard. There was a large tree growing in the middle of their field and there was grass and banks of earth to hide behind, patches to dig in and a small stream running through for fresh water. It looked idyllic. In fact, never mind Brack, _I_ would happily have moved in.

Katie and I walked around slowly, whilst Jill and Nicola chatted and Euan sketched. He wasn't doing the kind of sitting down drawing I'd imagined, but was moving constantly with a sketch pad and pencil, drawing bits of animals. By the time we came back, his pad resembled a dissection table – an eye here, a set of ears there and some paws in the corner with a curved rump floating in the middle. When we arrived home at the cottages, rattled by the journey in Jill's van, he immediately headed off back to his own house, presumably to assemble the parts into one enormous Frankenstein's Badger.

Jill left us at the door with a waved hand, and Katie and I went inside. I was thoughtful, slow. I could imagine Brack at the sanctuary, living a happy foxy life amid the heather growth and ferns of the paddock. Getting to be natural with a pair of girlfriends. But when he greeted me as I let him out of his run, rubbing his furry face against my coat and yipping, I knew I wasn't quite there yet.

'One day soon,' I whispered to the fox, who had stretched elastically, like a cartoon, and followed me back to the house. 'You can go and live there soon.'

Katie was sitting at the kitchen table when Brack and I went back in, with her feet up on the opposite chair and the old photos that she'd peeled from the fridge in a heap on the table. 'Who's this?' she asked.

'I'm not sure. We think it's someone who used to live here but we're waiting for Jill's mum, who apparently knows everything about everyone, to get back from Greece to ask.' For want of something else to do, I put the kettle on again. When Katie went back, which I devoutly hoped would be soon, I wasn't going to drink tea for a month. 'It's just interesting to see how the house used to look before it was a holiday cottage.'

'Have you tried looking her up?' Katie picked up the photo of Stella cooking in the kitchen and looked from the modern tiled walls and floor with the over-large range oven to the picture of the small hob, lino flooring and walls that looked like they were bare plaster. 'She might like to come and see what the place looks like now.'

'I did have a quick try. But there's not much about these cottages online, all I get is property listings and the rental details, and a bit about planning.'

Katie sighed. 'Did you do censuses?'

'I wouldn't know where to start. And I don't have any of those family research membership thingies. There didn't seem much point.' Both of my parents had been only children. Their deaths, when I was ten, had been the reason that I'd had to be brought up by Gran, my mother's mother. She had also been an only child. My family was rarer than giant pandas and, apparently, about as keen to breed.

Katie sighed. 'Give me your laptop.'

'What?'

'*I'll* look. Come on, Tam, it's practically what I do for a living!' Katie shook back her hair. 'And I might as well earn my keep while I'm here.'

A Dominic-shaped cloud seemed to pass over the sun, as we both remembered why she *was* here.

'You belong to genealogical sites?' I'd forgotten that about Katie. She worked in the hospital, counselling people who were being tested for genetic conditions like Huntingdon's, so she'd had everyday access to Dominic and I had to squash down my wonderings about how long they'd been seeing one another before he'd finally decided to teach me a lesson. When he'd packed up and moved in with her because of my 'behaviour'. Designed, I'd always suspected, to bring me back to heel, make me realise what I was missing, when he ostentatiously took her to very smart parties and on holidays to places I'd always wanted to go. He'd made sure everything was documented all over social media, so I couldn't miss what was happening. But of course I couldn't say that to Katie. How could I broach the subject that her shiny new boyfriend was not just a manipulative schemer, but was using her to try to make me jealous, make me reconsider? Katie was – well, Katie was physically his ideal girlfriend, but she was a middle-class girl with a large family from whom he'd had to work hard to isolate her. No echoing loneliness about Katie. No physical insecurities. And, most importantly, no deceased relatives leaving a large house and a small fortune. If I had been suitably contrite, Dominic would have 'had me back' in a heartbeat. And made me pay, in every sense of the word, for my disobedience.

'Professional membership. Sometimes we have to trace family members.' Katie swung the laptop around and opened it, pushing it over to me to unlock. 'For rare conditions.'

'Gosh.'

It was odd. I'd always thought of Katie as a brash, over-confident blonde. That was pretty much where my interest in her had begun and ended, although I must have felt some sympathy for her to have given her my new address. Had it been sympathy? Or guilt? Anyway, I'd never really considered her as a *person*. She'd just been a blonde, female-shaped threat held over my head by Dom for so long, with all the hospital parties and all the times he'd casually mentioned popping down to the lab. All those times he'd invited her to the house for parties that were meant to be 'family only'. He'd flaunted her to keep me in line until she'd become the Cruella de Vil in my story. And yet, she was just an ordinary woman. Rather better turned out than me, of course, better dressed and with naturally blonde hair, but really, just another victim.

'Does Dominic still go to a lot of parties?' I asked, randomly.

Katie looked up from the screen where she was busy filling in fields on a search engine. 'Sometimes.'

'Without you?'

'Well, I'm often working and he has to socialise, after all, he's got such a hard job, he deserves his downtime.' She sounded as though she had practised those words. Probably used them to her friends, her mum. Anyone who asked why Dominic rarely came on visits.

'And has he started to mention a woman yet?'

This time the glance was sharp. 'What do you mean? He meets lots of women, of course he does.'

But I could see her mind working away. She was looking at the laptop screen but her eyes weren't moving, she wasn't reading. She was thinking.

'Nothing. But it's just the way he works, Katie.'

The look she gave me now was shrewd, but her voice was quiet. 'I know how he works, Tamzin.' Just a soft acceptance. I had to remind myself again that Katie wasn't me, that the way she reacted to Dominic wasn't the same, the expectations she had of their relationship weren't the ones I'd had. That his abuse of her would have a different shape.

'Will you go back to him?' I asked, equally quietly. 'Really? When you know what he's doing to you?'

Another pause in the typing. 'I love him,' she said simply. 'Now, what was the name of the people who owned the house before you?'

'Watson, I think.' I went back to my tea making. She knew. She *knew*. And maybe that was enough. 'They bought the house when the farm was broken up, and I bought the cottage after Mrs Watson died. So they must have owned it for about fifty years and just rented it out. Though I'm not sure who to, it's hardly awash with things to do out here.' I thought of Euan's spartan living room. 'Maybe it was a holiday home for monks.'

'Okay.' Katie typed more words. I stared out of the kitchen

window, down the length of the garden and out to where the field beyond curved away to form the valley. Euan was out there again, at the end of his garden, standing motionless. I knew he was just absorbing the scenery. Noting the flight of the birds that dipped to pick insects off the ground, the sturdy plod of the cattle through the mud patch under the tree. I wished I could see life the way he did. And then I remembered that sketch of me, where I looked happy and free and – lighter, somehow. I wished I could see *myself* the way he seemed to. 'Yep, this cottage was owned by the Watsons continually, from the end of 1971 up until you bought it.'

'I already know that, though.' I tried to pull myself back. Picked up the photograph of Stella in her wedding dress, looking happily defiant, in 1971. Laid it alongside the pictures taken in 1973 and could see the change of expression, even under the sepia tint of years. No longer bright-faced and radiant, she'd lost some of the shine. She was definitely thinner, more careworn and there was a cautious look in her eyes. She'd been happy when she got married, happy when she'd had her picture taken in the garden in that long, patterned skirt. But in those later photos she looked sad, and I wondered what had happened. *Survivor knows survivor*, Euan had said. Was *that* what had happened?

'Stella was their daughter, according to the census,' Katie said, waving at the screen. 'She was married in December 1971 to an Andrew Gregg, and they lived in this cottage. She had been a typist but gave up work to get married.'

I found myself holding the photograph of that wedding scene so tightly that the edges folded under. 'Then what happened?'

'These are official pages, not the *Daily Mirror*,' Katie said waspishly. 'They give you facts, not gossip. Anyway, they lived here until... well, it was a holiday cottage by 1981.'

I swung myself into the chair opposite her. 'Well, that's a bit disappointing, I was hoping for rather more than that. Cottage-based scandal or something.'

She gave me a stern look. 'I've only had the information for about ten seconds, Tam, give me a chance.' Her immaculate nails tapped along the keyboard again.

'I'm just going to pop Brack out for a walk.' The nose nudging my ankle was my way out of a day locked in a tea-loop. 'He's been in his run for a long time.'

A single eyebrow raised. 'And, of course, Euan is out there, right now, isn't he?'

I bobbed up and looked out of the window again. Euan was still standing at the end of his garden. 'That's incidental.'

'Oh, come off it, Tam. I've seen you two giving each other those sideways looks. You're a free woman and he's – okay, well, he's a bit odd, but he's good looking. Not *Dominic* good looking, but not bad. And he's on TV, sometimes, and he's got a house.'

'None of those are essentials, you know.'

'Maybe not, but you and Dom split ages ago, you ought to be over him by now.' Tap, tap. Did Katie realise what she was saying? Any hurt there might have been had been so submerged under the depth of relief that it barely even registered on the Richter Scale of Relationship Endings.

'Going out,' I said shortly, and, with Brack tracking at my heels, we went out of the front door. Katie's perfume had clearly heard of subtlety and decided against it, so outdoors was something of a relief.

The air was thick with birdsong and sunshine. Brack started digging in the grass verge in front of my car, where Jill's van had disturbed the earth, and I hesitated for a moment. Should I go round the back and walk through the paddock? Then I wondered if I'd only thought that because Euan was there, and I started wondering if I *did* want to attract his attention. I started walking

up the track, despite the fact that Brack clearly had his sights set
on something crunchy and was reluctant. I would *not* even *think*
about Euan. Quiet, gentle, slowly spoken Euan, with his green
coat and paint-stained hands, with his living room that contained
no real sign of being lived in. As though his entire life was
contained by painting, so all he needed was a chair, an easel and
good light. Did he even have a phone? I wondered what he'd been
like ten, fifteen years ago, at college when he'd met his wife. Had
he been a party boy, dancing and drinking the night away and
painting by day on no sleep, or had he always been this serious,
lonely character – maybe that was what had attracted Sarah, the
lure of the quiet, dark man who lived for his art?

I realised that I'd walked on a hundred yards thinking about
the man that I'd decided not to think about, and Brack was still
scrabbling about in the long grass by my garden wall. I turned
around to call the fox to me, and there was Euan, just outside his
front door now, watching me.

I had to turn round and go back. Brack was taking no notice
of my attempts to attract his attention, the worm-digging exercise
was far more captivating than the prospect of a trot up the lane.

'What did you think of the sanctuary?' Euan asked as I got
close enough for him to speak without raising his voice. He wasn't
moving and he'd stopped looking at me, he was watching the fox
digging with the kind of concentration that looked as though it
wished it had a pencil.

'It was lovely.' Brack raised his head as I spoke, but then saw
that I'd come back, and went on scratching a hole in the grass
bank. 'All the animals were so well cared for.'

'Nicola works hard.' Euan flicked a quick glance at my front
door. 'Where's Katie?'

'Looking up the people who lived in my cottage.'

Neither of us was moving, either closer or away from one

another. As though we were trying to keep the conversation going, in an odd and piecemeal sort of way, without really meaning to. 'Oh.' He dug his hands into his pockets and sort of shifted about. 'Do you want to come in and see that rabbit picture that goes with the fox? You didn't really get the chance this morning.'

I opened my mouth to say that I was supposed to be taking Brack for some exercise, but one glance at the frantically scrabbling fox made me realise that this would sound like an excuse. And I realised, quite suddenly, that I didn't want an excuse to go away. 'I'd love to see it. But I've got Brack with me.'

'Will he follow you?'

'Yes, but maybe not inside somewhere strange. Besides, if he comes in, he might pee.'

'On my vast collection of soft furnishings.' Euan didn't smile, but there was a lightness to his tone that acknowledged the ridiculousness of his words.

'It soaks in. Honestly, you really don't want an adult male fox running around through your house if you don't have to.'

'We'll cross that bridge if we come to it, shall we?' Euan stepped forwards. 'I'll leave the door open.' With that, he vanished back inside.

I looked at Brack, who glanced up at me with soil in his eyebrows. 'I'm going in here,' I said to him, and pointed. I had no real idea why I was talking to the fox as though he was my chaperone. 'You can come if you want.'

Once I'd made my intentions clear by going in through Euan's front gate, Brack left the digging and trotted after me. There was half a worm hanging from his jaws and rather a lot of earth coming along with him. Despite his really tiny feet, Brack could make quite large tracks across a clean floor when he'd been digging. Inside Euan's house, he looked around cautiously, crouched close to the floor, and then slunk off into the corner behind the single chair.

I *really* hoped he wasn't peeing.

'The rabbit is here.' Euan was in the kitchen, where he had the framed rabbit painting propped on the table. From the tips of its pricked ears to the arrested movement of its paws, the rabbit looked lifelike, caught in a moment of nostril-flaring, sensing of danger. Which, given the fox picture would, presumably, be hung close by, was probably appropriate.

'It's absolutely gorgeous, Euan.' I tipped my head to change the angle, and the rabbit seemed to move along with me. It must have been a trick of the light and the way the animal was painted, but it almost looked as though it turned to keep me in sight. 'I really, really don't know how you make them so lifelike.'

When I glanced up, Euan had a complicated expression on his face. Pleasure and pain mingled, an almost reluctant smile. 'I practise,' he said. 'A lot. I don't really have much of a life, you see.'

'Well, I guess that's—'

'And I've got a TV programme coming to do a bit about me and I wondered if you'd let me hide out in your house when they come because I hate doing these things. They always want me to talk to them while they're setting up and I just want to keep out of the way and I need someone to keep me company.' The words rattled out of him as though someone had pulled a sentence-trigger. When he stopped talking, the silence felt profound.

'Oh,' was all I could really come up with.

'It's fine, it's fine, it was just a thought because there's nobody else really to ask. Well, there's Jill, I suppose, but they sometimes take a long time to do these film things and she doesn't really like being away from the girls too much – I think she suspects that they'd have some kind of huge party for the entire neighbourhood and she'd get home to people sleeping in the bath and having to sponge clean the carpets. Not that that's always a bad thing, I mean, you must have a lot of experience with sponge cleaning things...' he finally ran out of justifying breath and ended on a little gasp.

'Just stop talking, Euan,' I said mildly. 'Give me a chance to think.'

'Oh. Right.' He blinked slowly a couple of times, looked down at the rabbit on the table and then left the room. I wasn't sure if I'd upset him, but I had just needed him to stop the strained word-barrage.

He came back a moment later, carrying something, and I looked up and away from the table and met his eyes. 'I'd like to, I think,' I said slowly and carefully. 'Keep you company during the TV thing. I'm just – well, I find being around a man a bit... I get a bit nervous.'

Euan looked at me steadily, and still didn't speak. I wondered if he'd run out of words. Then he held out the package he'd got in his hands and said, very slowly, 'Remember, all that it cost you to accept, it cost me to ask.'

Survivor knows survivor, I thought, and felt guilty. It wasn't just me having that sharp dig under the ribs and the fizz of uncertainty in my stomach. He knew what it was like too.

Was I going to drag Dom through life behind me like an anchor, weighing me down and stopping me from ever having any fun?

'I'd love to keep you company,' I said again, and the words gabbled out as fast as his had. 'Honestly.'

Our eyes met. I couldn't read the expression in his. It looked a little like relief but there was maybe a touch of guardedness too – he would be dragging an anchor at least as big as mine, after all. And then we both smiled at the same time, a grin that brought a light of mischief into his eyes and I hoped that mine showed something of what I'd been weighing up and discarding too.

'We're a proper pair, aren't we?' Euan wiggled the package he was holding. 'Here. It's better you have it.'

It was the drawing that he'd done of me. He'd done a little more to it, I could see now, although when he'd had time I had no idea. When I'd thought he'd been drawing badger parts, probably. He'd altered the lines of my face, somehow, to make me look happier. Younger. It gave me more movement and a kind of carefree joy.

'Wow,' I said, looking down at my own face. 'That's amazing.'

'You don't feel...?' he stopped. Blinked. Started again. 'I didn't want you to feel intruded on.'

I frowned and looked at the drawing again. 'How? It's not like you've drawn me getting out of the bath, is it?'

Another steady look. 'If I were taking photographs of you, without you knowing, that would be intrusive, wouldn't it?'

Slowly I began to see what he meant. 'Well, it would be odd, certainly. And a bit creepy. *Especially* if they were of me getting out of the bath. But a drawing is – well, it's not entirely me, is it? I mean, it's partly your imagination; how you see me and all that. For a start, I don't think my hair has ever looked quite that tidy, and I'm pretty sure I squint when I smile like that.' I tapped the drawing. 'So as long as you aren't going to start drawing me with boobs like beach balls and wearing two tassels and a thong, I think we're good.'

He'd gone a bit pink now. 'Um.' He coughed and blinked and raked through his hair with his hands. 'I... err... I don't do that sort of picture.'

'Yet,' I said, darkly and then started laughing. His expression suddenly made me wish I could draw, that I could show him how *I* saw him, as he'd done for me.

'Well... I may have done some saucily flirty pigeons once.' He started to laugh too now. 'But I don't really do people. In any sense.' The laugh faded to a smile. 'But you're different.'

'Am I?' I asked and then realised how disingenuous it sounded. '*Everyone* is different, though. Otherwise mankind would just be this one very predictable blob.' I tipped the picture to catch more light. It was me and yet not me; the me I would have liked to have been. Attractively windswept, laughing. I looked *lighter*, somehow.

The look he gave me now held a half-amused promise of things to come. I think I returned the look, but I wasn't sure, I'd become so used to policing my expressions that spontaneity no longer felt natural.

'Anyway. I'd better get Brack out from behind your chair. You might want to open the doors and windows for half an hour or so, he can be a bit *redolent*.' I walked back into the living room. The sun had moved over the cottages now, making the kitchen the bright sunny room, and my eyes took a second to react to the shadows. 'Yep, there he is.'

Brack was still in slinking mode, tucked away under the low chair, cat-like.

'I'll stay here until he's out or he might just carry on hiding,' Euan said, and I realised that he really did understand the wildlife that he drew. He properly knew them, with their irrational fears and twitches and their desire to hide from mankind. *Survivor knows survivor*. He was practically wildlife himself. 'And you're sure you're all right? To be around for the shoot with the TV people? There's a *lot* of waiting around and I can't really draw and I end up just sort of – well, standing there. Everyone knows everyone else and it's a bit like being on your own at a party. You don't even get a drink and to look at someone's bookshelves,' he added sadly.

'Yes, of course.'

We were on our way through to the front door and, for a journey of about five metres, it was taking us a very long time to get there. My feet felt weighted with the desire to stay, to talk. But the presence of the smelly fox and the sun that peeped through the open door made me want to be outside.

At last, we stood just inside the door. 'When are the TV company coming?' I asked. 'I will probably have to nail Katie inside the house while they're here, if they're male. Even if they're not, to be honest, she might come over a bit *Love Island*.'

Euan smiled. 'A couple of weeks' time.' He raised a hand and gently touched my arm. It was a butterfly of a touch, no more than the brush of a passing breeze. 'Do you think she will still be here then?'

I thought of Katie, sitting there in my kitchen, pretending she was just having a few days away. 'I don't know,' I said. 'I hope not, but I don't want to push her out, she'd only...' I stopped.

'Only go straight back to him?'

'I *was* going to say she'll only be knocking on your door.'

Euan widened his eyes. 'Oh, Lord. I'm sure she's lovely, but she's a little bit carnivorous for my liking.'

I felt a sudden surge of relief. Euan didn't fancy Katie, it was nice to have the confirmation.

'Besides,' he went on, 'she's rather lost the element of surprise in that outfit she's got on.'

'It is a bit "turning on the light and leaving the curtains open", isn't it?' I found I was grinning now. 'It's just how she is. She doesn't believe in hiding her light under a bushel.'

'I'm not entirely sure that just one bushel would cover it.' Euan was grinning back. 'But I'm not that kind of man.'

His hand was still on my arm. I could see it, but his touch was so barely-there that the sensation wasn't making its way through my shirt. I wanted to return it. I wanted to touch him, suddenly the urge to stroke his cheek or squeeze his hand was almost insurmountable, but I didn't dare move. Like an approach to a wild animal, I knew any untoward movement would make him shy away. So I stood, as though I wasn't aware of the sensation of warmth from his fingers.

'You'd better take Brack out,' Euan observed, as the tip of a snout poked cautiously from under the chair. 'Like you said, pee is to be avoided.' And as cautiously as the touch had begun, it was over, his hand sliding into his pocket as though he'd never made contact with me, but his smile was more relaxed now, wider, and making little creases appear in the grey streak of stubble alongside his mouth.

'Plus Katie will be wondering what I'm doing here.' I moved into the gap of the open door. As though he'd been yanked by the tail, Brack shot out from his hiding place and into the open air. 'I'm sorry about the smell.'

'I'm sure I'll get used to it.' Euan waved a hand. 'And the fox's, too.'

I felt my grin widen, then I turned away so he wouldn't see, and headed out up the track after Brack's nervous running shape.

A few days passed. Katie and I settled into a little routine in the cottage. I'd get up early, take Brack for a walk, then paint some walls or rub down some woodwork. I really wanted to put some effort into getting that awful fire surround out, but the cracks in the plaster were now forming a useable map of the London Underground and it was beginning to look as though removal would have to be a professional job. I painted my bedroom instead. I'd given up on Forest Green and painted it Sweet Lavender. It was pinker than I'd thought, and gave the morning light a slight 'internal organs' quality, but it would do for now.

Katie would get up late, whereupon I would leave her to her searches, surrounded by the photographs of Stella spread over the kitchen table. I'd head outside, gardening, walking, and getting away from the smell of the paint and Katie's perfume. Euan was mostly only visible as a rustle in the hedgerows and an occasional 'hello' across a field, a flash of sketchbook and a figure on the horizon. The bright spring was sliding downhill into a damp early summer, with showers blowing through on a fresh breeze that bent the newly leaved branches and stripped the last of the blossom from the hedges.

Katie showed no sign of leaving. There were long, half-overheard telephone conversations which I presumed were with Dominic, during which I gleaned the information that she'd taken extended leave from work, and there seemed to be a certain amount of discussion about 'change' – things needing to, specifically. But the alacrity with which she answered the phone when the call came from his number, and the way she'd leave the room to talk to him, coming back with a half-smile, told me that she hadn't made the break and maybe never would.

She was also deeply into researching the history of the cottage. She'd dug up records from the farm the place had been, showing that the row of four cottages had been built in 1840 to accommodate the extra workers the farm had needed and their families. When the farm had contracted, selling some land and moving from arable into a small milking herd and sheep in the 1950s, the two outermost cottages had been pulled down, but it hadn't saved the farm. In 1970, the derelict farmhouse had been sold for building stone and the pair of remaining cottages for housing, the land having long gone to assorted local farmers. She wasn't having much luck with tracking Stella, though.

I looked out across the field at the end of the garden. People had lived here, worked in that yard doing things – I was a little sketchy on the details of nineteenth-century farming practices, but I was fairly sure they involved pitchforks and lots of big boots. Now it was just Euan and me, a field of sparse vegetation and a herd of moochily grazing cattle.

So it was a nice change to the routine when Jill drove up in her van late one morning. 'Just coming by to check up on my handiwork,' she said cheerily. 'And cadge free cups of tea and see if you need any other bits done. It's all gone a bit quiet in town.'

I put the kettle on. Katie still hadn't wafted her way down the stairs yet, but the combination of the kettle and someone's arrival usually got her out of bed, so I prepared three mugs. 'Well, I *was* thinking about painting the spare room,' I said as Jill dragged a chair out and sat down. 'But I have to wait for her ladyship to vacate first.'

'Might be a way of getting her out.' Jill rested her chin in her hands and stared out of the window. Another splatter of showery rain plastered itself against the glass. 'Tell her you need to decorate.'

Neither of us acknowledged the dust sheet in the living room. It flapped an audible reminder as another gust came down the chimney, but we both ignored it.

'Maybe.' I couldn't frame the words to Jill, but I knew I didn't want to hustle Katie out. I was getting a tiny frisson of vicarious pleasure from knowing that I was, somehow, keeping her away from Dominic. 'How's business?' I asked.

Jill started telling me about how the weather had put a stop to outside jobs, it being too windy to safely be up a ladder, when there was a looming presence at the kitchen window and a tap at the back door. I got out another mug. 'Come in, Euan.'

'I saw Jill.' He came in and stood on the mat. 'Wanted to talk about some work.'

'Oh, goody,' Jill said. 'It was worth dragging myself out here. I hope it's big and expensive.'

'I need some more racking built up in the loft space. For storing pictures.'

Jill sighed. 'Well, it's indoor work and it'll keep the girls in whatever that shampoo is that they use that costs about a tenner a bottle.'

'Have a cup of tea.' I handed him a mug. Overhead, I detected the thump of Katie, who clearly, having heard Euan's voice, was deciding to make an appearance.

From out at the front, there came the sound of a car on the track. We all raised our heads, like grazing deer scenting a predator. 'It's not your TV lot, is it?' I asked Euan.

'That's next week,' he said. 'You haven't forgotten, have you?'

'That I'm keeping you company? No, I'll be there.'

Jill grinned to herself, but I saw it. I was about to make a remark when the car outside slowed down and we heard the unmistakeable sound of a door opening and voices. I walked through to the front room, where I could peep out of the window. 'It's a taxi.'

'Out here?' Jill and Euan had followed me, like a Greek chorus, and we were all hunched behind the curtains. 'Why would *anyone* taxi out to here?'

Then I saw who had got out of the taxi on the far side, and my blood prickled in my veins. 'It's Dominic.'

He was leaning against the taxi, arm on the roof, talking casually through the driver's window and it struck me suddenly and forcefully that he knew we were watching. He was posing, ever so carefully, to look his best. When he straightened up and I saw that black gaze catch at the window behind which Euan, Jill and I were all sneakily peering out, I knew I was right. Dom wanted to be seen.

'Your ex?' Jill whispered.

'Yes.'

'Do you want me to go?' Euan asked, in a slightly panicked tone.

'No.' Without thinking I touched his shoulder. He didn't move but there was a moment in which we were both very aware of the fact that we were touching. 'He's not here for me. I'm the past, the discarded one. He's here for Katie.'

As though we were a besieged army watching the opposing force about to attack, we all stared out again. The taxi was turning around, making a hard job of it in the mud that the track had become, and sliding and bumping off the verge. Dominic didn't even acknowledge its presence. He was looking at the cottages. Katie's car was parked between both. I'd changed my car since we'd been together, so he didn't recognise it. I saw him flick a glance over my gravelled front garden and up across the neat lines of the house, then move in a determined way to Euan's front door. He looked for a moment at the 'No Callers' sign, which had been repinned so often that the corners were tattered into lace, then he knocked.

'I don't know why I bother with that sign,' Euan said in a defeated sort of tone. 'No. Callers. It's self-explanatory.'

'Why *is* it there?' I tried to distract myself from Dominic's appearance.

'Because when I'm working, I won't answer the door,' Euan said simply. 'Saves me bobbing up and down all day.'

'To the enormous number of people who come knocking out here,' I replied, dryly, and he smiled.

'It's precautionary. And pointless, evidently.'

Dominic, having received no answer to his knocking, stood

back and looked up at Euan's windows, shook his head and then moved purposefully around to my gate. I felt my heart start to grind in my chest and hesitated, unsure as to whether to pre-empt his knock by opening the door. Euan and Jill moved along with me at my shoulder, like an uncertain backing group behind a singer with stage fright.

Dominic was poised to knock when I threw open the door and I got a tiny amount of pleasure at the startled look on his handsome face as he stood with his hand raised to a group of three on the doorstep.

'Hello, Dom,' I said as calmly as I could.

He was utterly taken aback for a second. I saw the shadow of suspicion cross his face, then a quick frown and then the smooth, controlled expression was back on his face almost before anything else registered. 'Ah. Hello, Tamzin. Is Katie around? I think we need to talk.'

Katie had just begun a wafty descent of the stairs. I heard her misstep behind me on the steep flight. 'Dom?'

There was a tone in her voice that I knew well. I'd used it myself so many times. A mixture of pride and fear and inevitabil-ity, and also just a tiny bit of awe that this incredible man was anything to do with her.

He stood, framed to perfection in the doorway. Neatly dressed, not too showy but having taken obvious care; his hair not so long as to appear unkempt, but not so short that it would make his features harsh. The peripatetic sun directly above added shadows that made his bone structure look impeccable and his eyes look darker than dark. Before I'd met Dom, I'd always thought you could 'read' people through their eyes. But then I'd realised that people could act with their eyes, just like the rest of their bodies. That darkness hid another darkness, one that it had taken me far too long to see into.

'I thought you might want to come home,' Dom said, talking over my shoulder to Katie. 'But that you didn't know how.' There was just the right amount of humility in his tone, carefully balanced with reason and forgiveness. It made my flesh creep.

'I said I just needed some time.' Katie carried on down the stairs but I was pleased to see she didn't rush straight into his arms. Even now, *even now*, with all that I knew about him, I could feel that tug. That desire to be enveloped in his arms, secure, desired.

I glanced down at the mud-streaked floor, and had words with myself.

'Well, it *has* been nearly a fortnight.' Dom shifted his weight, clearly wanting to be invited in, but still pretending to play by the rules. But there was that chill of threat around the edges of his words I knew so well. That creeping frostiness that told you that, if you didn't acquiesce, you might as well prepare to be eating alone, sleeping alone, to just being a presence in the house whilst he ostentatiously 'lived' around you. Until he decided you'd been punished enough and then he'd suddenly thaw, be warm and loving and generous until you decided that you'd obviously imagined the previous ignoring or misunderstood him. He'd been stressed, worried, working too hard, tired. It couldn't have been anything you did, because *look* how much he loved you!

Until the next time.

Euan was really close to me. Standing alongside me, not speaking but looking at Dominic as though he too could see through the trappings of civilisation to the spite and control that lay within. Jill was looking from Dominic to Katie and then to me.

'Is he the one?' she whispered.

I just nodded. I didn't want to speak. Didn't want to risk attracting Dominic's attention while the stand-off was continuing. Katie wasn't coming any further down the stairs and Dom was doing his best vampire impersonation – not being allowed in until permission was granted. They'd made eye contact over my head and Dom was not letting it go.

'Perhaps,' Dominic said, still over my head, 'we could go for a walk and talk. Away from—' and he waved an arm to indicate the massed ranks of prying ears all still standing on the doorstep, as though we expected him to suddenly charge in and sweep Katie away.

Without a word, without even a look in my direction, Katie finished her descent of the stairs and wove between Euan and I with her back straight. She flounced out of the door and kicked the leading edge of it as she went, so it slammed shut in our faces.

We stood for a second longer, then Euan and Jill turned to me. 'Well, he's good looking, I'll give him that,' Jill said. 'But, blimey, Tamzin! You were with him how long?'

'Three and a half years, give or take a millennium.' I dropped my head. I didn't want to meet their eyes and see the accusation in them. Now I knew what he was, it was so obvious – how could I ever have fallen for it? Stupidity? Desperation?

'And he never asked you how you are, or anything.'

Euan didn't speak but I felt his arm against me. Not *around* me, that intrusion wouldn't be Euan's style, just... *there*.

'He doesn't care. I'm the discard. I literally don't exist to him any more.'

Euan was scrabbling in his pockets now, and went off to lean against the table, sketching. I wondered if it was to give him an occupation so he didn't have to look at me.

Jill blew out a long breath. 'Wow. I thought Sy was pretty horrible and all he did was quote in bad Latin and never help in the house.'

'Well, he did call your daughter Persephone,' I added, reasonably.

'Oh yeah, true. But only after I'd vetoed Antigone. Sheeeeesh,' she whistled. 'That guy looks like a one-man Mafia.' She gave me a brief hug. 'I'm glad you got away, Tamzin,' she said quietly.

'*I'm* glad I got away, especially with Gran's inheritance intact. I think that was the only reason he really ever wanted me; he knew she was elderly and rich and I was the only heir, and then once he realised I would put up with – I mean, Gran was lovely and everything but she was very old-fashioned and she never really prepared me for...' my voice dropped as my mind was full of memories of Dom's sheer mind-bending force of control, '...men like him,' I finished, weakly.

'But he didn't get his hands on any of your money?' Jill's voice was low and urgent. 'Please tell me he didn't?'

'Oh, no. It was just after Gran died that I started seeing through the mask. Up until then, I would have done *anything* to make Dom happy.' There was a hot ball of burning shame deep inside me when I remembered some of the ways I'd tried to turn him back into the caring, involved person he'd been when we first got together. 'But when he only wanted to talk about the money, and he never asked if I was all right – Gran had looked after me since I was *ten*! I missed her more than I missed my mum and dad.' I suddenly realised that I'd been blurting, while they had silently watched me, and I forced myself to shut up.

Jill sighed. 'And then he moved on to that poor lass.' She jerked her head towards the forcibly closed door.

'She's stronger than me. She seems to know the score a bit better,' I said feebly.

'No reason to cast her adrift, though.' Jill frowned.

'You can tell someone, but they can't hear when they're being love-bombed into deafness,' Euan said, suddenly and surprisingly from the table. 'You just think "well, they're not like that with *me*", and then you're kind of proud that you were the one to make them change and when you realise that they haven't, you're in too deep. And you don't want to prove the others right.'

Jill turned her frown onto him. 'Euan?'

I remembered what he'd told me, about being warned about his wife. About being a man attacked by a woman and not daring to speak up. 'Yes, well.' I cleared my throat. 'Katie is different. She's obviously starting to see through him, but he'll probably talk her round.'

'Maybe you could pack for her now?' Jill asked hopefully. 'I could get started on the painting.'

'He sent the taxi away.' Euan handed me the piece of paper he'd been sketching on. 'He knows she'll go home with him.'

'Yes, it's that kind of certainty that makes you want to shove a potato up his exhaust and put laxatives in his tea, isn't it?' Jill made a face. 'He made all my hair prickle.'

'That's because you have a normal and well-developed sense of your own worth.' I looked down at the sketch Euan had done and laughed. It was a very accurate and very identifiable drawing of a toad with Dominic's face.

'And yet. Sy,' Jill said and grinned. 'Even those of us with fantastic senses of our own value make stupid mistakes, Tamzin. Don't beat yourself up.'

I went to thank Euan and found that he was looking down at me. His eyebrows were raised and he had a twisted set to his mouth, half-hidden under the copious stubble, as though Brack had just sprayed his way through the room. It was a look of complicity. A look that said, 'You can't understand if you've never been there.'

So I just smiled at Jill. Euan was right. She couldn't know and hopefully she never would.

'Where have they gone?' said Jill, either not seeing our

exchange of looks or not understanding them. 'He doesn't look the sort to go roaming the outdoors. Not in those shoes.'

I looked out of the window. An explosion of rooks had gone up from the trees at the top of the lane and were clouding the wind-wracked sky. 'Up the track, I think.'

'Good, we've just got time to nail all the doors and windows shut.'

I glanced down again at the hasty sketch Euan had done. Dominic really did make a great toad. There was something about the wide mouth and slightly protruding eyes that had the essence of toad about it. 'I should frame this,' I said. 'To remind me.'

Euan nodded and then he smiled. It was a proper smile, one which had more than a hint of mischief about it. I wondered if he'd thought that there had been a danger that I might not truly have been free of Dom. That I might still have been holding a tiny torch against the day that he turned back up again and I could throw myself at him, begging forgiveness, and my response at the drawing had wiped out that fear.

'Oh, oh, they're coming back!' Jill pulled her head away from the window and crouched down below the sill. 'That didn't take long.'

And then I remembered. I remembered how Dom had this way of treating you as though any unpleasantness on his part was all in your perception. How he'd been doing whatever it was for your own good and now you'd seen sense, everything would be back to the way it had been. If you never upset him again, then he'd be the loving, attentive partner he'd been at the start.

He didn't tell you that you'd need to work harder and harder at 'not upsetting him', until you didn't know which way was up any more.

Katie and Dom were hand in hand. She was smiling, he was

bending his head forward as though he was explaining something to her in detail. I felt that needle under my ribs again, the
poke of the guilt that I hadn't had the strength to end things with
Dominic, cut all the crotches out of his trousers and write
'WANKER' in Tippex on his car bonnet.

Katie opened the front door and ushered Dom in ahead of
her. He stepped into the living room and seemed surprised to see
the three of us still there, which was a bit rich considering it was
my house. 'Oh. Hello again, Tamzin.'

He ignored Jill and Euan. He'd clearly assessed them as not
being glamorous, rich or successful enough to need to impress
them, or maybe the stony expressions on their faces put him off
trying to enrol them into the Dominic Boston Fan Club. I gave a
little inward grin of glee – when Dom discovered who Euan was,
he was going to be so angry that he hadn't at least tried to make
an impression on him. Dominic liked famous people, in the same
way that Elizabeth Taylor liked diamonds. Katie tripped off up
the stairs without a second glance at any of us.

'Hello, Dominic.' I was pleased that my voice came out
neutral and steady. Underneath my heart was dragging in my
chest, each thump as painful as though my blood had turned to
acid.

'This is your house?' The contempt leaked out a little bit
around his words. 'It needs a lot doing to it. I'm surprised at you
buying all the way out here in the countryside when you were
always such a town girl. But then, by the look of you, you've
clearly adapted.'

Jill was silent, stunned, I think, by the rudeness. Euan had his
head down. Perhaps he was hearing an echo from his own past in
the general scorn and condescension of Dom's tone.

'Well, it suits me,' I said, my tone still as beige and smooth as
a caramel, but infinitely less sweet. 'And Brack.'

'Oh, you've still got that dreadful smelly thing, have you?' Now Dominic included Jill and Euan in his smile, inviting them to join in abasing me in my choices of pet. *Clearly*, his smile seemed to invite them to say, *anyone who keeps a three-legged animal that's given to peeing in corners and smells like burning tar and battery acid is hanging on to their trolley by their fingernails, and I'm sure you'd agree.*

Neither Jill nor Euan smiled or said anything. Even I didn't rise to the bait, and was proud of myself for my lack of riposte. I didn't need to justify myself, and that was a pleasant realisation.

Running out of ways to try to get a rise out of me, Dominic began sauntering around the living room as though he owned the place, tipping books to read the spine, doing that 'down the nose snorting' that implied his total dismissal of my choice in reading material and soft furnishings. He probably wanted to appear highbrow, as though he were repudiating my entire life, but actually he sounded like a small horse slightly out of breath. He lifted the dust sheet to look at the wall underneath, and the resultant curl of his lip was visible even from behind. Eventually, he got to the portrait of Brack hanging on the wall opposite the window.

'Oh, you *do* actually have something nice!' He stood back as though he were appreciating the *Mona Lisa*, tilting his head. 'This is good work. D'you know, I'm sure I know the artist of this one, I *think* I went to the opening of his gallery... Kensington, I think. Katie will know, I'm sure she came with me. Chap called Dorian something. Really must get back in touch with him, he was going to do me some watercolours for the hall.'

'It's mine.' Euan stepped into the conversation, back straight and the pride in his work not allowing Dom to go on with attributing the painting to some other artist. 'That's my painting of Tamzin's fox.'

Dominic's smile only faltered for the briefest moment. 'Really?' I could almost see his brain struggling to switch tracks and retake control of the situation. Then he shrugged and inclined his head. 'Your style is very derivative of Dorian's.' He waved a hand in casual denial of any artistic merit, despite his previous words, and it was just so *Dominic*, so exactly how he worked, that I found myself starting to giggle.

'Just shut up, Dom,' I said, and it felt so good. 'Before you dig yourself an even deeper hole.'

Dominic reacted as though the fox in the picture had suddenly lunged forward and bitten him. The expression on his face was one that I had wanted to put there so many times that the quiet triumph gave me a warm feeling and made the giggles intensify. If *only* I could have left him with those few pithy words and this feeling. If *only* I'd been this strong eighteen months ago.

Euan was standing beside me, back straight, head up. Not at all the self-effacing person he'd been a few moments ago. I could feel him vibrating slightly with an energy I couldn't place. Not anger, I didn't think, but more a kind of vitality. 'Yes,' he said. 'I also think you should stop talking now.'

Dom's face was a picture that I really needed to get Euan to paint, I thought. It looked as though his brain and his mouth had slipped cogs and were whirling about behind the scenes, trying to mesh together sufficiently to form words that would take us down swiftly and efficiently. But nothing was happening. He stalked away to the far side of the room, obviously trying to stand on his dignity, but his dignity was trying to get away even faster than he was, so it was like watching a man trying to jump on a moving frisbee.

Into this walked Katie, carrying her tiny suitcase, and Dominic seized on the interruption with the gratitude of a starving man walking into a picnic. 'Ah, there you are, darling, I was wondering what was keeping you so long. I think it's time we left—' He stopped there. I had the feeling that the words *these philistines, who know nothing about art and are merely pretending, to their own miserable lifespans* were bubbling about but didn't quite dare emerge.

'Just a minute,' I said. I bustled forward and grabbed Katie by the arm, hustling her on in front of me by her elbow or risk having her shoulder dislocated. I got her into the kitchen and kicked the door shut. 'You can't go with him,' I said. 'He's a coercively controlling, narcissistic, self-important little *shit*.'

Katie looked at me levelly. 'He's promised things will change,' she said. She didn't acknowledge my incisive dissection of Dom's character. 'He's realised how important I am to him, and he's willing to work on things.'

'No, no, he isn't,' I hissed. 'This is what he *does*! Come on, Katie, you're a clever woman, you know how he operates, you've seen it for yourself.'

Katie gave me a complicated look. 'Thank you for your vote of confidence,' she said. 'But I have to give him a chance.'

'Okay, okay.' I let go of her arm. The kitchen window was suddenly illuminated by the sun coming through between the navy-black of the shower clouds. It struck us both like a floodlight and released the smell of last night's bolognaise from the woodwork. 'Just... I'm here if you need me. Remember that. And,' I lowered my voice a little bit more, '*don't let him change you.*'

Katie gave a curious little smile. 'Thank you,' she said softly. Then she turned, dramatically threw open the kitchen door and the group of three, who were standing in a state of elastic tension on the other side, recoiled. Jill was looking from Euan to Dom like a fight referee. Euan looked defensive, head up and shoulders back, whilst Dom had clearly got the measure of things and seemed set to sling a few more carefully handcrafted insults disguised as observations. Dominic was the master of the cotton-wool packed scalpel blade.

I suddenly realised that I didn't want Dom to get the better of Euan. I didn't want to see the expression on Euan's face that had so often decorated mine – that look that said, 'I know I'm better than you think I am but I just can't prove it,' and swiftly degenerated into, 'I am exactly as pathetic as you believe me to be,' once Dom got a few more take-downs under you. I didn't want Euan to have to relive his past.

Although he did seem to be holding his own quite well at present. Compared to Dom's city honed slender shape, built mostly out of good suits and power lunches, Euan's skin had a sun-tinted healthy look. Slightly burned across the bridge of his nose and peeling a touch over his cheekbones, but healthy. He was taller than Dom, not bigger but better put together, like a LEGO set built by a professional. Everything just *fitted*. Dom was a handsome face but had the body of a doctor who spends too much time under hospital lights and eating quinoa and spelt salads to keep slender. Euan stayed slender by walking the hills in all weathers. It was quite a contrast, and it finally burst the bubble that Dom had had me in.

'Goodbye, Dominic.' I held the front door open. I even gave a cheery little smile as he passed me, although the whiff of his cologne was giving me memory-flashes that made the smile droop a little round the edges. 'Katie, I'm always here if you need me, you know that.'

Katie looked like a little girl who'd won the Pass the Parcel big prize at a glamorous party. Slightly baffled, but quietly triumphant. 'Thank you for everything, Tamzin,' she said as she went out.

'Just remember,' I said quietly, pretending to air kiss her cheek. 'That's all. *Remember*.'

She looked into my eyes, just briefly, before they finally went to her car. There was an expression hidden deep behind the victory. A look that I knew I'd had many a time. *Fear*. Fear of losing this amazing, successful, handsome man who'd talked you into believing that he was your everything. That he loved you so much, no one else would ever match up. That you weren't really worthy of him, but he was prepared to lower himself, to help you to raise yourself up to his standards. That he was only telling you your dress was hideous, you'd gained weight, you needed a nose job and to dye your hair, for your own good, so that people wouldn't laugh.

I'd fallen for it once. Now it just made me want to laugh at his assumption of highbrow taste and refined culture. After all, I'd seen his Bon Jovi albums.

Then they were gone, Katie driving away with a flourish that looked like bravado.

I closed the front door slowly, to Jill's whistle.

'My God, Tam, he's *dreadful*,' she said. 'But it's a good lesson to give the girls. If he ever comes back, can I bring them round to observe him from a distance? If they promise not to poke him with sticks?'

I felt like a balloon that someone had let all the air out of. Deflated and wrinkly. There was just something about Dominic's presence that made every room feel as though someone had drawn the curtains when he left. Euan patted my shoulder.

'You got out,' he said. 'He can't hurt you any more.'

'I just wanted to puncture him,' I said. 'Just take him down a bit.'

'Think Euan did that with the picture thing.' Jill looked at the fox portrait. '"I think I went to his gallery opening..." What an utter tit.'

'Maybe I'll have a gallery,' Euan said suddenly and surprisingly. 'One day. Er.' He suddenly got hit by an attack of reticence. 'Not London, though. York, maybe. Or Pickering.'

'You could have a London gallery,' I said, suddenly fierce. 'New York, Milan – the world is just waiting for you.'

'Er, I don't think it is. Actually.' Euan still sounded diffident.

'Well, it could be,' Jill said, reasonably. 'Capitalise on your TV fame. You are very good, and you know it.'

We all looked at the picture of Brack, as lifelike as though I could see his sides moving with the little panting breaths he took when he was warm, mouth half open, which, with his white markings, made him look as though he was smiling. Shiny, black, splinter-of-coal nose and those bright, knowing and slightly mad eyes.

'You are.' I backed her up. 'Seriously.'

Euan shrugged but I could tell he was pleased. *He* knew he was good, but he seemed to care about our opinion, which was lovely.

'Tea,' I said. 'I am seriously going to have to take up gin or absinthe or something, just for a change.' I went through to the kitchen.

'As long as you give up cushions first.' Jill picked up the little file of what Katie and I had been calling 'cottage stuff'. 'I'm still worried about your addiction to those. By the way, Mum should be back end of next week,' she said thoughtfully, flipping through the photographs. 'And then I can ask her about the people who had this place without her getting distracted by biceps.'

'Do you think I should have stopped Katie?' I asked suddenly.

Jill put the folder down. 'How?'

'I don't know! Barricaded her in the bathroom?'

'Wouldn't that make you as bad as him?' She pushed at my hand. I'd been filling the kettle and it was beginning to overflow. 'Everyone has to make their own decisions, Tam. You kind of have to bite your tongue, even when you see your daughter going out with a face full of make-up so obvious that it comes into a room three minutes before she does,' she finished, with a tone of bitter humour. 'She wanted to go with him.'

'Only because he's fed her some line about things being different! Dominic can't change – he thinks he's perfect as he is and it's the rest of the world that needs to fall in line.'

'Then she'll either see that, or she won't. Put that bloody kettle on.'

Euan and I locked eyes. I suddenly noticed how his eyes were a greenish colour, little flecks of brown and gold dotted through like pebbles under water. 'We were just too close to see,' he said quietly.

'Well, I'm closer to dehydration.' Jill took the kettle from me and plugged it in. 'You two can carry on the "unspoken communication" thing if you must, but I'm going out to check that run. Two sugars, please, Tam, I've had a shock, having to encounter your ex.' And she flung open the back door to march off out between the showers.

'You dealt with it very well,' I said, having to turn away. The intensity in Euan's face was disturbing.

'It broke something in me.' His voice was still quiet. I took the teabags down and spent longer than necessary putting them in mugs. 'Like seeing through the conjuring trick. I saw how he did it.'

'Oh yes?'

Euan was standing very close again. He smelled of paint, of turpentine, of dust and the outdoors: rain and sun-baked clay. 'When you see how it's done, it breaks the illusion. I saw how Sarah did it too, in that second.'

I turned and there he was, at my shoulder. 'We aren't stupid.' Without thinking about it, I reached out and touched his cheek, where the grey line of stubble ran down under his jawbone. 'We just got taken in.'

'And we know better now?' He put his hand on my wrist, not to pull it away or hold it closer. Just... just touching. His hand was warm and there were callouses on his fingers, I could feel them pressing against my skin.

'I think so.' It was practically a whisper. I looked up, up into those green-gold eyes and his pupils widened until they were like mirrors. The roughness of his skin chafed my wrist briefly as he moved and then he was cupping my face in his palms, tipping my chin as though he wanted to see the light change on my face, as though he was about to paint me. And then his lips came down and I stretched up, meeting the kiss in the middle, in a breath-holding moment of heat.

I closed my eyes, felt the soft rub where his stubble brushed my cheek, the firmness of his mouth on mine, the press of his body against me. And then his arms came around me and he was holding me and I had my hands across his back, feeling that play of muscle against bone, and I opened my eyes again.

'All right, knock it off, where's the tea?' Jill sounded amused but her presence made us step apart, breaking contact with all the embarrassment of a pair of teenagers being caught by a parent. 'You two snogging is all very well, but it's bloody parky out there and I need a warm-up of a different kind. Unless you're both offering to snuggle me up in there with you.'

Euan raised his eyebrows at me. 'Clear to see you're a mum,' he said, mildly. 'We're adults, Jill. If we want to kiss, we shall.'

'Not at the expense of my cup of tea,' Jill said briskly and gave me a huge wink. 'But I'm fantastically glad to see you've both come down from the "I've been hurt before and must never love again" position, which, I have to say, never works.'

I wasn't sure if Euan was aware of what he did when he

reached up and touched his head, but I think it may have been involuntary and probably linked to 'love hurts'. 'I don't think she's being literal,' I said.

'Tea.' Jill nodded towards the kettle. 'And we'll work up to the absinthe from there, shall we?'

19

After Jill and Euan had gone, I took Brack for a walk up the lane, still a little dazed. Everything seemed to have happened at once – Dominic reappearing, Katie leaving with him, Euan and I kissing... I mean, what was *that* all about?

'I think I really like Euan,' I said to Brack, who was sniffing a daisy. 'Which is very confusing.'

Brack, fairly obviously, said nothing, but scratched a little hole next to the flower.

'I mean, I made such a cock-up with Dominic, how can I even trust my own judgement? Euan may turn out to be a complete mistake as well.'

Crunch, crunch went the fox in reply, his tail stuck straight out behind him with enjoyment at whatever dirt-covered invertebrate he was just eating.

'But he's just so sweet and kind and he's talented and good looking and—'

'—and he wants to point out, before he dies of hyperbole, that he's lying on the other side of this hedge,' said a voice, which made me jump and Brack suddenly flee a few metres further up the trackway, with something brown and wriggly between his jaws.

'Why...?' I started and then realised that my voice was still far too high up the startle register. 'What on earth are you doing?' I finally managed to get out in a tone a little less shrill.

'Drawing. There's a white-tailed bumblebee in some toadflax down here. And I'm not. I mean, I can be, but I have my moments too. Plus I'm solitary by nature.'

'What?' I asked, so genuinely confused that I wondered if he'd misheard me and we were talking at complete cross purposes.

'Kind and sweet and all that. And I like my own company too much, well, I need to, painting isn't a team sport.' There was a gradual unfolding, rustling sort of sound from the field on the other side of the newly leafed hedge and Euan straightened up, detaching parts of his jacket from the little snaggy thorns. 'It was just one of Sarah's many complaints.'

I now had to decide, in the turn of a second, whether I confessed to how I felt, or pretended that none of the previous monologue had happened. 'I really like you,' I said, unable to come up with a reasonable alternative.

'Well. The feeling is mutual. I hope you got that from the fact we kissed in your kitchen.'

'But after Dominic...'

'I know. We're both still a bit screwed up by previous partners. I was thinking of trying therapy, what do you think? I've got a card somewhere, from some professional. I mean, before we fully plunge ourselves into anything?'

I looked at the top half of him, his lower being obscured by burgeoning greenery. He had his hands in his pockets, old green coat streaked with mud and the sunburn that had reddened the bridge of his nose was beginning to fade to brown. I had never seen a man look more desirable. 'I think I ought to try that too,' I said. 'Because if we let what they did to us stop us from having a good, healthy relationship – well, then they've won, haven't they? And I'd rather burn the board, bury the counters and shred the scorecard than let Dominic win at anything.'

'That's... probably healthy,' Euan said, carefully. 'Wee bit more vitriol than I'd actually like, I have to say.'

'He dissed your painting,' I pointed out.

'True. Yes, actually, maybe we could lightly set fire to his trousers.' There was more gold than green in his eyes now, seen in full sunlight, tints of blonde and auburn were picked out in his hair by the backlighting sun. 'But I will always have this.' He pointed to his head. 'So Sarah kind of won that round.'

'But not the whole game, Euan,' I half-whispered. I reached out a hand, intending to touch his face, but a riot of sparrows suddenly burst from between us, chirruping their distress into the air as they hurtled skywards and away from these two intrusive humans.

Euan's attention was diverted by the crowd of little brown birds and he leaned back towards his sketch pad, his pencil already moving to capture ragged wing beats and tail angles. I smiled to myself, left him standing at the hedge, and went around the cottage to put Brack into his run. I needed to let Euan's words filter down from my brain and further towards my heart before we carried that conversation any further forward. He liked me. The word 'relationship' had been uttered and neither of us had run screaming. We were on the edge of something and I needed to process how I felt about that, particularly whilst I was still fully comprehending the awfulness of Dominic.

Brack trundled happily into his run and started digging furiously, in search of invertebrates. I made my way cautiously back towards the track. Maybe Euan had gone? Maybe he'd had second thoughts and loped off to hide with the badgers and the deer until I forgot about him? It was slowly dawning on me how much I enjoyed his company, bizarre as it sometimes was, and how much I had come to rely on his silent presence. 'Relationship' no longer felt like a word to be avoided, and I was glad to see him still sketching where I'd left him, as though he was waiting for me to come back. He probably hadn't even noticed I'd been gone.

'Euan,' I started to speak and his head came up abruptly, proving me right, although I'd been gone long enough for several sparrows to have attained immortality on the sketch pad. 'I think—'

At precisely the same time, a car turned onto the track. We heard the change of gear as someone throttled down to negotiate the steep turn and then the hill and we both turned in time to see Katie's car come hurtling over the ruts and potholes in an almost comic cloud of dust.

'Oh,' I said, straining my eyes to try to see who was driving.

'Maybe they forgot something?' Euan shielded his eyes from the sun and squinted in the same direction.

'I don't think Dominic has come back to pick up his empathy.' I started to move back towards home. 'Since he's managed for thirty-three years without it so far.'

We reached the front of the house. The car was parked, but nobody had got out. The engine was ticking as it cooled in a distressingly bomb-like manner.

I went round to the driver's door and found Katie, resting her forehead on her arms against the steering wheel. She was alone.

'What happened?' I opened the door and bent in. 'Are you all right?'

'Can I stay a bit longer?' Katie spoke without raising her head.

'What, *here*?'

'In the house.' Katie smiled into her arms, I could hear it in her voice. 'Idiot.'

'Well, Jill is going to do her crust about the painting of the spare room, but, yes, of course.' I crouched down now to bring me level with her. 'Katie, what happened?' I didn't quite know what to think. I didn't *seriously* consider that Katie might have pushed Dominic out of the moving car on the motorway, but a tiny part of me hoped that's what had happened.

Euan gave me a small smile and waved towards his own front door. 'I'll leave you two to – whatever it is,' he said.

'Thank you.' I touched Katie's shoulder. 'Really, what happened?'

She raised her head now. Her eyes were shadowed, but not red. She looked exhausted. 'You know I said he deserved that chance to change? Like he promised? Well, it lasted as far as Malton. Then he started telling me all the things that *I* needed to do. To make myself better, so he didn't feel ashamed to be seen with me.'

'Oh, Katie,' I breathed.

'And all I could think of – so this is entirely your fault–' she gave me a grin that wouldn't have shamed a gargoyle, '–was you telling me not to change. And I thought, bugger it, I'm not that bad, fairly sure other people quite fancy me and don't think I've got a "provincial accent".' She gave a snorted laugh that was heavy with suppressed tears. 'So I drove to York station and told him to get a train home. I told him that we were done.'

'Wow,' I said, impressed. 'I think you might be my hero.'

She put her head back on the steering wheel again as though her neck couldn't support it any longer. 'Yeah, well, I had to give him seventy quid towards his fare, so it wasn't quite the classy leave-taking it should have been, what with trying to find an ATM and Dominic whining about how I'd misunderstood, all along the platform.' Katie rolled her head so she could look at me out of one eye. 'But you were right. He never intended to do one damn thing to save our relationship, all he was going to do was try to make me so scared of losing him that I'd never dare raise any issues again.'

'That backfired, big time.' I was still quietly astonished. But then, as I'd always known, Katie wasn't me. She was stronger. Had higher self-esteem. 'I want to be you when I grow up.'

Katie made a sneery sort of noise in her throat. 'Grown-up isn't all that,' she said, half whispering. 'The worst I had to contend with when I was ten was the primary school netball team bullies. Compared to Dominic, being shouted at by Goal Attack for not cutting the oranges up properly is fairly minor.' Now she threw herself back so that she was upright in the seat. 'Actually, it's pretty minor compared to most things, but it was horrible when I was ten.'

I looked along the row, to where Euan was standing outside his front door, looking thoughtfully at the 'No Callers' sign, which was catching the breeze underneath it and pillowing upwards. He stared at it for a few moments and then, decisively, tore it away from its pins and shoved it into his coat pocket.

'What puzzles me,' Katie was carrying on, 'is how Dom knew where I was.' She raised her eyebrows at me. 'Because someone must have told him, and it certainly wasn't me.'

'Why do you think I bought a new car to come up here from Truro?' I was still watching Euan, who'd been distracted by something moving out in the field. The wind was flicking at his hair like an ignored girlfriend, but he was focused on detail. Utterly Euan. And something inside me whispered *yes*.

'I assumed you didn't want to be seen in a Micra in the wilds of Yorkshire?'

'He's put a tracker in your car, Katie,' I said wearily. 'I thought you would have worked that out ages ago.'

'Oh.' Katie stared at me, then stared at the interior of her car for a moment, then shot out of the driver's seat as though someone had poked her firmly from behind. 'Oh!' There was a look of disgust on her face. 'That's illegal.'

I just shrugged.

'So now I need a new car?'

The thought of having Katie staying whilst she tried out all the models of car available on the market made my stomach drop. 'You can get them removed. Apparently. I didn't because I didn't know if he was even still bothered enough to track me. But I laugh every day at the thought that, if he was, he's now tracking a nineteen-year-old lad who's just passed his test and is probably putting miles on the clock that will be puzzling the hell out of Dominic.'

'Right.' But Katie was still looking at her car as though someone had been sick on the back seat. 'Why a tracker, though? I always told him where I was going.'

'And you think he believed you?'

'I...'

I gave her a sympathetic shoulder pat. 'Let's go inside.'

'All right. But no tea, please. Gin, brandy, wine if you must. But let's dial back on the tea consumption.'

'Tamzin.'

It was Euan calling me. He was still standing motionless in his front garden, looking out across the cow field behind us. 'I think that's Brack, running out across the field.'

'It can't be, he's in his run.' I left Katie fetching her tiny suitcase from the boot and went across. 'I've just put him in there. It must be a wild fox.'

Euan shook his head without taking his eyes away from the field. 'Fairly sure it's Brack. It's the way he moves, y'see.'

'I'll check his run.' I wasn't particularly panicked. Brack had never shown any real urge to go native, apart from the occasional foray into local woodland. Up here, he'd been too traumatised by the change of location to ever stray far from me. 'Still think it's some local fox.'

But Brack's run was empty. There was a tiny portion of wire at the bottom of one of the sides, almost invisible, torn away from the staples. Jill wouldn't have noticed it on her inspection, as it was tucked behind undergrowth and she would have been looking at the structure as a whole, not for tiny little escape hatches. It was almost impossible to imagine that a full-grown fox could have squeezed out of there, but the hairs stuck to the wire proved the opposite.

'Brack!' I ran out into the field, calling. 'BRACK!'

Nothing. No sign of the fox, who had vanished into the gathering twilight over the edge of the field, where the hill dropped down into woodland.

'It was him, then.' Euan was there. 'This is the time of year when the vixens and cubs start coming out of the dens more. There'll be a lot of activity down in the woods just now.'

'I don't need you to David Attenborough the situation,' I said, 'I just need to find him. He'll get torn to shreds by the local big boys.'

'Won't he starve to death first?' Katie had come to join us.

I stared around. What had been a pleasant view up until now, short-grazed grass sloping gently down to meet the wild-with-birdsong hedge and then the popping greenery of the woodland, was suddenly impossibly vast and filled with peril. One small, hand-reared fox wouldn't last a night out here. He could hunt worms and bugs but not for the meat he'd need. He'd be attacked by other foxes for crossing their territory, hell, he'd probably get mugged by gangs of rabbits.

'We need to find him.' I started out across the field.

'But he runs away from me.' Euan didn't have nearly enough panic in his voice for my liking. 'So there's no point in me tearing around the woods on my own looking for him, it'll just make things worse. Could you put food in his run and try to tempt him back that way?'

'Katie, there's some meat in the fridge, can you scatter that about in the run, I'm going to try to find Brack,' I called across over my shoulder. Then, to my surprise, Euan was there beside me.

'He runs away from you.'

'Yes, but if I'm with you he'll be all right. And I know where the foxes are, he'll probably gravitate towards them, especially at this time of day when they'll all be out of the den, teaching the cubs to hunt.'

My throat was dry. I couldn't lose Brack. I *couldn't*. He'd given me purpose, been instrumental in Dom leaving. I owed that fox. And the thought of his inexperience with other animals, with roads, imagining him as one of the flat corpses scattered along the verges – I was almost paralysed with imaginings.

I found I was running down to the hedge-line. Over the hump of hill, I could see the streams of light from the cottage and I kept half an eye on them, hoping to see the jumpy outline of a three-legged fox creeping his way back home on the horizon. But there was nothing but the long shadow of Katie, probably with rubber washing-up gloves on, putting meat into the run.

The light was fading fast, almost imperceptibly, as day slithered into night. It was odd how the outlines of the trees became threatening as the light died; from picturesque shapes against the sky to gnarled and spooky and almost animate. I hesitated, stopped from plunging into the dark recess of the wood by a sudden atavistic fear.

'Everything in there is smaller than you and largely terrified.' Euan was still behind me.

'Except for the serial killers.' There were shadows, moving.

'And they generally don't need to hang around in woods for fifteen years waiting for clients, they just batter down your back door and kill you in your bed.' Euan paused. 'Actually, maybe I shouldn't have said that.'

Almost without thinking, I grabbed at his hand and laced my fingers through his. The feel of those callouses between his fingers, where the paintbrushes had worn a groove, was oddly reassuring and we plunged on together between the scrawny hawthorns that delineated the wood, with our clothes snagging and catching on the sharp, protruding thorns.

In the wood it was muddy underfoot. I was still wearing the trainers I'd been slobbing about in all day and they slithered and slid on the damp surface. Where it wasn't muddy, it was mossy, and like stepping on sponges. I found I was turning my head rapidly, side to side. There was still no sign of Brack.

'This way,' Euan whispered and tugged on my hand. 'There's a fox earth over the bank here.'

We crept through the knitted undergrowth, pushing aside newly leafed branches like a pair of explorers opening a new continent. Whippy little saplings flicked against my face, brambles dragged at my feet as we forced our way forward. Euan was still holding my hand, and I was glad of the reassurance and the balancing effect as I slithered in mud and tripped on tree roots. I opened my mouth to call for Brack, but a frilly little rowan caught me in the teeth and Euan 'sssshed' me at the same time.

'If you shout, you'll scare them all off. I reckon he's gone to other foxes,' he whispered to me as he helped me disentangle myself again from a bush with spikes like tent pegs.

'But the road goes along near here. He could be out in traffic,' I hissed back, half under my breath and not letting myself see mental images of Brack under the wheels of a car. He was small, drivers probably wouldn't notice him until they hit him and, unlike a dog, they wouldn't have to report it or even mention it. It was 'just a fox'. *My* fox.

My hand was sweating in Euan's. My stomach was a tennis ball of apprehension, and I was fighting the urge to run through the wood shouting Brack's name, although I would only have made it for about five metres before I fell over something, got tangled up and slipped in the mud.

'We're close to the earth now.' Euan's voice was a hair-prickle in my ear. 'Keep low.'

Since the branches threatened to take my head off if I stood up, I couldn't have got much lower without crawling.

'And let me go ahead. They already know me, so if they see me coming they're less likely to run.'

'Except Brack,' I put in, in a whisper that wasn't much of a whisper.

'Ssssh. All right. But he'll likely take his cue from the others; if they don't run, he won't. Just let me see if he's there.' Euan dropped to his stomach and began a snake slither up the bank, seemingly not caring in the least that the mud was sparkling with fresh rain and nearly liquid, propelling himself with knees and elbows. In a second, he was invisible, his green coat and paint-stained trousers blending in with the thrusting ruffles of nettle growth, the grasses and the tripwire brambles.

I hopped from foot to foot, the terrified burn in my stomach rising higher. *I can't lose Brack. Not after all this. Not after everything we've been through together.*

'He's there.' Euan wriggled his way back down from the top of the slope. 'There's a vixen and a couple of cubs sitting outside their earth. It's way outside mating season, so she's keeping him at a very wary distance, so he's just sort of prowling about and watching.'

I let out a little puff of relief. 'Are you sure it's Brack?'

Euan clambered to his feet, mud trickling from his jacket, and gave me a slightly pitying look. 'One, I've been painting animals since I was five, I can tell one hare from another and I'm not bad at rabbits and rats, and they are even less easy to distinguish than foxes and, two, how many three-legged male foxes do you think there *are* around here?'

'Yes, sorry,' I muttered, still jiggling on my feet. 'What do you think I should do?'

He even had mud in his hair. What was most attractive about this was that he really didn't seem aware of it. Relief was beginning to unfurl in my stomach.

'Go quietly up to the top of the bank. She'll see you and take the cubs underground. Brack's out of his territory, so he won't quite know what to do, which is when you dash in and scoop him up.'

'He'll pee on me.'

'And you're worried about that now?' Euan sounded lightly amused, but hadn't lost the slight frown of concern that had arrived when he'd told me Brack had run.

'No. Not really. Sorry, again.'

Euan gave my shoulder a tiny push. 'Go.'

And like the world's least convincing commando, I shuffled my way up the slight slope of the bank. I didn't go on hands and knees, but I bent double, trying to avoid the snatch and snare of branches. This far into the wood, there was so much under, over and just general growth that even moving forwards in a crouch was hard work. I had to pull myself up on a couple of branches to reach the top.

Euan was right, of course he was. Brack was there, sitting with every muscle taut, just inside a small circle of packed earth. A thin and, it had to be said, somewhat mangy-looking other fox was lying chewing something, but everything about her shouted that she was watching Brack closely at the same time. Two smallish kits were fighting one another over possession of a feather, jumping and rolling and making high-pitched snarling noises, launching tiny ambushes from behind their mother and being distracted by her twitching tail.

I had been going to creep my way closer, try not to alarm the vixen too much, so she slunk off rather than panicking, but my first step over the lip of the slope caught my foot in a loop of tree root. I plunged forward, face down, hitting the ground and sliding uncontrollably with my knees and palms stinging and mud splattering, until I came to rest just outside the fox earth, with the cubs' feather in my collar.

The vixen and cubs were gone, spirited away underground by the perpetual watchfulness of maternal anxiety. I hadn't even seen them go. Brack, alarmed by my arrival, had fled into cover but had frozen a couple of metres away, stuck in an attitude of curiosity. He knew my smell, he just wasn't used to me arriving horizontally, looking like an extra from *Who Dares Wins*.

I picked him up. Predictably, he peed on me. Brack hadn't liked being picked up, even as a tiny kit, and this had always been his go-to revenge. But, right now, I didn't care. I didn't care that I stank of the rich, dark, rank pee or that I was one long streak of mud from my nose to my knees or that I'd almost certainly torn my jeans and grazed my hands. I'd got Brack, who hadn't even bothered to struggle.

Euan came down into the clearing, causing Brack to freeze again and shove his head in my pocket. 'Well done.'

My dry mouth and throat seemed to have expanded. Relief was a pressure behind my eyes and deep in my chest and in the warm, furry little body in my arms. 'He's here,' I said, amid tears that the pressure was driving out. 'I got him.'

'Yes.' And Euan enfolded me in a hug that was ninety per cent mud and ten per cent fox pee. 'He's safe.'

Driven into darkness by the hug, and slightly squashed by the pressure of two bodies, Brack wriggled, kicking his one good back leg against my ribs. 'I need to get him home.'

'Better not put him back in the run, though. Now he's found out how to escape.'

'He needs to go to the sanctuary,' I said. 'I need to give him up.'

The narrow escape Brack had had brought it all back. That last time that Dominic and I had fought, the catalyst for the ending of our relationship. The vet had rung me to tell me that Dominic was there with Brack, asking to have Brack put to sleep and saying that he'd had to bring him because I was too upset. She'd known, clearly, that the situation wasn't all it appeared to be and had just wanted to double check that I'd *really* intended to have the fox put down and that Dominic hadn't misunderstood.

I hadn't even stopped to think. I'd driven straight there. Dominic had left, because of course he had, he wasn't even prepared to stay and hold Brack on his last journey. He had instructed the vet to kill the fox and, as far as he was concerned, him deciding it would happen was the same thing as it *actually* happening. Only the vet's diligence had saved the cub that day and I had swept home with Brack in an old cat carrier that the vet had lent me, on a tide of fury so white-hot that all Dominic's excuses, all his reasoning and his gradually fraying calm, hadn't mitigated it one fraction. We'd argued. And, for the first time, I hadn't backed down.

So he'd gone, and I'd been left with the knowledge that I couldn't keep Brack safe forever. One day, he would need to move on, and that knowledge had made me treasure the time I spent with him. Maybe a little of that feeling had helped me realise that my relationship with Dom really *was* over. He moved in with Katie that very weekend and left me distraught and unable to cope with more than eating soup cold out of tins and keeping Brack fed and clean. I still didn't know if he'd intended to make me beg, if the Katie thing had been temporary and designed to bring me to heel, because I'd put the house up for sale immediately and sent him back his things. It had been my only moment of strength in the whole affair. Because Brack was *mine* for as long as he needed me.

I'd let Katie have Dominic. Ignored the sense of guilt and slight relief that began to replace the sadness, and hoped that she would be stronger than I had been. But I'd known, hadn't I, that she'd suffer? That's why, on that last day before I left Cornwall, I'd given her my address and told her to find me if she needed someone to talk to.

Then I looked at Brack, who'd clearly decided that I wasn't going to let go, and had settled in my arms within the darkness of the hug that was still ongoing.

'He needs to go to Nicola's,' I said, slightly muffled by being against quite a large amount of Euan.

A brief pressure of arms across my back. 'It's your call.' Euan's voice rumbled against me. 'But I think you're right.'

Then, with Euan's arm around me to keep me stable, and Brack with his head under my collar and a distinct air of defeat about him, we stumbled and slid our way home.

20

I had been going to speak to Nicola the next day, but Euan asked me to wait. 'The TV lot will want to film me painting something. They always like there to be a cute animal to focus on, to avoid me having to be in every shot,' he said, as we stood in my garden few days later.

'You want to borrow Brack again?'

'It will make him very popular. And that will be a draw for the sanctuary.'

I looked at Brack, who was lying in the shade in his harness. I didn't want to risk him making another break for freedom, I'd only just got the smell out of my jacket. 'That's blackmail.'

Euan raised his eyebrows and grinned.

But I was full of a sense of relief. I didn't have to do anything about Brack, not yet. There was a legitimate reason for keeping him. 'Great. Now I'm a fox's pimp.'

'Tam!' Katie leaned out of the kitchen window. She was sitting at the table in there with my laptop again, redoubling her attempts to research the cottage to distract her from thoughts of Dominic. It wasn't altogether working, her occasional shouts of 'that bastard!' followed by the sound of things being thrown, kept drifting out to us. 'I've found something!'

I wasn't sure whether she meant something to do with the cottage, or something to do with Dominic. She kept searching for his name across all the platforms. Apparently, he'd already changed his status to 'single' and taken down the pictures of them together on holiday. A young blonde girl had started featuring on Instagram, apparently a 'work friend', and Katie had locked herself in the bathroom for half an hour as a result.

'What is it?' I asked cautiously. I wasn't in any hurry to dash in and find out, it was very pleasant out here in the garden in the sun. Euan, leaning against my wall to look out at the wildlife, looking attractively rumpled in a paint-stained shirt and with his feet bare again, wasn't hurting the feeling of pleasantness at all.

'The cottage was registered with the tax office as a holiday let, early in 1974.' Katie leaned her arms on the windowsill. 'So your Stella lady and her husband must have moved out by then. I wonder why her parents didn't sell it, though?'

'Maybe they wanted to go into holiday properties?'

'The weird thing is that I can't find where Stella and Andrew moved to. I've tried searching them through other counties' record offices, but there's no sign.'

'Maybe they emigrated?' Euan suggested. He was furtively sketching me, I knew. I could see him hiding the pencil whenever I looked in his direction, so I was pretending not to notice. But I did catch myself trying to look winsome and occasionally flicking my hair.

'You're right, that's slightly weird.' I wanted to keep Katie focused on the cottage history. If she could just get through this first week without contacting Dom, she might recover, especially if she could keep the level of anger up. I didn't think he'd be contacting her any time soon, not if he still owed her seventy pounds, anyway. 'And yes, emigration is a good call.'

'Or she could have divorced and remarried. Changed her name.' Katie squinted out into the bright garden. 'That's more likely.'

I wanted to think of Stella out there somewhere, making a new life. Maybe she'd lost that worried expression under the sun of a Queensland cattle ranch. Maybe she'd raised a brood of children with Andrew, miles from civilisation and surrounded by nothing but sheep in New Zealand. Or left him and turned to working with street children in a South American city. I couldn't bear the thought that she still had that haunted look around the eyes, now compounded by frown lines and a tight-lipped face as she shopped and cooked and cleaned in Tamworth or Doncaster with a new husband and a new name and nearly fifty more years' worth of unhappiness.

I looked down at my feet. I was standing, near enough, where Stella had been in that photograph of her in the garden. No forsythia bush, or vegetable patch, but everything else was more or less the same. 'I hope you're happy,' I whispered. 'Please be happy.'

'I found some old maps that show the way the farm went from a house and four cottages down to these two. I've printed them out. You'll have to make a scrapbook.'

Katie, obviously having said all she had to say, pulled her top half back inside to carry on the alternate searching and swearing. I was left standing out in the sun with Euan and Brack. Whenever I looked at the whiskery, inscrutable face, with its smiling markings and those amber eyes screwed up slightly against the light of the sun, I had that sinking, sick feeling of standing on the edge of a precipice. Maybe there was another way? Where I could keep him and... and... Nothing sprang to mind. Either Brack was happy and I broke my heart or I kept him here in solitude, obviously missing company and hearing the call of the wild trumpeting through his restrictions.

He might be smelly and awkward, but he was *my* smelly and awkward. I loved him. And I was slowly beginning to realise that I was actually quite fond of Euan too.

* * *

Three days later, the film crew arrived. It wasn't, as I'd been expecting, four vans full of men with equipment, just two blokes in a Land Rover. One I recognised from TV, a famous face in the world of wildlife programmes; king of the fluffy cute 'otters playing in rippling waters' and carefully downbeat voiceover of the sad moments. His name was Jonathan 'call me Jonty!' Williams and he was smaller, thinner and had less hair than the TV screens showed. The other man did things with equipment, largely silently. He was beefy, in his late fifties and grunted acknowledgement when 'Jonty' called him Mike.

Euan watched them setting up with the look of a man who is watching the gallows being built for his execution.

'Why do you do it? If you hate it so much?' I made him another tea. We were hiding out in my kitchen while they rearranged the furniture in Euan's living room to make it look like – well, like he actually *lived* there. Well, Mike was arranging and setting up cameras and sound equipment. Jonty was mostly flirting with Katie, who'd gone over to 'help'. She was flirting back in a way that made me very hopeful that her break with Dominic was permanent.

Euan sighed so deeply that the green coat rustled. 'Money,' he said and then hid his face in the tea mug again. 'Bills.'

'But the paintings...?'

'Take me months to get right. And then fetch, what, a couple of thousand? And there are some weeks where I just—' he rubbed his head, I didn't know whether it was an unconscious movement reflecting memory. 'When it's hard to paint,' he finally finished.

I just nodded. I knew that feeling. When sometimes the paralysis of the past came down over your head like a sweater with a too-small neck.

'Don't feel sorry for me, Tam.' He was still talking into the mug. 'Please. Makes me feel – well... like I'm not fit for any woman.'

'Euan.' I abandoned my own cup and went around the table to perch in front of him. 'You're not less of a man because you got beaten up, you know. Doesn't matter who did the beating.'

Now he raised his eyes and met mine. 'Thank you for that,' he said, quietly. 'Could we... I mean, do you think we could have a shot? Together?'

I looked at him, very seriously. He'd come to me straight from filming out in the field, where Euan had been stalking through the little copse at the top of the hill and, apparently, the sight of Jonty and Mike had frightened off all the wildlife for miles. So he was still wearing his 'animal spotting' clothes, the dreadful coat with the torn pocket, the mud-stained trousers and the boots. His hair had dead leaves in and the grey streak in his stubble was growing lopsided. But his eyes were golden and warm, even shadowed with tension.

'Well, we do have one advantage,' I said, picking up my tea again, but not moving from where I sat.

'Oh yes?'

'We don't need to move in together, just knock some doorways through.'

He hesitated and then threw back his head and laughed. It

was the first time I'd heard quiet, low-key Euan laugh properly and it was a big shout of a laugh. I'd guess he rarely did it, because it even made Brack, curled up in the corner of the kitchen, jump. 'Very true,' he said. He went on drinking his tea, but his unoccupied hand reached out and laid itself on my arm. 'And, let's face it, if any more plaster comes off that wall behind the fireplace, we won't even have to put any effort in, we can just walk through the gap.'

'I am sorting it,' I said, slightly defensively. 'I'm just waiting for the "sheeting" look to be the new trend in interiors. Or for Jill to have time to replaster, whichever comes first.'

Jonty appeared at the back door. 'We're ready for you and the fox now,' he said, then twinkled professionally in my direction. 'If your fox wrangler can tear herself away.' He headed back off up the garden and vaulted the fence into the paddock. I suspected Katie was watching.

'Over the top,' Euan said, slightly grimly.

'It's not that bad.' I put my mug down. 'And I'm here to hold your hand.'

Euan stood too. 'Figuratively?' he asked. 'Or literally?'

I reached out and gently removed some of the dead leaves from his hair. 'Oh, both, I think. Don't you?'

His body was firm with the fitness of walking miles across undulating fields, and the beardy stubble was soft against my face as he put both arms around me and held me while his lips made very definite contact with my mouth. It started as a soft and fleeting kiss but developed into something deep and hot until I was enveloped in a kind of pulsing darkness. I had my eyes closed but little purple lights kept bursting behind my eyelids and my breath was catching so far down my throat that it didn't feel as though it was leaving my lungs at all. If it hadn't been for the knowledge that Jonty and Mike were poised and ready for Euan out in the paddock, I would have hurled myself backwards onto the kitchen table and stripped.

'Better get out there,' I finally broke off to whisper. 'Jonty's wound up ready.'

'He's not the only one,' was the slightly gruff reply. 'Hell's teeth, Tamzin, you pick your moments.'

'Go on.' I gave his shoulder a slight push. 'I'm following with Brack. He's going to get all twitchy at the sight of the camera, so I'll need to get him settled. Go and be professional.'

'Professional. Yes.' Euan took a couple of very deep breaths. 'Right.' He turned and headed for the door, then stopped. 'Tamzin...'

'What?' I was hunting for Brack's lead amid the maps and papers that Katie had left piled on the side. When I looked up, he was watching me with a very slight smile.

'Nothing.' And Euan was gone, slipping out of the back door with the silent, fluid movement that reminded me of foxes, of deer, of hares running across fields with the wind.

I smiled to myself and carried on searching. Katie had started sorting papers chronologically; maps were interspersed with photographs and census results in a fault zone of layers sliding into one another. The picture of Stella cooking in this kitchen slithered to the floor and I bent to pick it up, twisting it to meet the light as I did so. Whenever I'd looked at this picture before, I'd concentrated on the kitchen, being most interested in its 'then and now' differences. Stella had just been the centrepiece, the reason for the photograph, in her enveloping apron and wielding the laundry tongs. With her stretched smile and her worried expression that looked, to my prejudiced eye, as though she'd been bullied into having her photo taken. Had I read my own past into hers?

But now, with my concentration and the glinting rays of the

sun coming full in at the window, I thought I saw something else on Stella's face. It looked very much as though there was a fading bruise on her cheek.

Survivor knows survivor.

'Please be happy now,' I whispered to the picture. 'Please be living in a thatched cottage with a brood of grown-up children visiting you every weekend.' My fingers were so tight around the flimsy card that they were bending it. 'Don't let him have won.'

'Tamzin!' Jonty was calling over the fence. 'We're ready for the fox!'

I found Brack's lead and snapped it on. He trotted along with me eagerly enough when I opened the door, with his nose up, wrinkling and flaring as he scented the air. Jonty was keen to make the three-legged fox a star, so his hoppy trot across the garden from the back door was being filmed from Euan's patio with a long lens. Fortunately, I didn't need to feature as more than a pair of legs. I had the feeling that my contribution to Brack's continued welfare was probably going to be airbrushed out of history by Jonty, and they'd make it sound as though Euan had hand-raised the fox, but I didn't really mind. Brack would be famous in his own way and if... no, not if, *when*, I had to tell myself sternly... *when* Brack went to Nicola's animal sanctuary, he would be a publicity magnet.

Out in the garden, with Euan being filmed sketching away, leaning on the fence that separated our properties, Brack looked restless. He kept looking up, scenting the air and prowling, obviously eager to slip his harness and leg it for the dangerous lure of other foxes and life in the wild. When filming was over and Jonty and Mike had packed everything back into the Land Rover and popped in for yet more tea, I knew it was time.

I rang Nicola, feeling as though I was betraying my best friend. After the call, I had to go and stand outside for a while, staring into the hedge and trying not to cry. It was the best thing. Of course it was. He needed more than I could give him. But I loved him. And I had nothing else.

'Hey.' Euan was suddenly there, standing beside me.

'It's going to be so empty without him.' I didn't look at Euan. I didn't want to see sympathy because it would break me into a weeping heap, and I worried I might go back on my decision.

Euan leaned his back against the garden wall behind us and followed my gaze. 'You could get a dog,' he said. 'I had a spaniel once. Sarah hated him.'

'I'm not ready for a dog,' I said. 'I need to get rid of the smell of fox first.'

'Hmmm.' Then he was in front of me, just a shadow with the sun behind him. 'It's the right thing, Tamzin. You know it is. For him and for you, but it just doesn't feel like it yet.'

'I know.' My voice was tiny and choked.

'We'll do it together. Tomorrow, you said?'

'Yes.' Still very quiet, the word came out with a few tears. 'I can't keep him safe any more.'

'Tamzin.' The bulk of the hug was comforting. The smell of the outdoors came more strongly from Euan than from the actual outdoors around me. His skin smelled of crushed grass and ditches and his hair of leaves and blossom. 'We can still visit him. He won't forget you, you know that.'

My only answer was a little squeak. I was crying too hard to find any words, but crying into Euan's green coat was infinitely better than crying alone.

'Come on.' Euan tugged at my sleeve.

'Where?' I gradually unpeeled myself from his front, wiping my face on my forearm and trying not to look as though I was composed entirely of snot and redness. I was so far past wanting to make a good impression on Euan that it wasn't even a distant memory, but I still had some pride left.

'Just come.' And he was away, walking off up the lane.

'But Katie will wonder…'

'Katie will think we've gone up to the woods for an undisturbed shag. Anyway, she's packing, didn't you see her? I think she's got a date with Jonty down in town and he's muttering something about wanting an assistant for the rest of the week, when they go down to Wales.'

I found myself hurrying after him, scuffling through the mud ridges of the track, where the tractors had left patterns in the earth like the marks of a giant snake's passing. 'But she's a genetic counsellor! What does she know about assisting a wildlife film unit?'

Euan stopped suddenly and turned around. 'You and I made complete changes to get away,' he said, quietly. 'Why shouldn't she?'

'Oh.' I stood for a second, listening to the cacophony of birdsong from the hedges and trees. There was no other sound, just nature, being loud. 'Yes. You're right.'

'Of course I am.' He gave me a dark sort of smile. 'It's nice to know I can be, now.'

One day, I thought, as we started off up the hill again, one day he'd tell me. In dribs and drabs, little fragments of the mosaic of a life, we'd share what had been done to us; what had made us into the people we were. But for the present, the people we were now was enough.

'This way.' Euan helped me squeeze through a hedge and we followed it down, the ditch now green with weedy water, down to where the channel poured into a gulley, dropping several feet in a waterfall of liquid mud. We crossed here and plunged into the wood at the bottom of the valley.

'Where are we going?' I whispered. There was something about this cathedral of trees, now they had leaves that blocked the sky, that made me feel I wasn't quite welcome.

'Just this way. Now, stop here.' Euan waved me into a space behind a particularly prickly holly bush, and motioned at me to keep down. He crept on a few paces and pulled a handful of something from his pocket, cast it out onto the mossy woodland floor a few metres ahead of himself, and then dodged back behind the bush with me.

'Very good,' I whispered. 'Lovely throwing action.'

'Thank you.'

'But *why*... oh.' Quietly, as though they'd been there all along and were just coming into focus, a badger and a fox appeared. 'It's like *The Animals of Farthing Wood*!' I hissed, delighted.

'Sssssh.'

The badger was looking at the fox in grumpy acknowledgement, like a resident of a town looking at a tourist. The fox ignored the badger and started rooting around whatever Euan had thrown, gobbling eagerly, until the badger, clearly worried that he was missing out, also began nosing through the moss and snuffling up edibles. After a minute or two, the badger stomped off to be surly elsewhere and the fox sat back and stretched. Then it yipped, a high, imperative call and, after a second, a succession of small furry heads popped up from the far side of the clearing. Three half-grown cubs and another adult fox leapt down from beneath the roots of a tree and joined the first fox, sniffing out any leftover scatterings and rolling after one another in the lengthening shadows of early evening.

'This is how Brack should live,' Euan whispered. 'And he can, at Nicola's. She's got the space, the other foxes.'

I watched as the darkness shaded their fur. Five foxes, eating, playing, communicating. Euan was right. This was what Brack would have. I shouldn't feel guilty, he wouldn't miss me at all, it would just be *me* missing *him*, and I could deal with that.

'Come on. We'll go back.' Gently Euan pulled me from the bush, raking my skin with holly prickles as I went, and we clumped our way back through the now-dark woodland and the mud. The moon was rising over the stomach of the hill as we emerged back into the field and two deer were highlighted by its white light. They raised their heads and looked at us, then bounded away in high leaps until all we could see were their pale rumps curvetting along the hedge-line and then vanishing through the undergrowth. The moors rose to the sky on the horizon, but I didn't see them as threatening now. They were just more scenery, more of the things that contributed to making Euan who he was.

The cottages stood proud on the hill as we approached. Euan's was dark and mine had lights out of every window, competing fiercely with the moon for illumination of the paddock. 'What did you throw down for the badger and the foxes?' I asked idly, as we walked down the trackway towards our homes.

'Mix of raisins and mealworms.' Euan flicked me a quick look.

'You've got *mealworms* in your *pockets*?' I moved half a step further away from him.

He shrugged.

'Yes,' I answered myself. 'Yes, of course you have. Of all the people I would expect to go around with maggots in their clothing, you top the list.'

'Well, at least you think about me. And that's good.'

'But *maggots*!'

He shrugged again. 'Lots of things eat maggots. And raisins, I feel you are overlooking the raisins.'

I stopped suddenly and burst out laughing. It was slowly starting to dawn on me how much I liked Euan. Obviously, kissing him had been a bit of a giveaway, but this was more than lust, more than a superficial enjoyment of the way he looked, and an admiration of his talent. It was an acknowledgement of his weird, offbeat kindness, so unlike Dominic's relentless desire to conform.

And he'd taken me to see the wild foxes. Just to make me feel better about having to let Brack go.

'What's the matter? It's fine, no more maggots. Well, not many. Well, *some*.' He was looking at me closely, bending slightly so that he could search my face with eyes that were very dark in the moonlight.

'You will come with me? Tomorrow? To... to drop off Brack? I think I need someone to make sure I don't chicken out.'

'Of course.' Simple. Matter of fact, as though it were unthinkable that he could have let me go through that alone.

'Well, I'd better go in. Katie looks like she's communicating with ships at sea with all those lights on, and it's my electricity bill, so...' I tailed off. I couldn't believe how reluctant I was to leave him. 'So I'll see you tomorrow.'

He reached out and touched my hair, very gently. 'There's time,' he said. 'Always time.'

'Yes.'

'And, perhaps, that therapy we talked about. To make sure we don't drag the past with us?'

'Yes,' I whispered again, enjoying the touch of his fingers on my hair.

He didn't say anything else. He just smiled and gave me a little nod, then walked round to his front door, a cool shadow under the beaming light of the full moon.

I went inside to help Katie pack and only slightly enjoyed her shrieking fit when a mealworm fell from my hair onto her duvet.

21

'You can come back any time you want, you know. I mean, I'll miss you. If you ever – I mean, if it doesn't live up to your expectations, or you don't enjoy it, you can come back here.'

Katie just gave me a pitying look. 'I'll be fine. I'm going to give Jonty a go, he might not be forever but he'll be a great way of getting Dom out of my system. And as for the job, well, I can get genetic counselling work again if I want to. But for now—' she closed the door and settled herself in the driver's seat of her car, 'a change is as good as a rest, isn't that what they say? Oh, and let me know what Jill's mum says about the people who lived here before. I'm *ridiculously* invested in your cottage story. I left the file of all the stuff on the kitchen table – you never know, you might get a book out of it!'

That's not a bad idea, I thought, waving until her car was nothing but a puff of dust hitting the distant metalled road. If I could find out what happened to Stella, make her story central to the cottage's history, it would give a book a shape. A beginning, a middle and an end. Yes, not a bad idea at all. All that research, all those things left behind; the tattered fabric in the old suitcase hidden away, the sweet wrappers and the photographs, they could all give shape to the story. And, hopefully, Jill's mum could flesh Stella out for me. Maybe I could even meet up with Stella and find out a bit more about how life had been here, back then. Yes. Something to work towards, something to occupy me.

I carefully didn't look at Brack, in his travelling cage under the table. I couldn't meet his eye, in case I saw any sense of betrayal there.

'Has she gone?'

Euan arrived at the back door. No coat today, just a linen jacket and jeans and, thankfully, shoes. He looked rumpled and lived-in and attractively solid, not unlike the cottage itself, come to think of it.

'Yep, she's just left.'

'Good. I mean, she's nice, but a wee bit on the predatory side for me. You and she were a bit "hawk and hare" – I might have to paint that.' He slouched in and leaned against the wall. 'Brack all ready? Suitcase packed?'

'Stop it. Yes, he's under here in his cage. He seems very calm about everything.'

'A new life.' Euan smiled. 'Are you ready?'

I took a deep breath. 'Yes.' And I wasn't just thinking of Brack. There were possibilities encompassed by Euan, possibilities that made me shiver in a pleasant way, especially with the way he looked here in my kitchen, as though he belonged.

'Right.' Then he lowered his voice. 'It's right. You know it is.'

I thought about the wild foxes out there in the wood. Having cubs and digging and foraging properly for food rather than just searching out lumps of meat in a run, that was what Brack needed now. Company. Communication that he understood.

'Yes.' My voice sounded small, and I had to shake away the tears that kept trying to break through. 'Let's go.'

* * *

Nicola was the no-nonsense type of person whom I couldn't have cried in front of if I'd wanted to. Her brisk capability was a great antidote to sentimental goodbyes, and Brack looked so happy to be decanted from his little cage into the section of the huge paddock that Nicola had cordoned off for him.

'We'll just give him this bit for now, so he can meet the girls through a safe fence,' she said, giving the very firmly attached wire divide a good wobble. 'Proper introductions and all that. We don't want fighting. Once they're used to one another, we'll take it down and they can all run together.'

Brack was sniffing up and down the fence line. One of the vixens cautiously tiptoed close to the wire and stared at him. Noses rose and sniffed the air and eyes met, then both Brack and the vixen slunk off in different directions to pretend to be interested in other things.

'That looks hopeful,' Euan said.

I couldn't answer. My throat had widened to allow the lump of tears to get as far as my tongue. My little fox. Whenever I looked at the adult Brack nosing his way now through a clump of grass in the hope of something crunchy, all I could see was the tiny damaged fox kit that I'd rescued from the men with dogs, bleeding and crying. His cold little nose under my chin, nudging at me for food when I'd got him home. Bathing the stitches on his poor, bald stump after the operation. Those trusting amber eyes, following me around the room when he'd been confined to a cage to stop him moving.

But now, here he was, adult, ready to move on. Scenting the air with his head high, turning towards the adjoining pen with the two vixens in again. Needing more than I could give him.

'It's all right,' Euan said, his voice very quiet. 'You're allowed to be sad for you. You can be happy for him at the same time.'

Life, in a nutshell.

I wanted to ask Brack if he'd miss me. If he'd wonder where the human who gave him lovely food and occasionally cuddled him tight had gone. I wanted to ask if he'd miss being stroked or curling up in front of a fire. But Nicola's pragmatism and Euan's confidence that it was the right thing wouldn't let me. It would be admitting that I'd domesticated Brack beyond survival, and I really hoped I hadn't.

'I know,' I said and my voice sounded small and weak. 'I know.'

'Give him a week or so to settle, then you can come back and visit him whenever you want.' Nicola sounded a little softer now. 'Honestly, he won't forget you. I've got a goose around here somewhere, raised by a family who found her as an abandoned gosling. They come up once a month and she'll flap in from wherever she is on the farm to nag them for titbits. She's been here for fifteen years.' She looked at Brack, who had peed confidently up against one of his fence posts. 'He'll always be your fox.'

Euan and I watched Brack for a few minutes longer. He didn't seem to feel at all abandoned. He dug several small holes, ate a worm and some of the scraps that Nicola and her team had put in the run to help him get used to his new home, and then strolled off into the long grasses, where he curled up in the sun and showed every sign of being unconcerned enough to sleep.

Euan was watching me as though he wanted to capture my every expression on paper. As though he were photographing me in his mind for later. 'Take me home,' I said, eventually, still with the tiny voice. 'Otherwise I may never leave.'

He took the keys from my outstretched hand and gently

steered me towards the car. I kept looking over my shoulder to see if Brack was going to leap to the wire and howl as I left, but he stayed where he was, tidily curled with his nose on his tail and just watched me go with a typically inscrutable expression. 'The house is going to feel empty,' I said.

'And smell nicer.'

'Well, there is that.' I glanced at Euan, fiddling with the driver's seat to get it far enough back for his legs. 'But he was out in his run mostly, until he escaped. So the worst of the smell has worn off.'

'I got you something.' Euan said it in a rush, almost as though he were worried about my reaction. 'Not to replace Brack, never that. But something to take care of.'

'Euan, you—'

'I just wanted to take that shadow away. Dominic left his shade on you, you know. I'm sure Sarah left hers on me, that's why I think therapy would be good. Like, it's nothing solid, nothing tangible that you can point to and say that's the effect they had, but just... just something. Shade. And you lose it a bit when you're caring for Brack so I thought... anyway. Yes.'

He's bought me a puppy, I thought, and felt my heart sink a little. I'd told him, hadn't I? That I wasn't ready for a dog yet. I needed a bit of time to get used to living without something constantly behind me. I mean, I'd love a puppy, of course, but – I'd *told* him. Not yet. And he hadn't listened.

Euan presumably put my quietness down to leaving Brack. He didn't try to jolly me out of it, he just let me look out of the window as he drove my car back to the cottages. I was thinking of Brack too, of course I was, but there was that little bit of me that was trying to work on my expression so that I wouldn't look disappointed. I wanted to believe that Euan listened. But a dog would mean he didn't. That he had his own beliefs about what I needed and he was going to impress them on me.

'Great. It's arrived.' Euan nosed the car onto the verge. 'I told them to put the box in my kitchen for now. Come on in.'

I didn't want to face the Bracklessness of my own cottage just yet, so I followed him. I couldn't hear any puppy-type sounds and my heart rose a little. Maybe a kitten? I could probably cope with a kitten.

On Euan's kitchen table stood a box of annoyance. It thumped, occasionally, in an irritated way.

'This,' he said, indicating the box, 'is for you. Open it carefully and be prepared to slam it shut again very, very fast.'

I regarded the box with a mixture of disturbance and terror. 'It's not poisonous, is it?'

Euan grinned. 'No. But it's cross.'

The box bumped across the table a few centimetres. I cautiously went over and lifted a flap. 'Oh, God, it's dinosaurs!'

Now Euan laughed. He came over and took the box from me, carrying it outside to Brack's now deserted run. 'They're ex-battery hens. Rescued from destruction by a lady I sometimes paint for. She's just had a new delivery and she's given me these three.' He held the box out to me now. 'For you. To nurse back to proper chickenhood. They've barely been outside in their lives and they really don't know how to chicken. That's where you come in.'

We opened the box and let the traumatised hens out. They were largely bald, but feathers were regrowing in patches, giving them the look of small velociraptors with a bad case of evolution. 'I don't know anything about hens,' I said, feeling almost as discombobulated as the chickens evidently were.

'You didn't know anything about foxes either,' Euan said brightly. 'And they don't need too much in the way of input. Food and protection and that's about it. Plus, you get eggs.' He looked dubiously at the motley crew, with their pimply skin and scraggy feathering. 'Probably. Eventually, anyway.'

The three hens stood as though shocked by the outdoors. I'd had to tip them out of the box and they hadn't properly righted themselves. One sat as she'd landed, wings half outstretched and crouched as though she expected an explosion. The other two seemed traumatised by the feel of earth under their feet.

I knew how they felt. *Survivor knows survivor.*

'Thank you,' I said, turning to Euan. 'For everything.'

He did the half-shrug thing again and a couple of slow blinks. 'I thought – well, they don't take too much looking after.'

So he had listened. Not just to my words, either, but to what ran underneath them.

We stood together outside the run. The boldest of the hens pecked experimentally at the wall and took a few shuffling steps forward. The other two watched her as though waiting to see if some terrible fate was about to descend, but not reassured when it didn't.

'Jill said she'd come up and get the run into shape for them tomorrow.' Euan carried on looking at the chickens. 'I had to tell her what I was planning, I hope you don't mind. I just thought it was best if I ran it past someone else in case I was doing something stupid.' His attention on those birds was so rapt that I could only assume it was because he didn't want to meet my eye. That caution, that lack of belief in himself, nearly broke my heart, and as my heart was already still swollen and sore from leaving Brack, that feeling came to the surface riding on a raft of tears.

'Euan.' It was a whisper. But something in it made him tear his eyes away and then I found myself wrapped in his arms, in his jacket, in *him*.

'Because I don't trust myself any more,' he whispered. 'I

second guess and I avoid and I am just so *afraid* all the time. That was what Sarah did to me, but I am trying, I really am, to get over it.'

There was nothing else I could do but hug him back, hard. Hoping that my feelings came over in the embrace and the tears and that, if he could read a wild animal well enough to paint it, he could also read me.

We stayed like that for quite some time. Even the hens got bored eventually and, with weak little scutters and the occasional flap, took themselves off to the safety and security of the enclosed house part of the run, which Brack had ignored in favour of sleeping in the grass. I hoped Euan was taking as much comfort from me as I was getting from him. Something in the solidity of the hug gave me a renewed hope for the future – and that tiny fizz of potential that Katie had set off with her research into the cottage was helping.

I could write a book. I *could*. I could. Contrary to what Dom had always told me, I was beginning to feel I could do *anything*.

22

I can't sleep. I'm just, oh, I don't know. I want to tell someone, but who do I tell? Jeanette and Jackie both look at me funny now cos I go everywhere with Andy. He says they're just jealous because they are with Dean and that Paul lad with the lazy eye and neither of them can drive and Andy's got his own car. Andy takes me to the coast and we sit on the sand down at Scarborough and he's got this book of poetry that he reads to me and he holds my hand and tells me that I'm his little Star-Girl. Makes me all shivery just remembering.

He makes me feel like I've done nothing. Like I've got nothing to talk about because he's so clever and he just *knows* stuff. He was reading this poem and I asked who wrote it because it's all about a boat on a lake or something, I didn't really understand some of it, and Andy told me it was Wordsworth and I remember him from school. So I said that he wrote stuff about the Lake District and he came over and got married just near Scarborough and could we go up to the church and see? Then Andy got a bit funny and slammed the book shut and said it was just a stupid poem and he didn't want to go into any stuffy old churches on such a nice day. Well, it made me feel a bit strange at first. Like I was when I first met him, all shy and not knowing what to say, and then Andy went all quiet and I said I was sorry a few times but it was like he couldn't hear me. He just kept staring out at the sea and I didn't know what to do. So I told him that he could kiss me when we got back to the car, if he wanted, if we could park somewhere that we could be sure no one who knew my parents could see, and he cheered up then. He got really chatty about his job, how the boss is getting to really rely on him and he's sure he's going to get promoted to senior mechanic soon and he'll get a rise and how he's thinking it would be a good time to settle down.

Then we parked in this lane. And we kissed for *hours*. Well, not hours, because I'd told Dad I'd be home by nine and I know he doesn't really like me going with Andy even though Andy's always really nice and polite and respectful to him and calls him 'sir'. He even brought Dad a bottle of his favourite whisky last time he picked me up. So, we're there, and we're kissing and I can tell Andy wants to put his hands down the front of my blouse and do *stuff*, but I won't let him. And then... well, and then Andy says, 'We should get married'! And I was so astonished, I think I gawped like a carp. I said something like, 'But I promised Mr Harris when I took the job that I wouldn't be leaving to get married for *years* and I'd need to save up a bit first,' and Andy just laughed. He laughed and laughed and he said, 'You won't be working when you're my wife. Being married to me would be your new job,' something like that, anyway. And the way he said it, all kind of low and hot, like Ryan O'Neal in *Love Story*, made me feel all prickly and kind of odd, like I really wanted him to kiss me again.

So, Andy's going to talk to Dad. He said he wants to do it all official, to ask for my hand and everything. I just *know* what everyone is going to think. I mean, we've only known each other a few months, but Mum told me what men like to do to you and how I'm absolutely *not* to let anyone put a hand on my ha'penny until I've got a ring on my finger because we don't want any more shame on the family like when my cousin Margaret had to go away to the country for six months and came back a widow with a baby. And I promised her that I wouldn't, but – well. But if I tell them that I just really, really want to marry Andy; that he's so kind and he loves me, well, he must love me, he calls me his Star-Girl and he wouldn't say *that* if he didn't love me, would he? He looks a lot like Ryan O'Neal, and Mum and I cried *buckets* at that film, so I know she will be on my side.

Besides, I know their secret, and if they won't let me marry Andy, I'm going to tell them that I know. It's really funny, actually, but I know they won't want anyone else to know, and that's the real reason that they moved to Thornton from out near Helmsley way, because they *had to* get married because Mum was expecting me. I only found out by accident when I was talking to Gran before she died. She was getting a bit rambly and not always sure who she was talking to and she said, 'Course, you never had much of a wedding, did you, Eileen?' cos she thought I was Mum. Then she went on about them announcing their engagement on the day the old king died and I thought she was mistaken, being old and confused and all. But then I thought about it and some of the things that Mum had let slip, like everything being all draped in black when Dad proposed to her and how she thought it was a sign. She stopped and then pretended she'd made a mistake and she'd said everything *should have been* draped in black, but I knew. The old king died in the February and I was born in July. And I came top of our year in maths, I could work that one out.

So anyway. I might be getting married to Andy! I borrowed some of Mum's magazines this evening, I told her I wanted to look at the recipes, but really I wanted to look at the wedding fashions special...

23

Jill arrived next morning in a van laden with equipment and her mother.

'Thought I'd bring up some paint charts so you can choose some proper colours, with official guidance,' Jill said cheerfully, putting the kettle on without thinking about it. 'And I want to make that run completely fox-proof, but from the other side, if you see what I mean, now you've got hens.'

I was sitting at the kitchen table, the sun hadn't made it over the roof to the back of the house yet, so it was slightly shadowy, but that suited me. My first full day without Brack, and I didn't want it to be a day where I was outdoors, missing him. Inside, with the weather not quite knowing whether it wanted to be summer or to reprise winter, that was fine. I didn't feel the lack of the little furry follower so much. I'd phoned Nicola already, to be told that Brack was eating well, had touched noses with one of the little vixens and, if things continued to go well, Nicola was going to let him run in with them tomorrow. He didn't, she said in a tone of slight but kind amusement, seem to be pining for me too badly.

'Oh, and this is my mum, Janet. Mum, this is Tamzin who, fairly evidently, lives here now, or is a really audacious squatter.'

Janet did not at all look like a woman who would even entertain the idea of her daughter having a toy boy and, apart from the tan, I wouldn't have guessed at the 'Greek' element either. She looked like an older and more rounded version of Jill, with cropped grey hair and a comfortable cardigan. She looked around the kitchen and then came to sit opposite me at the table.

'Yes, I remember this place,' she said. 'My mum grew up friendly with Diana Williams, she lived on the end when she was a girl and Mum used to take me to visit Diana when I was little, she lived with her mum then, in Pickering.' Janet glanced around the room again. 'After the place got pulled to ruins. They used to tell me about weekends, when they were at school and Diana's dad would let them help on the farm, well, I say "help", it was probably mostly giggling at the farmhands. It will have been just after the war, place was already going to pot.' She sighed. 'And then when it was a holiday cottage and they needed a housekeeper, well, I already felt like I knew the place after hearing Mum and Diana go on.'

'Sorry.' Jill swung around with the tea mugs in her hand. 'Mum does like to talk. I should have primed you. Tea.' She doled the mugs out onto the table. There was an extra one.

'Katie's gone,' I said, nodding at the mug.

'Oh, it's not for her.' Jill sat confidently next to her mother, cupping her hands around her mug. 'It's for him.'

At that precise moment, Euan appeared, passing the window and giving a little tentative tap at the back door. I stared.

'Is this some kind of psychic connection?'

Euan rustled into the kitchen in the green coat. He'd obviously been out somewhere drawing because he had moss staining along one shoulder and the hems of his trousers were damp. His hair was dishevelled and full of unspecified pollen and he'd never looked more attractive. 'We use phones,' he said mildly. 'Jill and I do talk, you know. I don't exist in stasis when I'm not around.'

He picked up the spare mug and sat beside me. The kitchen felt full of life and people, and I realised I wasn't missing Brack as much as I'd been afraid I would. Maybe that was why they'd chosen now to do this, to take my mind off things? I looked at them, Euan with his paint-stained hands wrapped around his mug and Jill making 'that needs fixing' faces at the wobbly chair leg underneath her, and felt a little detonation of warmth inside me. I had friends. More than friends, in Euan's case. People who cared.

After my time with Dominic, the isolation and his insistence that he was all I could rely on, it made little bubbles of potential fizz through my bloodstream. There was a life without him. And here it was.

'Go on, Mum,' Jill said. 'Are there any biscuits, Tam? I have to keep her sugar levels up or she starts talking about knitting patterns and other people's grandchildren.'

'Top shelf,' I said, although I didn't know why, Jill knew perfectly well where the biscuits were and was, in fact, already halfway to the cupboard. 'But yes, Janet, please tell me everything you know about this place. I'm fascinated.'

I didn't want to raise the potential of writing about the cottage. Not yet, while it was such a new idea.

Euan had dropped his head forward and was picking dried cerulean blue off a fingernail. 'We're interested in Stella,' he said and opened the cardboard file that Katie had compiled of all the cottage information. The pictures of Stella were no longer filed away in that nebulous date order, they were on the top of the sheaf of papers, and one slipped out. 'Did you know her?'

Janet looked down at the picture. It was the one of the wedding, Stella with her proud, reckless face and her carefully formal bouquet, next to the narrow-faced young man in his tight suit. The orangey wash that age had given the photograph made the event look sunny and glowing with possibilities. She sighed.

'Stella Watson,' she said. Her tone was absolutely unreadable. 'Yes. She was, what, six, seven years older than Diana and me, of course, but round here everyone knows everyone and she used to babysit me and your uncle Don when we all lived in Thornton, growing up.' Janet turned the photograph, as though, hologram-like, it would enable her to see Stella's face more clearly. 'Nice girl. It was terrible, what happened.'

A sudden clutch of cold around my heart. *It was terrible, what happened.* Those words did not lead me to expectations of a wonderful long life, lived among those who loved her. 'What did happen?' My voice sounded a bit cracked, and I took a mouthful of tea.

Janet made a noise as though she were sucking her teeth. 'Get the pictures out,' she said. 'I'd like to see all of them.'

I had the feeling that she wanted to build the tension. Janet had taken the comfortable stance of the born storyteller about to launch into a tale, wrapping her cardigan more snugly around her and putting her tea carefully within reach. I wondered if her exposure to Greek culture had made her appreciate the dramatic, as we dealt out the photographs like dealing a deck of cards, spreading them in front of her. Some of the old sweet wrappers came with them, adhered with static almost as though they were still sticky with chocolate. Janet smiled.

'Oh, she did love her sweeties, our Stella.' She picked up the Bar Six wrapper and stroked it thoughtfully. 'Not seen these around in a while. Wonder if they still make them?'

'Mum...' Jill put in, warningly, 'do not get sidetracked into the history of confectionary you have known and loved that is no longer produced. Before we know it, we'll be up to our armpits in nostalgia about the size of Curly Wurlies and we'll have to stand you outside until you calm down. I brought you over so that Tamzin could hear about her cottage, not your obsession with the Milk Tray man.'

'Your gran used to pay her for the babysitting in bars of chocolate.' Janet still sounded dreamy, as though she were back in the sixties, a young child. 'They were pricier then. Mind, the Watsons always had a penny or two put away and Stella was their only.'

We were all quiet as though we were listening for Stella's ghost to rattle at the cups on the side. She was here with us, as much part of the cottage as I was now, Janet's words drawing her out of the ether. Under the table, Euan leaned his leg against mine and he gave me a sideways smile.

'It was a bit of a scandal, her marrying that Andrew Gregg, apparently.' Janet tapped at the wedding photo. 'She'd have been – what?' She turned the picture over and saw the 1971 date written on the back. 'Nineteen or so. They'd hardly known each other five minutes so we all thought she was, well, in the family way, as they used to say back then.'

'You're allowed to say "pregnant" now, though, Mum.' Jill swished her tea around in her mug. 'Was she?'

Janet shook her head. 'Doesn't look like it. *I* think it was that Andy Gregg, rushing her up the aisle because he thought he'd get his hands on her parents' money. Thought he was on to a good thing when he met our Stella, him a bit of a bad lad over from Leeds. Met her at a disco in Pickering, next thing they're engaged and, like I said, married in such short order we reckoned there was a happy event on the way.'

'Pregnant, Mum,' Jill said again, in a weary way.

'And it seems a fair few others thought the same as I did, cos her dad bought them this place. We thought that he'd give it as a wedding present, but he kept it in his name and gave them a trifle bowl from Browns. It was a lovely bowl, mind, but I think Andy thought they'd get the house. There was a bit of a dust-up at the reception, I seem to remember.'

'Were you at the wedding?' I asked. The comforting pressure of Euan's leg and the permeating smell of linseed coming from him were very pleasant. I tried not to think about maggots in the pockets.

Janet shook her head. 'My mum and dad were, though. Friends of the family, you see. In those days you invited all your parents' friends when you needed to make the numbers up, and Andy didn't have any family. So he said,' she added, darkly. 'There was some talk that he'd been in borstal over Bradford way, but we never knew. Nobody from his side came to the wedding, anyway.' She smiled down at Stella's happy face. 'Poor lass. She'd had a bit of a sheltered upbringing, her dad had a car and they were the first to get a colour telly. Reckon she fell for a bad boy because she didn't know better.'

I had a sudden moment of fellow-feeling for Stella. My grand-mother's advice on men had been a bit thin on the ground and had tended towards making sure they had clean fingernails and used the right knife and fork in restaurants. It had made me a prime target for Dominic, as it seemed, if Janet was right, Stella had been for Andrew.

'Aaaaaaaaanyway...' Jill said, taking the wedding picture from her mother's hand and pushing the photo of Stella in the garden in front of her. 'Stella and What Happened Next.'

'I was coming to that.' Janet settled herself more deeply into the chair and gathered her storyteller's cardigan around her as though this was about to become a Ghastly Tale. 'So, they lived up here in this cottage for a couple of years. Andy worked down at the garage in Kirkdale, the one everyone went to for a quick cheap car and not too many questions asked, if you know what I mean, but at least it was work. Nobody saw much of Stella – well, she'd come into Kirkby on the bus on market day to get her shopping but she was always a bit quiet, apparently. Even her mum and dad didn't get to see her much, but I reckon they were sitting back and waiting for the grandchildren to arrive. And then, one day—'

She stopped and took a mouthful of her tea. Janet was a masterly storyteller, we were all leaning forward across the table, our elbows almost touching in our eagerness to hear the rest.

'Well, one day, must have been September, October, back in seventy-three, Andy comes dashing into the little shop that used to be down on the corner.' Janet pointed vaguely in the direction of the main road. 'He's covered in blood and he says there's been an accident and Stella has fallen down the stairs and to call an ambulance. Says he came in from work early, she was on the landing, him coming in surprised her and she fell. Backwards.'

We were all, suddenly, silent. I could feel my heart and the pulse of blood in my veins. The photographs on the table looked heavier. Euan moved away from my leg but raised his head and caught my eye.

'What happened to her?' My voice sounded small.

'Ambulance took her off to the cottage hospital, but they had to move her through to York. She was in a coma for five weeks.' Janet traced the shape of the pale-faced girl in that last photograph in the kitchen.

'And then?' I felt hope trickling through me, much as the sun was now beginning to slide over the roof and lay a tiny slice of light outside the window.

'Oh, she died.' Janet picked up her cup again. 'Terrible for her mum and dad, of course. They couldn't bear to let this place go, so they started renting it out for holidays. When old Mrs Watson got too frail to do the housekeeping herself, that's when I took over. The Nettersthwaites lived next door then, of course,' she added, inconsequentially, since none of us knew who the Nettersthwaites were.

I wanted to get up and go and stand at the foot of that narrow, steep staircase. Up until now, it had just been an inconvenience – annoying to pass in the night on the way to the bathroom, irritating to try to get furniture up without gouging stripes in the plaster. But now, all I could imagine was that young girl falling backwards to land sprawled and broken on the living room floor.

'Well, of course, we all had our doubts about young Andy's story but – well, she was never a disloyal girl, you could never have said that about her, naïve, yes, but never one to badmouth. So we'd never heard anything... *untoward*, but we all filled in our own gaps.'

'And you think...' I tailed off. We were, around this table, all filling in our own gaps.

'Police had him in, asked a few questions but once they let him go and he realised he wasn't going to get a penny out of her parents, he was off like a scalded cat. Nobody could prove anything, but we'd got our suspicions, so he didn't hang around here. We heard he'd joined the Merchant Navy and settled down in Portugal or some such.'

I looked down at the picture of Stella in the garden. That poor, bright girl. Whether it was an accident or whether he'd pushed her, or whether the whole 'falling downstairs' was a cover story for something even worse – she had still died. Not much older than Jill's eldest daughter. Suddenly, all those photographs gained a shadow.

Jill made a face. 'Have to say though, Mum, Tamzin found all these bits hidden around the house. I think that calls your house-keeping skills into question – I mean, that's nearly fifty years down the back of the water tank and up on the beams in the attic – didn't you *dust*?'

'They were quite well hidden.' I felt I had to defend Janet. 'Really tucked away. Not in places that you'd clean in the normal order of things.'

'And I wasn't in that much.' Janet sounded almost dreamy, looking down at the scatter of pictures on the table. 'Once a week, just to open the windows and air the place out, and then to do a clean through when people had been in. But the cottage wasn't on any websites, the Watsons weren't up to technology. Mostly went to friends of friends, that sort of thing, can't have been more than a dozen times a year.'

I looked around the bright, sunny kitchen. 'They couldn't bear to part with it,' I said quietly. 'Her parents. I wonder if they knew.'

'Things were different back then, though,' Janet said. 'A husband giving his wife a thumping on a Saturday night if he was drunk and she'd not got his dinner – it was all normalised. Common. Nobody thought much of it.'

I remembered the way Dominic had spoken to me sometimes. The way people had rolled their eyes or looked away when he'd put me down in public or made a joke at my expense. 'People don't like to get involved, I suppose,' I said. 'Poor Stella.'

'And it *might* have been an accident,' Jill put in bravely. 'Maybe he really did come home and startle her into falling.'

I looked down at the photograph of Stella in this kitchen. Standing awkwardly, the laundry tongs in her hand and that faintest of bruises on her face. *Survivor knows survivor.* 'I'm pretty sure he had something to do with it,' I said. 'But, if there was no evidence, what could anyone do?'

'Andy died overseas somewhere.' Janet finished the last of her tea. 'Went yellow, apparently,' she added, inconsequentially.

We all went quiet. So, it was over. Nothing anyone could do any more, except hold that memory of Stella, now everyone who had loved her was gone.

Euan's hands were busy. He was sketching something on a bit of paper he'd pulled from a pocket with a stub of pencil, just a few lines and then he wrote something.

'What do you think?' he asked, pushing the paper towards me. 'I mean, at the moment it's just Cottage Two, Bracken Ridge Farm Lane, but...' He'd drawn an outline of the front of my cottage, just walls, door and windows, and standing in front of it was a girl. At first, I thought it was me, but when I looked again it was Stella. Stella as she had been in the early pictures, defiant, head up. Happy. And above the front door he'd drawn a sign and written 'Stella's Cottage'. 'I did think you might call it Brack Cottage but maybe...?' He tailed off again.

'Stella's Cottage,' I said thoughtfully. 'It's an improvement on Cottage Two, certainly.' I looked around. Jill was nodding slowly, and Janet gave me a smile.

'She'd have liked that, I think,' she said. 'She must have loved the place or her parents wouldn't have kept hold of it. I mean, takes a lot to keep visiting the place where your daughter got so badly hurt that she died, but her mum must have felt – well, close to her here.'

We sat in silence for a minute. Outside, the birds sang and the sun shone and the breeze flickered through the grass. I found my eyes were tracing the ceiling beams; along the wood and down to the permanence of the thick cottage walls. I thought of the cosy little rooms upstairs and how proud Stella must have been to have lived here. How much she must have loved this little place.

'I think it's a really good idea,' I said, picking up the sketch.

'Stella's Cottage. Yes, I like it.' I looked at the smiling face, the suggestion of movement that Euan captured so well. 'And I think you should paint this,' I added, surprising myself with how fierce I sounded. 'I'll hang it up there, opposite Brack's portrait.'

'You'll have to put up with the postman calling you Stella,' Jill pointed out pragmatically.

'I'm "that bloke off the telly",' Euan said. 'So you might prefer "Stella" to whatever else he may call you.'

I looked at Euan's face, familiar now and a face I was beginning to enjoy having around, with its half-bearded, can't-be-bothered-to-shave grey stripe and the subtlest of paint flecking. At Jill, comfortably making tea again. At Janet, lost now in memory as she leafed through Katie's file of information on 'Stella's Cottage'.

Then I remembered Dominic and his parting words, some glib phrase about how I was doomed to a life of no friends bar a smelly, disabled fox, holed up in my little shoebox of a terraced house. How that was all my life would ever be, unless I invested my money in those high-earning schemes he had in mind. How I'd fritter it all away on stupidity and animal charities until I was forced to come to him for loans. The things he'd called me.

'I can think of worse things to be called than Stella,' I said.

24

I only went to the disco in Pickering because Jeanette thought that Mike Winters might be there. Course, we all tease her something rotten about him – 'is his brother Bernie coming along too?' and all that, but she really fancies him and she'd heard from her brother that he'd been thinking of going down the disco. Jeanette would usually go with Jackie, but she's off to Wales with her family to visit her grandad, so she asked me if my dad would let me go with her instead.

Dad didn't like the idea. 'How are you going to get home?' he kept saying. But, if I promised to be on the ten o'clock bus, to stay with Jeanette all evening and not to drink any alcohol, in the end, I could go. Oh, and I wasn't to 'plaster my face with any of that rubbish' either, so I took all my make-up round to Jeanette's, and my new maxi skirt, and I borrowed her new boots because I've only got my shoes that I wear for work and my plimsolls. I was feeling really glam when we got to the disco. The boots were a bit too small and made me walk funny, but they looked so cool, and the skirt had been made by my mum but nobody knew that, and anyway it was just the people that I'd been to school with, and some of the girls who went to typing college with us, and the boys from the farms and that kind of thing. Nobody special. Nobody who mattered.

And then, there he was. Like... like this film star in the middle of all these ordinary people. He was just *so good looking*! He was wearing a *suit*! All the other boys were in their normal clothes, slacks and things, and there was this person in a natty suit, all done up and drinking actual *wine*! Course, soon as we got there, Jeanette goes off looking for Mike, cos she's heard he's in the room round the back snogging Sandra Banks, but then *everyone* snogged Sandra Banks first off, so Jeanette wasn't worried. She was just going to hang round outside and be all 'oh, hi Mike, fancy seeing you here' and cool and stuff and get him to light her cigarette, so she'd left me sitting there. I'd got a glass of squash, cos I'd told Dad I wouldn't drink or anything, and they're playing some really good music but you can't dance on your own, can you?

I saw this new man talking to a couple of the boys from the shop. They all kept looking over, but they wouldn't be talking about me, I mean, I'm just Stella, Jim Watson's girl to everyone here. They all know my dad, they all know that he's quite strict with what I'm allowed to do, so they don't even bother trying to get me outside for a snog and a grope. They know my dad would get to hear about it and then they'd be waiting for the knock on the front door and someone having a 'word' with their dad. So when this new bloke comes over and sits down next to me and says, 'I hear you're called Stella. That's a very cool name, do you know where it's from?' and he starts telling me about how it's like some foreign word and it means 'star' and how it suits me – well. I couldn't say much, cos I was practically drowning in my squash, my hands were shaking that much.

His name's Andy. And he's got a *car* and his friend is getting him a job over at the garage outside Kirkby, cos he's really, really good at fixing things. And he is so good looking! I still can't believe that he wanted to talk to me! Then, when I had to get my bus and I couldn't find Jeanette because she'd gone off out the back with Dean, Andy walked me to the bus stop. He was such a gentleman. Never tried to grab my hand, never even went in to try to kiss me or anything like that, he just waited until I was on the bus and then said he'd see me here again next week, and he'd remember me because I was just like my name, I was a star, all bright and shiny. I nearly forgot to wipe off all the make-up before I got home, but at least I'd got my long skirt on so Dad couldn't see I'd still got Jeanette's boots on. I had to go down her house on Sunday to get my shoes back, but that was good because she wanted to tell me all about Dean and I couldn't help but tell her about Andy.

So we're both going back next Saturday. I hope, hope, *hope* Andy will be there again. I wonder if I can get Mum to run me up a new skirt in time? She's got this ace swirly velvet dress that she said she was going to cut up to make me something new and it would make such a *fab* skirt...

25

A week later, Euan and I paid our first visit to Brack.

The sun had come out with all the force of June behind it and bounced almost audibly off every metal surface all the way to Wood House Farm. Although that might also have been the fact that I was slightly hung-over.

'All right?' Euan touched my hand. He was driving and the blinding white light wasn't affecting him in the slightest, which annoyed me.

'That second bottle was a mistake.'

'You think so?' He gave me a grin, taking his eyes off the road, where little gobbets of gravel were being thrown up to ping off the car bodywork far too loudly.

'Last night, no.' I remembered what had followed the second bottle. The moist, hot tangle of limbs and breath. The realisation that we were *each other's* neighbours and didn't have to be restrained and keep the noise down. The even more astonishing realisation that quiet, part-time grump Euan was actually very, very good in bed. 'This morning, yes. Why aren't you hung-over as well?'

Euan swung the car down the lane to Nicola's sanctuary with a bump and wallop of suspension that almost caused my breakfast to manifest into my lap. 'Because I'm an artist. We specialise in sitting up all night drinking absinthe and producing paintings of the tortured state of our inner thoughts. No time for hangovers.'

'Plus you're about four stone heavier than me.'

'And that.' He grinned again. There was a relaxed look to him this morning and I wondered whether that had been occasioned by our new physical closeness or the fact that, as he had admitted last night, he'd not had sex for four years. I'd told him that having a sign that said 'No Callers' on his door was probably the reason. Then we'd practised again to make sure we'd got it absolutely right.

'And only if your tortured inner thoughts look like a goldfinch on a branch.' He'd got up early to make me tea and toast and not come back and I'd gone downstairs to find him working on the sketch of Stella outside the cottage, complete with a backdrop of autumnal trees.

'What can I say? I'm uncomplicated and not that tortured. Anyway, we didn't have any absinthe.'

We drove into the little parking area and got out. There was nobody about, not Nicola or any of the vet students or work experience girls who normally padded about behind wheelbarrows. Everything looked flat and baked under the weight of the sun. Euan held his hand out to me. 'Let's go and find him, then.'

The paddock was, once more, undivided. The grass was long and there was no sign of any of the foxes, no movement, no long shadows. My heart dropped a little. I'd hoped, in the tiny part of the back of my mind that wanted Brack to pine, just a tiny bit, that he'd have heard the car and be pacing by the wire, eager for my arrival. Instead, there was nothing. Just a huge bumble bee droning a refill among some straggling yellow flowers and the newly minted leaves on the big tree ruffling their skirts in a trace of breeze. The smell of fox was sharp. It poked me in the hangover with heart-melting memory – a smell that should have been unpleasant, but the familiarity meant it was associated with soft fur and love.

'Is he even in there?' I had a momentary vision of Brack escaping. Lost, feeling deserted, streaking his lumpy stride across the hilltops. Searching for me.

'Call him and find out.' Euan leaned against the post and rail fencing that outlined the paddock. 'And here. Throw some of these.' He dug in the pocket of his reasonably smart trousers and handed me a few mealworms.

'Really? Do you have maggots in all your pockets?'

He made a non-committal gesture and I had to smile. Life with Euan was going to be a life of this kind of thing. Unexpected maggots, sketches of wildlife on every available surface, days in fields in the rain. And the nights... well. Things could be worse.

'Brack!' I called the fox's name. At first there was no reaction. Then I saw grass bending and parting, forming a line between the shade of the big tree and the fence. Stems flickered and seed heads twisted and then there was the familiar red face and white grin staring at me from the undergrowth. 'Hello, little fox,' I whispered.

Brack gave a little yip and dashed up to the wire, pushing his muzzle against my hand through the taut metal. His coat shone in the sun, his white patches gleamed and there was a kind of focused intensity in his eyes that I'd never really seen before. He looked like a wild fox now, but a wild fox who was quite happy to eat mealworms from my hand and stretch himself along the fence so I could stroke him.

'He looks happy,' I whispered to Euan, feeling that tiny pull of grief again. *Happier than he did in a house or a small run. Happier than he was with me.*

Euan nodded. 'He's living the best life for him,' he said. 'But, if it hadn't been for you, he wouldn't have had any life to live at all.'

His words made me feel a bit better. Still sad, still missing the little fox who'd followed me everywhere in the house, who'd curled up next to me on the sofa. But I had Euan to do that now, of course, although I hoped he'd keep the similarities to sitting beside me, rather than following me everywhere. I'd had enough of that from Dominic.

When the last of the mealworms had been gobbled down, Brack sat by the fence and looked at me in his direct, inscrutable way. Paws neatly together, tail curled around, as though he wanted to show me how content he was with his new home. No need to hide in the undergrowth, or creep behind the shed that formed their bad-weather shelter, he was at ease and relaxed, and I felt even better about my decision to send him here.

After a few minutes, there was a soft coughing sort of noise from the long grass and a small vixen combed her way along the pathway Brack had trodden. She stopped suddenly when she saw Euan and I, head up and ears cocked as though she was about to run. Brack just flicked his ears, acknowledging her arrival behind him, but he didn't move, and eventually she tiptoed her cautious way nearer, nosing the ground for any dropped remnants of mealworm with one eye on me in case I was about to make a sudden rush.

'Brack's got a girlfriend,' Euan observed, voice low, as the vixen greeted Brack with a cheek-to-cheek nuzzle, once she was sure that there was no trace of foodstuffs left.

We watched as the two foxes trotted off into the shelter of the grass towards the shade offered by the tree in the middle of their paddock. Brack didn't look back once. It didn't make me sad now.

He had all this space, this chunk of Yorkshire wilderness; he had security and safety in the proper environment for him. And he had company. It was all I'd ever wanted for him.

And, as Euan put his arm around me and pulled me against his shoulder for the walk back to the car, I thought that Brack and I hadn't done so badly out of coming to Yorkshire at all.

* * *

We had a proper party, the day we renamed the cottage. Jill wouldn't let me hold it until she'd taken out the fireplace, replastered the wall and painted the whole room, so it took a few weeks to get around to it. She showed me how mixing the Militia Grey with the Wicked Stepmother Forest Green gave rise to a pale sage colour, which I loved, and we spent a companionable couple of days painting it onto the living room walls. Oddly enough, I'd actually come around to liking the grey, but Jill had commented that it would be like living with a World War II tank division, so, sage it was. It looked classy and crisp when we did the woodwork white, I'd completely gone off pale yellow.

The majority of the cushions went off up into the attic room where, combined with the oversized flamingos on the walls, they made the place look like an opium den. Downstairs, Euan helped me to put fairy-lights around the beams and he carefully hung the portrait of Stella on the newly renovated wall. He'd painted her looking relaxed and happy, with a background of beautifully laid out garden. 'She seemed to like the garden,' he said. 'It just felt right to paint her out there.' He'd painted her in that long skirt with the swirly pattern, but not posed as she'd been in the photograph, instead she was sitting on the grass, arms around her knees. Her hair was being gently tweaked at by a breeze, the cottage was visible, square and dependable in the background. A long-stemmed flower – Jill told me it was a delphinium, but I hadn't got that far in my gardening book yet – lay in Stella's lap. There was a reason for it, something artistic to do with leading the eye and all that, but I left all that to Euan. All I knew was that the colours were bright and summery, and Stella was smiling. I hoped it was how she would want to be remembered.

Then came the day of the party. Jill and the girls came, along with the mysterious Sy. I'd built a mental picture of him as a long-haired Byronic figure, possibly with a dreadful ponytail and beachwear. When he turned out to be short and balding, like a bank manager with a natty taste in ties, I laughed for about half an hour. Katie and Jonty came up from London, bringing expensive champagne, and even some of my paint-selling shop owners turned up, bearing home-made wine and an air of disappointment that I didn't live in a magazine spread.

The cottage was full to bursting. We set drinks up in the garden, opened all the windows and put music on in the living room. 'Who's going to complain about the noise?' Euan said. 'I'm responsible for most of it.' People chatted and mingled, although Jill knew everyone already, and Euan kept taking people next door to show them his paintings, so the party sort of spilled out over both cottages, until everyone was everywhere and the hens went and sat in their house with their newly regrown feathers all fluffed up in annoyance.

In the midst of it all, we hung the new sign: 'Stella's Cottage'. No fanfare, no ceremony, just Euan and I, hand in hand whilst the chat went on around us. The sun had gone down, the air was warm and smelled of the hay drying in the field, of flowers and wine, as we stepped back to admire the effect.

'Do you think she would have liked it?'

Euan put his arm around me. There were still some flecks of

paint in his hair, but I didn't comment. It was Euan. It was who he was. 'I think so.'

Then we went and sat on the fence and watched the night drop down around us. The barn owls came and flew their evening route down the valley, whilst behind us in the cottage, one of Jill's daughters started to sing along to the music. The pure, high notes drifted after the owl, into the darkness. Voices rose and fell, someone laughed, another cork popped. Stella's Cottage was alive, full of people having fun.

It was, I thought, not a bad way to be remembered.

MORE FROM JANE LOVERING

We hope you enjoyed reading *A Cottage Full of Secrets*. If you did, please leave a review.

If you'd like to gift a copy, this book is also available as an ebook, digital audio download and audiobook CD.

Sign up to Jane Lovering's mailing list for news, competitions and updates on future books.

https://bit.ly/JaneLoveringNewsletter

Explore more funny and warm-hearted reads from Jane Lovering.

ABOUT THE AUTHOR

Jane Lovering is the bestselling and award-winning romantic comedy writer who won the RNA Novel of the Year Award in 2012 with *Please Don't Stop the Music*. She lives in Yorkshire and has a cat and a bonkers terrier, as well as five children who have now left home.

Visit Jane's website: www.janelovering.co.uk

Follow Jane on social media:

facebook.com/Jane-Lovering-Author-106404969412833
twitter.com/janelovering
bookbub.com/authors/jane-lovering

ABOUT BOLDWOOD BOOKS

Boldwood Books is a fiction publishing company seeking out the best stories from around the world.

Find out more at www.boldwoodbooks.com

Sign up to the Book and Tonic newsletter for news, offers and competitions from Boldwood Books!

http://www.bit.ly/bookandtonic

We'd love to hear from you, follow us on social media:

facebook.com/BookandTonic

twitter.com/BoldwoodBooks

instagram.com/BookandTonic

Milton Keynes UK
Ingram Content Group UK Ltd.
UKHW041258080224
437499UK00008B/80

9 781800 482555